A RIVER IN THE TREES

Jacqueline O'Mahony

riverrun

First published in Great Britain in 2019 by riverrun
This edition published in 2019 by

riverrun

An imprint of

Quercus Editions Limited
Carmelite House
50 Victoria Embankment
London EC4Y 0DZ

An Hachette UK company

A CIP catalogue record for this book is available
from the British Library

Paperback 978 1 78747 355 3
Ebook 978 1 78747 352 2

10 9 8 7 6 5 4 3 2 1

Typeset in Monotype Fournier by CC Book Production

Printed and bound in Great Britain by Clays Ltd, Elcograf S.p.A.

Praise for *A River in the Trees*

'Gripping . . . O'Mahony is very good at surprises . . . The atrocities and betrayals during the Troubles are revealed in a series of violent, gripping chapters interspersed with some fine poetic passages . . . O'Mahony's pace never falters in a first novel which shows great potential. Her unflinching and brave examination of the lives of women is bracing – sad and funny' Martina Evans, *Irish Times*

'Ireland has once again been flung into discussions about national independence, 100 years on, and this elegantly-penned novel offers some historical perspective. But while it's backlit by the struggle for Irish sovereignty, the pith of it is the struggle of two women, separated across a century, for their own personal sovereignty' Anne Cunningham, *Sunday Independent*

'The reader is won round to the quietly desperate struggle of a woman realising she hasn't lived the life she could and should have had . . . O'Mahony's prose remains supple and expressive throughout; she finds the emotion in each moment without forcing it. She's definitely one to watch' Eilis O'Hanlon, *Irish Independent*

'Gripping . . . Hannah's story has gravitas and pathos . . . Ireland has changed drastically for women over the last century, and *A River in the Trees* does succeed at bringing that century-long transformation to life' Róisín Kiberd, *Sunday Business Post*

to Mike

We shall not cease from exploration
And the end of all our exploring
Will be to arrive where we started
And know the place for the first time.

TS Eliot, *Little Gidding*

PROLOGUE

1919

THE MEN CAME THAT night, very late. By the time they arrived they had all been sitting for hours in the kitchen, hardly speaking. Hannah had cleaned and trimmed the lamps for the morning and when she'd done that she set to ripping up the old sheets and turning and sewing them so the thin worn part was on the outside. It was a dull job, but the needle on the Singer clicked quietly and steadily and the sound and the feel of the foot pedal working perfectly like a poem almost soothed her. Her mother and her sister sewed the cotton for a dress by hand. Her father sat by the fire, smoking, with the guns under his chair. They had put a single candle in the window and there was something terribly lonely, it seemed to her, about its small brave light against the huge darkness beyond.

They waited. Near the end she thought she would be sick from the waiting, but when she finally heard the boots in the yard she wanted the waiting back: the fear hit her like a slap. She stood up; so did her father. Her mother moaned and put her head on Eily's shoulder. Her father opened the kitchen door, and the men came in, bringing with them the smells of the night and the earth and the rain. They were so out of place in the kitchen that for a minute no one could speak.

Then one of them stepped forward and shook her father's hand. He turned towards her mother and touched his cap. When he spoke he had the strong accent of the Gaeltacht; the English didn't sit easily on his tongue. She knew then that he was O'Riada; her father had said that he was from down the country.

'God bless you for the hospitality,' he said.

'God bless the work,' said her father in return.

Hannah had moved to stand next to her father. The man looked from her father to her and she got such a shock at how beautiful his face was that she had to drop her eyes to the floor. With all that happened afterwards, it was that moment that stayed with her: the seeing him for the first time. That was the moment, she would think, much later, when it all began and finished, all at once.

I

2019

SHE WAS A GHOST, now, in her own life. That's how she thought of it. She was a ghost and the baby was a little ghost that travelled with her, all day long. They both went about their business, every day, two ghosts. Sometimes she had to stop herself from putting her hand out to hold the baby's small cold white hand. She could touch her, almost, she thought; she could almost see her, out of the tail of her eye, if she didn't try to look at her straight on. She was with her, always. She would never again, she thought, be free of her.

She had to get free.

She looked at herself in the car's rear-view mirror. Her eyes, glazed with tiredness, looked back at her, dully, sullenly. She shifted on the seat. Her breasts were sitting on the high mound of her stomach. The skin on her stomach felt pulled tight and thin, and her breasts were nuzzling each other like little overfed animals. The band of her bra was damp; its straps were cutting into the thin skin of her shoulders. She sat up straighter and pulled her stomach in:

she might be on her own in the car, driving in the near dark, but still – her breasts were touching her stomach.

She'd been putting on the weight, steadily, over the last few years, ever since the pregnancies. She was thirty-eight now, so she'd given up the cigarettes, of course, but she still drank wine, and, oh god, the cheese, the bread, the butter, the crisps – down they all went, chug chomp chug chomp. Until just recently, surely, she'd looked fine with everything squashed in behind the Wolford pants, the Wolford body with the terrible poppers that rubbed and rubbed, the skinny jeans under the flowing top. The weight had gone on slowly, steadily, and she'd thought of herself as a thin person for so long that it was hard to reconcile herself to the other possibility. But when she looked at photos now she saw her head jutting forwards like a pigeon's, a slight double chin underneath, the cheeks turning to jowls, almost, the hated stomach sticking out, the legs, even the legs, like fat carrots. I'm a skinny person trapped in a fat person's body, she thought to herself now. She'd heard a friend say that once and had liked the swing of it. But it sounded flat when she repeated it to herself, in her head. It sounded like a big fat lie.

She'd been driving for three hours and the tiredness and the enormity of what she was doing made the fat suddenly seem unbearable, unmanageable. She could not be the heroine of her own story if she was a fat person. She could only, really, have the courage to face the future if she could fit into size 25 J Brand skinnies. There was really no point trying to do all of this as a fat person. She remembered Caroline saying all those years ago that hitting nine stone was the beginning of the slide towards obesity. They had laughed, but they had both believed it.

'I'm a fattist,' Caroline used to say, between slow drags on her cigarette. 'I don't care. I am.'

Really, Ellen had no interest in fat people, and she refused to be one of them. I will be thin again, she told herself, I will have control over all this again, soon.

SHE SAW A PETROL station ahead of her on the road and pulled in. In the lovely gloaming of the dusk it glowered like a squatting toad. She turned off the engine and for a second listened to its ticking as it cooled down. It sighed and fell silent. She loved this car. She had the same car in London. My car is more intelligent than me, she used to say. She'd made sure when she was planning all of this that the car rental company had her car available: she wanted to make the journey in something familiar. I love you, car, she thought, and then immediately, Maybe I really am losing it. She gave the steering wheel a small shake. She closed her eyes and felt her left arm give a jerk. She looked up, opened the car door, and got out.

She went into the garage.

There was a woman of about fifty behind the till. Ellen ignored the sandwich rolls behind the counter and the crisps arranged in glorious pyramids by the door.

'Could I have twenty Marlboro Lights, please,' she said. She cleared her throat – her voice had caught a bit on the last word.

'Twenty Marlboro Lights,' said the woman, not looking at her.

She spun around, instantly businesslike. She had short hair and it was flattened down at the back in a kind of crop-circle pattern. She had brushed the front, but not the back, thought Ellen, or the back just wouldn't sit right for her – it was a bad cut. She had huge, strong-looking flanks that strained against too-tight, cropped trousers. Ellen loathed cropped trousers but these ones were especially terrible: they were ruched at the bottom, and white. If you were going to go cropped, they had to be perfect raw silk Capris and you had to be a Jackie O size 6 to pull those off. A sudden wave of sadness hit her. She thought of the woman working in this garage to earn the money to buy the trousers. She imagined her picking them out in the shop, trying them on in front of the mirror and doing quick little half-turns with her toes pointed down and her hands on her hips and deciding, yes, these are the pants for me – they called them pants here, of course. She imagined her taking them home and taking them out of the bag and putting them on her bed and carefully smoothing them out and standing back to take a good look at them.

Really, it was nearly too much to bear.

'That's twelve euros and seventy cents,' the woman said.

'They've gone up since I last bought them,' said Ellen.

'Ah, sure,' said the woman, expansively. 'It's only pure madness now, the price of everything.' She handed her the cigarettes. 'Are you here on a visit?'

That was the problem with dealing with anyone from here – they acted like it was their duty to interrogate you. When she was young she used to think that as an adult she'd have some witty reply at the ready when she was questioned, that if someone asked her a question like, 'Where are you going?' she'd be able to laugh a silvery laugh and answer, 'Wherever the road takes me,' and spin on her heel and head off, an international Marlboro-Light-smoking woman of mystery. But it was impossible not to answer. She was from this place and she knew the rules and to have not answered, or even to have not answered fully, generously, would have been like slapping the woman in the face.

She handed over her credit card.

'I'm over from London for a few days. I've driven down from Dublin.'

'That's a fierce long way,' said the woman, looking at her. 'But we're blessed now with the new road, we don't know ourselves. I'd say you could do it in nearly three hours, could you?'

'That's it,' said Ellen. 'Just the three.'

'Where are you headed?' said the woman.

'Lisarna,' she said, and put the cigarettes in her bag. She didn't have a lighter, she realized.

'You haven't far to go,' said the woman. 'But sure there's nothing there. Are you visiting someone?'

'I'm looking at a house that's for sale,' she said.

'All the way from London to look at a house in Lisarna,' said the woman with exaggerated wonder. 'You're looking at the right time anyway. The cigarettes are dear but the houses are cheap.'

She shook her shoulders with pleasure at her own joke and handed Ellen the machine with the credit card in it.

'Could I get a lighter as well? And that bottle of wine, too – the Pinot Grigio. The one with the screwtop.'

She had made it come out as a question, like she was unsure about what she was saying and might change her mind.

'Sorry about that – will you have to put it all through again?'

'I will,' said the woman. 'But sure, what else am I doing.'

She redid the transaction, putting the wine and the lighter in a thin white plastic bag.

'Now,' she said, leaning across the wide glass counter to hand Ellen the bag.

'Thanks,' said Ellen.

'You're grand,' said the woman. 'Enjoy Lisarna. They'll be delighted with you.'

Ellen laughed. The sound of it surprised her.

'Bye now,' said the woman. 'Mind yourself.'

She turned to the sandwich roll counter and began to rearrange the display. She didn't look up when Ellen walked out.

She walked to the car, clicking open the doors. Beep beep, they said in hello. She got in and took out the bottle of wine, and opened its screwtop and drank from it like she was drinking water. The wine shot through her like electricity. She picked up the pack of cigarettes. Off with the plastic wrapping, out with the lovely silver foil. The cigarettes shone before her like little white soldiers. She took one out and put it between her lips. It felt dry and smooth and perfect.

She looked back at the shop. The woman was looking out at her, and seeing Ellen looking, she raised her hand in goodbye. There was an awful loneliness about her, standing in the frame of the door with the hard false light behind her, her hand held up in a hopeful salute. Ellen turned her head away too quickly, pretending that she hadn't seen her. She would not say goodbye. She had said so many goodbyes now that even the most insignificant ones made her recall the feeling of all the others, goodbye after goodbye after goodbye, and her drowning in the slipstream of them all as they rolled over her like a slow wave. All the people I let go of, and all the people who let go of me, she thought – too many.

Too much has happened to me. I've seen too much.

She picked up the lighter and lit the cigarette. She inhaled and then, exhaling, she turned the car to face the black road.

S HE COULD FEEL HER father watch her as she did her work. Her head was bent forwards a little and her cheeks were hot from the effort of stirring the heavy porridge but when she turned he smiled at her with his shy half-smile full of approval. 'You were always calm and steady in your doings, even as a child,' he had said to her one Christmas night when he had had too much whiskey. 'There was always a drawing stillness about you.' They had had a great crowd that Christmas night and there had been singing and talking into the morning. A hard frost had set in late in the evening and when the visitors had finally left the heat of the kitchen they'd whooped and laughed with the shock of the cold as they'd crossed the starlit yard; she could bring to mind the whoops, still, though the easy pleasures of that night seemed strange and childish to her now.

'Hello, Dadda,' she said.

He was standing in the doorway with the stairs behind him and she was at the range, by the window. The morning light that she loved was all in a pool about her.

'You're at the porridge already,' he said, as though he were surprised.

She had been making the porridge for the house since she was tall enough to reach the range. When she was smaller than that she would come into the bedroom sometimes and wake him and say, 'Will I light your cigarette for you, Dadda?' and he would give her the Woodbine and she'd run down the stairs and put it to the embers of the fire, and puff at it until it began to catch, and then she'd run back up the stairs with it well lit and into the room she'd come with it held high, a trail of sweet blue smoke spooling out behind her like a thin ribbon. Her mother had stopped her lighting the cigarettes when she got bigger. She said it wasn't done for girls to be smoking. Only shop girls would be seen with a cigarette, she'd said.

'They'll all be down in a minute, roaring for the breakfast,' she said. 'I'm better off having it done early. Do you want some tea, Dadda?'

She didn't wait for his answer, but poured the tea and milk into a mug and then cut him a thick slice of the bread and buttered it. She put it on a plate and carried it and the tea over to the table. He sat down.

He put his big hands flat on the table on either side of the plate. The skin on them was cracked and sore-looking; the nails were thick and ridged and cut too short. She picked up the jar of honey and put it in front of him.

'Put some of the honey on your bread,' she said, and he picked up the jar.

It had always been the best time of the day, she thought, the morning, when it was just the two of them in the kitchen, and not a word wasted between them. She turned away from him and started to stir the porridge again.

'Was there any news last night?' she asked. It was better not to be looking at him now.

'Michael O'Sullivan called,' he said.

She knew that: she had listened to the voices through the floorboards of her bedroom. It had been very late but still light; on these long hot June nights the darkness, when it came, was more blue than black. Last week, she had taken the horse down to the river at nearly eleven o'clock and the land had been washed in a silver light that made the night look like it was daytime turned inside out. She had seen a trout jump in the river. It had dived in and out of the still silver water in a perfect arc, almost soundlessly.

'Did he say anything?' she asked.

'He heard they were seen near Skibbereen on Tuesday,' he said. 'And that they stayed out by Coolmore on the Wednesday and the Thursday. So they're headed for us all right. They'll have to come here before they make for the pass. They'll need a couple of days' rest and food and then sure, what can they do but head for the mountains. They have to get over and into Kerry and meet the rest of the lads there.'

'If they left Coolmore on Friday, they'll be here tonight,' she said.

She turned around and he started and looked up at her; he had been looking down at the table, as if in a dream.

'Tonight, or tomorrow,' he said. 'We'll get word first. But we have to be ready now, girl.'

She nodded.

'Do we have plenty of food?' he asked.

'We do,' she said.

'There's no need for any worry,' he said.

'I'm not worried, Dadda,' she said, and she wasn't. She was ready.

'Aren't you my great girl?' he said.

It was what he used to say to her when she was a child. He put his hand out to her. It was such an unexpected gesture that for a second she did not move. Then, though she did not want to, she took his hand and he squeezed hers, hard.

'The whole country's gone mad,' he said. 'It's all right for the rest of them up in Dublin. We've to pay for things in blood down here.'

She took her hand back.

'It'll be all right, Dadda.'

She wanted to say more. She wanted to say, I've enough of keeping the head down, keeping quiet, passing notes in the lanes at dark. We should be out in the fields fighting instead of waiting, waiting here like half-dead people. She'd had enough, now, of the waiting for things to start. She had been waiting for things to start, for something to happen, it seemed to her, for as long as she could remember. Certainly since she'd left school the days had hung heavily on her, and too often she wandered the house saying to herself, almost without realizing it, what will I do now, because each day was like a fence she had to climb over.

It was easy enough to get through the morning, because she had to take the horse out, and do jobs around the place, but the afternoons and the evenings – the summer evenings, especially, with their long beautiful light that thrummed with a hinted-at other life – were the worst. Then the hours stretched out in front of her after the dinner and there was nothing to do but sit in the kitchen and sew a bit of stuff or lie on her bed in the stillness and wait for sleep to come. What will I do now, she would ask herself, over and over, and there was never an answer to be had, she knew, even as she asked, but, Wait and see. Wait, wait.

'Don't say anything to Mammy until we get word for definite,' her father said. 'There's no point worrying her for nothing.'

She didn't answer. She picked up his empty cup, and took it to the sink and went back to the porridge.

There was a bang on the stairs; it sounded like someone had fallen down. The three boys came into the kitchen, laughing and shouting and shoving each other.

'He pushed me down them stairs,' said Ciaran in fake outrage, aiming a kick at Eoin. 'The big fecking bull that he is.'

'Be quiet,' shouted her father, and his voice broke on the shout. 'Do you think we want to be listening to your guff at this hour of the morning? Sit down and eat your breakfast and lucky you are to have it.'

It was such a shock to hear him raise his voice that the boys instantly fell silent; Liam, who was six, and still the baby, started to cry quietly.

'Eat your breakfast, boys.'

Their mother came into the room with her arms above her head as she pinned her hair up, her mouth set in a line. She sat opposite their father at the long table and ran her palm along the tablecloth in front of her, patting it, smoothing it out.

'It's early in the morning for shouting,' she said coolly.

'Will you have a cup of tea?' her father said, not looking at her mother. He was red in the face as if he had frightened himself, too.

Her mother gave a little forced yawn.

'I will,' she said. 'And Hannah, will you cut me a thin slice of the bread and put a small bit of butter on it. No big old chunks like your father has.' She looked around the room and put her hand against her face. 'Where's Mary?'

'She's out in the yard, Mammy, doing the hens. She'll be in once she's seen to them,' said Hannah, cutting the bread and pouring the tea and putting it all down in front of her.

'Isn't she a fine hard-working girl?' said her mother. 'Weren't we blessed the day she came to us?'

In answer to her own question she gave a small sniff and took a slow, careful sip of the tea.

'Eily's still in bed,' said Hannah, and she gave the porridge a few unnecessary stabs of the spoon.

'She must be tired out after the town yesterday,' her mother said.

'I'd say shopping for stuff for her new dress was exhausting all right,' said Hannah, and Eoin laughed.

'What's funny?' said Liam.

Hannah could feel her mother looking at her.

'Nothing,' said her mother. 'Nothing's funny. Bring that porridge over, Hannah. You'll have it turned to stone.'

There was a half-knock on the door, and then Denis came in, shuffling and bowing and making a great show of taking his cap off and flattening his hair.

'Good morning, all,' he said, wiping his face and looking at no one. 'Good morning, Mrs O'Donovan.'

'Dia dhuit,' said her father. 'The cows are out?'

'They are,' said Denis. 'They're gone mad from the heat. 'Tis only boiling out there, boiling I tell you,' and he gave a mad grimace of a smile.

He'd come to work for them when he was thirteen and she was nine. Ten years he had been with her father now, and well treated he had been every year of it, paid decently, and fed from the table if he wanted it. He had a room to sleep in off the yard by the pigs and he kept it as tidy as a barracks, her father said: he hung the few clothes he had on a nail he'd hammered into the wall, his boots he polished every Sunday before Mass, he made his bed as soon as he got out of it in the morning. Once a week Mary gave him a bowl of warmed water and he shaved in front of the bit of mirror he had on his shelf.

Her father had taught him all this, because before he'd come to them he'd worked for a pair of old bachelors who'd taken him as a child from the industrial school and kept him like a dog in an outhouse. Her father had seen inside the outhouse once, when he'd brought Denis home after he'd met him walking back from the dairy in the driving rain carrying the empty churns. He'd had to climb in through a small window high up in the wall: the door hadn't been opened for years, he'd said, and that was how Denis had to get in and out, day and night. And the smell of the place was unbelievable, because Denis didn't know to relieve himself outside, and he'd soil the clothes he was wearing and sleep in them and then stand up in them in the morning – he knew no better, and anyway, said her father, knowing better would have done him no good since all he had were the clothes on his back. The old bachelors starved him and beat him, said her father, and god knows what else, and when one of them died he'd gone with the donkey and cart to the farm and broke down the door to the shed and brought Denis home with him. The priest had given him the go-ahead, he'd told the remaining brother, and they'd all whooped when he'd told them that, for it was a lie, and a big lie, too – the priest would not have gone against the farmers, who were of an old family, and had a substantial farm. But he hadn't had a word of argument back from the old bachelor, who knew when he was beaten, said her father, and since that day Denis had been with them. Ten years now the formality of the morning ritual had been a source of daily torture to him, thought Hannah, watching him shuffle from one foot to another, but her mother would have him greet the family at breakfast as if they were in a great house and he were their agent. Poor Denis, she thought, suddenly, fiercely, and him stuck here in this kitchen like all the rest of us.

Her father stood up.

'I've to go up to the long field,' he said to her mother. 'We'll be gone all day. Will you send Mary up with the dinner?'

He used a different voice when he spoke to her mother: it became tighter, strangled-sounding. It is as if he is afraid of her, thought Hannah. What is there to be afraid of? What can she do?

'I will,' she said, and sighed.

She was a great one for the sighing, a great one for the sighing and the yawning and the sniffing. She had to finish every sentence with a sigh like she was exhausted. Hannah longed to shout at her, Is it tired you are, Mammy? Or are you sick? Is that why you keep sighing all the time?

She walked over to the table with the pot of porridge held out in front of her. She put it on the rack on the table and started to ladle it into the bowls.

Her father put on his cap. He leaned down and kissed the top of Liam's golden head.

'Will you be good?'

'I'm always good,' said Liam, in surprise. 'Aren't I?' and they all laughed then at his round open face and the tension that had been in the room since her father's shout lifted a bit.

'Goodbye to you all,' said her father.

'Goodbye, Dadda,' said Hannah, above the noise of the boys, and he smiled his sudden, brilliant smile at her. Then he went out the door ahead of Denis.

She could hear them calling to each other across the yard, and then there was a shout of sharp laughter and the dog barked happily in response.

After they had gone there was silence in the room for a minute.

The thought came into her head and without waiting for it to settle, Hannah said, 'Will I take a tray up to Eily?'

She saw the surprise on her mother's face and then the confusion as she searched for a suitable answer. It would nearly be worth taking up the tray to make her mother feel beholden. Nearly.

She looked up at the clock and because she knew her mother was watching her she opened her mouth in a small O, and frowned.

'It's half seven,' she said. 'I've to take the horse out.'

She carried the porridge pot to the scullery sink. She took the great black kettle from the fire, carried it to the sink and half filled the pot with boiled water. Mary would scour it when she came in from the yard. She pulled her apron off over her head in a single swoop and hung it on the hook on the back of the scullery door. Then she untied the old bit of ribbon that was holding up her hair and shook it out down her back.

Her mother said she looked like a tinker with her hair down her back.

'I'll see you after, Mammy,' she said.

She went out the door and gave it a good bang behind her to cover her mother's sigh. She could hear the horse stomping in the stable across the yard, and she set off across the cobblestones without looking back at the house.

III

ELLEN WAS ON THE road to Lisarna now. She was smoking the cigarette and inhaling as hard as she could, her whole body was shaking in response. She hoped she wasn't going to be sick. She took another couple of swigs from the bottle of wine, a short one, and then a longer one. She'd had more than half the bottle already, which felt like a bit of an achievement. She took another drag of the cigarette. It had taken her ages first time round to get the hang of smoking. She had had to work at it, assiduously, for weeks. And the wine – she'd had to build up slowly to being able to drink as well. By the time she'd met James, of course, she'd been fluent in both. She and Caroline had, by then, been fully engaged in the great drinking and smoking project.

James. Her skin flushed, like it had been nettled; she had to open the window of the car to let some air in. It was hard to drive now: the taste of the cigarette and the wine in her mouth and the smell of the heavy wet air and the sound of the people's voices here was too much for her, suddenly.

She felt a great anger rise up in her. I can't handle anything anymore, she thought. I've become this fat person who keeps her head down and tries to get through the day. I've become someone who apologizes before she does anything. I'm afraid of everything now. Ever since the baby, I'm afraid of the whole world.

She took a big drink. Some of it spilled out of her mouth and ran down her chin and neck. She let her head fall back. Underneath this fat I am still the person I was, and I will be the person I was, again. I will keep smoking these cigarettes and not eating crisps and I will get thin. I will drink white wine when I want. And James and I—

She was going to be sick. She pulled over to the side of the road, too fast. She got out of the car in a half-stumble – she left the engine running, the door open – and crouched down on her haunches and retched into the grass. Some of the sick got on her shoes and she rubbed at it with a fistful of grass. It left a green stain. She fell back and sat down heavily, with her head between her knees. She put her head on her warm breasts and let her stomach roll out.

What am I doing? she thought. What am I doing? It's too much for me. She began to rock backwards and forwards then, holding on to bunches of the thick wet grass with both hands.

Her mind was racing away from her now and her breath was coming fast and shallow. She was beginning to float away from herself. She banged her fists on the ground. She had to hold on to something to slow her thoughts down, like she'd been taught. The first time she saw James. The first time she saw James, and she headed for that memory like she was a swimmer in a dark sea looking for a light from the surface.

She was in a taxi with Caroline, in America. In the years after, it was that moment, the seeing him for the first time, that had stayed with her. They were driving slowly along the main road in the city – there was traffic, and it was raining, and dark, and the city lights seemed to be sliding down the car windows. She and Caroline were going out – they were always going out – and she remembered exactly, always, the date she first saw him, the day, the time even – 8 p.m., Friday, 5 October. Even now, it was as easy for her to remember as her birthday.

She was wearing that crazy short dress – that dress! She wouldn't get it below her hips now! – and those high boots and she can pull the memory from her mind like she's pulling a book from a shelf. She sees herself and Caroline as they were then, when it was all just beginning. She was looking out the window of the taxi and there he was, standing on the other side of the street facing her, and she said to Caroline, 'Look at that guy,' and to the taxi driver, 'Stop, we're getting out here,' and then they were jumping out of the taxi, laughing, running across the street in the rain, looking for him in the crowd. People were pushing in and out of bars, shouting and laughing. They went into bar after bar and every time they left someone would shout after them with great good humour, 'Girls, stay, don't leave us.'

They found him in the fifth bar.

He was standing back from the crowd, with little gaggles of girls watching him from a distance and the more brazen ones, in twos and threes, standing closer to him and talking to each other too loudly. They went straight up to him and, as always, Caroline started to talk first. She was clever, and funny, and confident, and outrageous, and you could see that he was surprised, and then pleased, and then he started to smile that slow smile she would come to know meant he was enjoying himself. She just looked at him.

He was the best-looking person she'd ever seen in her life.

'He's like someone from a film,' a friend had said in disbelief the first time she saw him, and it was true – he was like someone from a painting, someone from a poem.

In the beginning, there had been no other way to think of him apart from in relation to the way he looked. Afterwards, when she loved him, she sometimes forgot what he looked like and then it was like opening a present when she looked at him properly again, at his eyes, his nose, and his beautiful mouth, his beautiful mouth. Afterwards, when she was with him, she would see other people jolt when they saw him and she would feel proud, then, of his shocking beauty.

But that first time she saw him she just stood there, silently, and looked, and felt her heart open up until it filled her chest, and stopped her breath, almost.

HER BREATH WAS SLOWING now. She sat up and pulled in her stomach. She could taste the sick in her mouth, and the smell on her hands was awful, and her shoes were ruined, really, but she was all right. She stood up against the car and when she'd steadied herself she got back in. Her mother always used to say that she was tougher than she looked. She's tough out, that Ellen, tougher than she looks, she'd say, when she was sure Ellen was listening.

She took hold of the steering wheel.

I'm still going, Mammy, she said to herself, so maybe you were right about that, anyway.

She turned back towards the road then, and drove into Lisarna.

SHE'D BOOKED A ROOM at the only hotel in the town. She parked the car behind it and pulled down the mirror and looked at herself. The last ten years were written on her face. She looked terrible; she looked like she'd been sick in a ditch. She took out her hairbrush, and powder compact and lipstick, and tried to fix herself, but she had great black circles under her eyes and her face looked swollen. She went to the boot of the car and opened her suitcase, and pulled out a vast cashmere shawl and swathed it about her shoulders. She changed her shoes for boots with too-high heels. She closed the case and pulled it out, stumbling a little under its weight, and locked the car and walked towards the hotel, with her chin up to hide the wobble of fat under it.

There was a woman her mother's age standing behind the reception desk, stabbing with some viciousness at a computer keyboard. She looked up at Ellen, and nodded.

'I'll be with you now,' she said, and continued typing.

The carpet was terrible: dark red and brown, and that awful swirly pattern was a horror. There was too much heavy furniture about and a distinct smell of mushroom soup. But to the right was a handsome enough looking bar, and to the left was a dining room with the tables already set for breakfast. They were laid with thick white cloths and silver cutlery and white china.

'So,' said the woman, cheerfully.

Ellen turned back to her. The woman was wearing very bright pink lipstick – some of it was smudged on her teeth – and she had short, neat hair swept behind her ears.

'Sorry about that,' she said. 'I'd love to throw that computer out the window.' She looked at Ellen. 'We're checking in, I take it?' she said.

'Yes,' she replied. 'Ellen Edwards.' She was very drunk, she realized. She put her hand on the desk to steady herself.

'Oh, that's right,' said the woman. 'Now.'

She put a form on the desk and Ellen bent over it with a pen; she could feel the woman studying the top of her head.

'How was the journey?' she asked, eventually.

'Grand,' said Ellen. 'Long. The drive down is the worst part.' She hoped she didn't smell of vomit. Maybe the mushroom soup would cover it.

'Oh, I'd say so,' said the woman.

There was a tiny pause.

'Is it work you're here for, or . . . ?'

Ellen looked up at her. The woman had let her voice trail off, and she kept her eyes down.

'I'd say business,' said Ellen, trying to sound formal and in control. 'The family house is after coming up for sale and I thought I'd come and have a look at it.'

'Isn't that great?' said the woman. 'That you have the interest, I mean. Where's the house?'

'It's the O'Donovan farm,' said Ellen. Would this woman never let her go? In London, she thought, she would be in her room by now, without having exchanged more than a couple of sentences. 'Out by Coolarn.'

The woman raised her hands like she was trying to put a wall up around Ellen's words.

'They're my cousins. My mother was an O'Donovan. God, here you are all the way over from London and we're cousins. Isn't it a fierce small world?'

'Isn't it?' said Ellen, gritting her teeth. 'Fierce small.'

'That's great altogether,' said the woman. 'I'm Dorothy Flood,' she said, holding out her hand for Ellen's. 'O'Donovan.' She gave a bit of a jiggle of excitement and then said, with a sudden seriousness, 'I'm only thrilled you're here,' as if she'd just decided how pleased she was about the whole thing.

Ellen gave her a small tight smile. She was determined to say no more. She pushed the completed form and her credit card across the desk. Dorothy Flood held out a key to her.

'It's the best room we have,' she said.

'Thanks very much,' said Ellen.

She had wanted to say 'Thank you so much' and had stopped herself: that was the English way. There was a different way of saying things here. The tiredness was making one of her eyes twitch – she was winking now at the woman, who was pretending not to notice – and the smell of vomit, and cigarettes, seemed to be getting stronger and was rising up off her, surely, like heat.

She pulled the handle up on her suitcase. The smart click it gave cheered her a bit, and she said, quite sharply, 'Goodnight, Dorothy.'

She had to wrestle back a bit of control over the conversation – she wasn't going to start calling her Mrs Flood.

'Goodnight, Ellen, and god bless,' said Dorothy.

She went to up to the room, went in, and sat on the edge of the white bed, facing the window that looked out on the street. It was dark in the room, though there was a street light outside the window. She had thought that once she'd come this far she would feel something. But she didn't feel triumphant or happy, or even at peace. She felt, really, nothing at all. She'd lost the thread of the narrative she'd been telling herself for the last few months and all she felt now was an absence; there was an empty feeling in her throat, like a hunger.

Tá ocras orm. The hunger is on me.

She lay down on the white bed and turned her back to the window.

Every love story is a great love story in the beginning. The wonder of that beginning – she could almost taste it, still. And every love story changes, and the changing is a kind of end. It's the beginning of the thing that stays with you. She'd had too many endings, she thought, and not enough beginnings. She closed her eyes against the light.

Goodnight, baby, she said, in a whisper. She put her hand down flat on the empty space on the bed just in front of her and patted it. Goodnight.

Within minutes she was asleep.

THEY GOT WORD THAT evening, after the dinner. The boys were doing their homework at one end of the table. Her mother and Eily were sitting at the other end, pinning a pattern to the fine cotton that was to be for Eily's new summer dress. Eily was full of talk about the dance she was going to on Friday, and her mother was leaning towards her to listen and laughing and nodding, oh, oh yes, at everything she said. Dances and dresses – that's all that's in their heads, thought Hannah, the laughter making her twist in her chair.

Last week it had taken Eily three hours to get ready for the dance. Tom Feeney was going to be there, she'd heard, so she'd wanted to wear the good linen dress that had to be washed and starched and ironed the day it was washed, and ironed again just before she put it on, and she'd made sure that her stockings were washed too and dried in the morning air and her hair washed in rose water and plaited damp and then brushed out so that it fell in perfect golden waves around her face. Halfway through getting ready she'd declared she was too exhausted to go on and she'd undressed again – Mammy's fingers fumbling over the tiny buttons all the way down her back – and had lain down her shift and her stockings and Mammy had had to bring her a bowl of soup to the bed to revive her. When she was recovered she'd dressed again – the buttons! – and gone on with the preparations. 'Is it getting married you are?' her father had asked from the bedroom door. 'Is there a wedding happening that I don't know about?' but her mother had shouted at him to go away because Eily's mouth had begun to tremble querulously and it was left to Hannah to catch his eye and wink at him as he turned to go down the stairs.

The memory of that day, and the dance that followed, made Hannah have to swallow a shout now. Eily had danced all night with Tom Feeney. He had wanted to see her home, even, but Eily had said no – next time, she had said, laughing. Hannah had not danced at all. Only Frankie McCarthy had come to talk to her, and it had become clear after a couple of minutes of terrible conversation that he was talking to her only to find out if Eily was set on Tom. It was because she looked so cross, Eily had said to her as they'd cycled home. 'You stood there all night with a face on you that would frighten sheep. And you could do something about the hair, Hannah,' she'd shouted back to her as she'd sped away from her down the hill in the dark. 'Brush it, or have it cut, or something.'

If she wasn't careful, her mother had said the morning after, on hearing Eily's report of the night, Hannah would see Eily – with her golden hair and her ready smile – married before her, and it would be the long wait she'd be in for then, because no one would want the older sister who'd been passed over.

She was sitting by the low fire, pretending to read an old *Ireland's Own*. There was nothing else to read – there were no books in the house, apart from a cookery book by Mrs Beeton that had been a wedding present to her mother, and prayer books, of course, but there was nothing new to look at, nothing to divert her from herself. Blindly, she turned the pages of the magazine. She felt dull, and stupid, and lumpen, much like she'd felt at the dance, and then images began to surface in her mind of Eily laughing and dancing and the look on Tom's face as he watched Eily spinning in front of him and his smile and the easy way he had. It wasn't that she wanted anything to do with Tom Feeney, who came from a nine-acre farm up the mountain and smelled of cow dirt, but it was the way he had smiled at Eily. No one has ever smiled at me that way, she thought, and no one will, if things go on like this.

She stood up. She had to get out of this kitchen. She would say that she was going to bed – anything, to move. Her father was smoking by the back door, facing out across the yard. She was about to speak, and then she saw him shift uneasily. He stubbed out his cigarette under his boot and pulled up his pants around his hips, and then he called out into the night at the same time as he stepped back into the kitchen.

'Who's there?'

Someone was outside. The air seemed to go still for a minute; the evening itself seemed to hold its breath, and wait. Then Jimmy from the dairy stepped into the frame of the door. He was holding on to his new bicycle. He looked around the kitchen.

'Good evening to you all,' he said.

'Come in, Jimmy,' said her father, turning away from the door and walking into the kitchen. He paused and turned back. 'Leave the bicycle outside.'

Jimmy rested the bicycle against the side of the open door with great care, and came in, beating his terrible hair down with his hand. Hannah could feel him looking at her even as her father read the note that he'd handed him. She kept her eyes down. She'd no interest in Jimmy from the dairy.

'By god, it's warm enough in here to rear piglets,' he said approvingly, and he beat his hands together and puffed his cheeks out.

He was as young as her, but he spoke like a man of fifty: this was only one of the things she didn't like about Jimmy. She kept her eyes on her father, and gave no sign that she had heard what he'd said.

'We've news here,' said her father then, folding up the note very carefully as he spoke.

He was looking at a point in the ceiling; his cheeks were flushed with shyness. Hannah couldn't look at him. She could not remember a time when he'd addressed them like this; he had never, she was sure, spoken to them as a group before. She felt unsteady with the discomfort and the excitement.

'This is about that business in Skibbereen last week.'

He was looking at her mother and speaking to her directly now.

'The column split up after Skibbereen, and most of them headed through the pass, and made it into Kerry. But three of the lads are still on the run.'

He walked over to her mother and held the note out to her. She turned her head away, shaking it, no, and she put one hand tight over her mouth and the other hand across her chest and on her shoulder. Her father let his hand drop back down to his side.

'The countryside is crawling with Tans now, Noreen,' he said. 'They've blocked the roads around Skibbereen. They're searching the bogs.'

'One of them was injured a while back in Garrymore,' said Jimmy, sounding delighted, like he was reporting back on a match he'd seen that evening. 'He was shot in the leg and he has a bit of a limp now. And Jesus, another one went half mad they say and started crying for his mammy after the lorry exploded and it all started. He had to be dragged away from it. That's why they didn't make it to the pass. They were too slow.'

He winked at Hannah's brothers, then looked at Hannah out of the side of his eye to make sure she was watching him. She looked back at him until he looked at her straight on, and then she held his gaze, with all the disdain she could muster, until he dropped his eyes. He looked away from her, blinking.

'The lorry they blew up was carrying the general from the train station to the barracks,' he said. He sounded sombre now. 'And by god, they say they blew it to heaven. There were bits of bodies everywhere. The birds will be eating the flesh off the trees in Skibbereen for days to come yet.' He paused to let his words land. 'The general himself was thrown clear of the lorry and O'Riada finished him off with a shot to the head, close range.' He pulled out an imaginary gun and took aim. 'Pow pow,' he said, softly, reverentially.

'They're on their way here,' her father said, sitting down. 'They'll be here tonight, or tomorrow night.'

He put his hands down flat on the table like he was trying to keep it from floating away from him.

Her mother made a noise, 'Ahhh,' and stood up. 'No, no, no,' she said, too loudly. 'Is it simple you are? We've five children. Let them go somewhere else.'

Her face was dark red, and she was crying, but in anger: her face

32

was contorted and her mouth was flecked with spit. She's ugly with the anger, thought Hannah, watching her with fascination. They were all watching her. It was hard to look away.

'Noreen,' said her father. 'We have to take them. There's nowhere else for them to go between here and the pass.'

'I don't care!' shouted her mother, crying now and wringing her cardigan in her hands like it was wet and she was trying to dry it out. She walked over to her father. His head was down low, over the table, and his arms were spread out wide to the sides. She put her hands on the table and her face down in front of his so that their noses were almost touching. He didn't move.

'Do you hear me? They'll not come here. Do you want us all burned in our beds? Let the Tans have them.'

She stood up. She was opening and closing her fists, fast.

'Now,' she said, breathlessly, almost to herself. 'Now.'

Liam started to cry. Hannah walked over to him and put her arm around his small shoulders, and he hid his hot face in her thin dress and cried so that soon she was wet through to her leg.

Her father was looking at her mother like he was seeing her for the first time.

'They're coming here,' he said. His voice was very quiet. 'Go on now, Jimmy,' he said, not looking at him. 'They can come here. We're ready for them. You can tell them that.'

'Right, so,' said Jimmy, too cheerfully.

He took a quick side look at her weeping mother, craven interest flickering on his face, then went to the door and took hold of the bicycle. He wants to say goodbye holding on to the old bike, thought Hannah. She turned her back to him and picked up Liam.

'Goodnight all, now,' he said.

'Goodnight, Jimmy,' said her father, and the room was silent then, but for Liam's muffled sobs.

When her father spoke again, his voice didn't sound like his own. It sounded like a voice he was trying out.

'Go on up to your bedroom now, boys, and stay up there. Don't come down no matter what you hear. You stay up in that room. Do you hear what I'm saying to you?'

'I'm not finished my homework,' said Ciaran. He sounded like he was going to cry.

'Take the lamp upstairs with you,' her father said. 'You can finish the work in the bedroom. We can't have the master saying you didn't do the work.'

Hannah stayed standing perfectly still in the middle of the room as the boys left. She wanted desperately to sit down but she was afraid to move, so she stayed standing there, stupidly immobile, hardly breathing. The kitchen was dark without the light of the lamp; the darkness had stolen her breath, she thought, had taken it for itself. She put her hand up to her eyes. She was close to falling over, she knew, and then the boys' bedroom door banged shut, and she jumped at the noise. She opened her eyes. Her mother was walking very slowly back to the end of the table. She sat down heavily next to Eily.

Eily put her hand on her arm and said, 'Mammy.' Her mother's eyes were tiny red pinholes in her terrible white face.

Eily turned to her father.

'Look what you're after doing to her,' she shouted.

'Ah!' shouted her father.

He raised his hands in the air like he wanted to push them all away

34

and then he suddenly stood up, shoving back his chair with such force that it fell onto the ground. He will strike someone, thought Hannah. He kicked the chair away from him and began to walk to the open door.

'Hannah,' he said, as he walked past her, without turning around, 'get the room ready, and the food, too.' She saw him look down at Eily. 'Do you want to wake Mary to help you?'

'I can do it on my own,' she said.

Mary would be no help to her; she was afraid of the chickens in the yard.

He was out the door now, nearly.

'I'm going out to the shed to get the guns,' he said, and then he was gone into the black night.

Without looking at her mother or Eily, Hannah turned towards the range.

V

S HE WOKE AT HALF past five in the morning feeling as lonely as she'd ever felt in her life. It was already completely bright in the room; the savage light was beating against the wall in front of her. There was nothing as depressing as that hard, flat, empty early morning Irish light. It stripped everything bare; it made you feel bleached down to the bone. It was hard to get away from yourself in this kind of light, she thought. There was lovely light in Italy, and, of course, in Paris you were bathed in a glow from morning to night. But no, she thought, I had to come here and be blinded at half five in the morning.

She was lying on her side, with her hands between her thighs and her knees bent up towards her chin; she had barely moved all night. She stood up. She was still wearing her boots, even. Her jeans were cutting into her and when she took them off and looked down at herself she saw that they'd left ugly red marks on her body. She took the rest of her clothes off then, and turned to look at her reflection in the long mirror on the wall. She could almost read the writing on the imprint the jeans' button had made high on her stomach. There was a bright thin band of scarlet running under her breasts and around her back from where her bra had bitten into the soft flesh. I would burn these clothes if I could, she thought, this bra with its cruel bones, these too-tight knickers, these stiff, hard jeans. She picked up all her clothes and threw them across the room. She turned back to the mirror. With both hands she took hold of the hard roll of fat that hung over her hips and shook it. 'Uggh,' she said out loud, quietly. She didn't look at her face.

She unzipped her suitcase. It was full of the smell of home. She took out her beautifully folded clothes, and put them on the bed, then turned her shoes out of their shoe bags. She'd packed high heels! Silver ones! They were new; she turned them over and looked at their perfect, creamy soles. They were the shoes of the season: T-bar, conical heel, sold out across London. No one here would know that. No one here would care. She looked out the window at the white sky. It amazed her that only yesterday she'd been in a world where she'd considered silver high heels a necessity. She felt the old panic begin to descend again but she'd had sleep now and she was able to pull herself up. In America people went across the Rockies in wagons, she said to herself. They had to fight Indians. They had to eat each other to keep going. So keep going, Ellen.

She put the silver shoes back in the shoe bag and the shoe bag back in the suitcase and zipped it closed. She put her clothes away in the dresser, and when she'd finished she straightened up, too suddenly. She felt like she might fall over. She went to the bathroom and turned on the shower and when it was as hot as she could bear she got in and sat down on the floor and let the water hit her on the back of the head.

When she got out she dried herself and started to put on fresh

37

make-up, but her face was puffy and, really, if you didn't take the make-up off properly the night before it was a waste of time trying to do it in the morning – her skin wouldn't take it. She thought of all the articles she'd written about that: cleanse properly! Don't forget to tone! It was one of the easiest of beauty pieces to write, because no one could argue with the merits of washing your face. Whenever she'd been faced with a blank page, which had been, of course, too often, because she never planned ahead, she'd relied on the cleansing piece as a filler. On deadline day she would call the PRs she was friendly with and have them send over images of new products and underneath each she'd copy out the description she'd been sent, cutting out a few words and adding in lots of exclamation marks, and then she'd put the whole thing on a page with a picture of a celebrity in the middle. Lots of pictures, and lots of colour, and exclamation marks! – that was the key. The editor, a man, never questioned her: he considered the beauty page to be women's business and left her to it.

In the beginning, it felt like she had played a great trick on everyone. She had to do so little, and for that she was paid, and she got all the free beauty products she could use, and it was glamorous, too, she told herself, to be the beauty correspondent on a national newspaper. But after a while she began to tire of it all, of the windowless office, of the work itself, which was dull, deadening. And she was lonely: Simon left for work before she woke and she could go through a whole day in the office without speaking to anyone, really. The hours often weighed heavily on her. On some particularly dark days she felt like she almost didn't exist, that she was some kind of shadowy figure who inhabited the edges of reality. She had no real friend; she spent her time amongst people she'd known for, at most, a few years, and they all knew only a carefully edited version of her. She had never felt fully alive after leaving Ireland. She had never been fully herself, again.

She went into the bedroom and sat on the edge of the bed, naked. She looked down at her body. I am about to cry, she realized, and as soon as the thought came into her head the tears filled her eyes. She could cry, these days, almost at will. She lifted her head up and cleared her throat. Stop, she said in her head, so firmly that it was as if she'd said it out loud to herself. There's no one here to help you. Help yourself. So she stood up and put on the dressing gown and phoned Simon.

He answered after one ring.

'Good morning,' he said.

'Good morning,' she replied. 'How are you?'

'Good,' he said, cheerfully. Then he gave a small, measured, sigh. 'OK.' He's remembered he's talking to me, she thought, he doesn't want to waste his good cheer on me. 'How was the journey?'

'I made it anyway,' she said. 'The drive was the worst part. I got carsick towards the end and I had to throw up. It was carsickness and exhaustion combined, I think.'

'Poor Bunny,' he said, absent-mindedly.

In the beginning he had called her Bunny in affection; now it was what he called her all the time. He only called her Ellen when he was annoyed with her, or trying to convince her of something; her name, now, was a reprimand. He had forgotten, she thought sometimes, that she had ever been called Ellen. He had renamed her.

'Do you miss me, Simon?' she said, suddenly.

It was like picking at a scab, asking that question.

'I do, Bunny,' he said. 'But you only left yesterday.'

'Are you relieved I'm gone?'

'I'm not answering that question now,' he said. 'I just hope when you come back you'll be in much better form. Much better.' He paused. 'Yeah?'

She hated that yeah. It was a bullying yeah designed to elicit the yeah he wanted in response.

'Don't say yeah,' she said. 'You know it drives me mad.'

That's the wrong thing to say now but I don't care, she thought.

'Oh, for god's sake,' he shouted. 'Fine. I'm going now. I'll talk to you later.' He paused. 'Right?'

'Right,' she said, as coldly as she could, and hung up.

He hated being hung up on. He would ring her back now, she knew, saying don't hang up on me, so she threw the phone across the room and it ricocheted off the curtain. Her heart gave a jump like a baby kicking in the womb. I'd take my chances with the Rockies and the Indians any day, she thought.

She went to the mini-fridge that was on the floor under the writing desk and knelt in front of it on the hard carpet and took out the Toblerone and the jelly beans in the glass jar, and the bag of crisps and the chocolate bar in the gold wrapper, and sitting on the floor, with her legs sticking out in front of her like a doll's, she began to eat. She ate the crisps first, and then all the rest of it, as quickly as she could.

THE DINING ROOM WAS nearly empty. She went to a table set for two in the corner. There was an *Irish Times* folded on the table and she sat down and turned it over and pretended to start reading it. Dorothy hove into view within minutes.

'Did we sleep well?' she asked, with great good cheer.

'Very well, thanks,' said Ellen, and then added, 'It's a lovely room.'

'That's great,' said Dorothy. 'Now, are you ready to order? You must be starving. You had no dinner.'

I'll have five sausages and hot buttered toast and two eggs and bacon burned crispy and a pot of tea for two, she said to herself.

'I'll have the porridge with skimmed milk, please, Dorothy, and a herbal tea.'

'Oh, you're very good,' said Dorothy, in a kind of stage whisper. 'We have to look after the figure, don't we? Isn't it a struggle for us?' She looked at Ellen, too sympathetically for her liking. 'I can't resist a sausage myself,' she said, sadly, and she patted her high, round stomach. 'And chips. Homemade ones. Chips and sausages,' she said, with reverence.

Ellen smiled at her. She'd forgotten how much the people here loved to tell you things about themselves. It could almost fool you into thinking they were friendly. She knew that this information was offered as a kind of sop; it took these people years to talk to you properly. All of this was just a kind of dance that allowed everyone to go about their business with an almost formal kind of civility.

Dorothy snapped her pad shut.

'Are you going to the house today?' she asked.

'I am,' said Ellen. 'The agent is meeting me here at nine.'

'Is that John O'Connor?' asked Dorothy, too brightly.

'It is,' said Ellen.

'I'll keep an eye out for him,' said Dorothy. She put her head on one side and looked at Ellen sharply; she had bright, darting eyes like a robin's. She's clever enough, thought Ellen, cleverer than she lets on.

'I'll tell him we're related so he behaves himself.' She winked at Ellen suddenly, unexpectedly. 'I'll be back with the porridge.'

VI

THE NEXT MORNING, AFTER they'd arrived, she took the breakfast up to them. It was so early that the cows had yet to start roaring by the gate to be let out. O'Riada was sitting on the floor, with his back against the wall and his head hanging down; she wasn't sure if he was awake or asleep. The other two were asleep on the blankets she had put on the ground. He looked up, and she could see now that he was young – not much older than her, she thought. He was tall and broad across the back and when he looked at her it was with an expression of such energy and interest and intelligence that for a moment she just stood there and smiled at him like a simpleton. Then she put the basket with the breakfast down on the floor in front of him.

'Thanks,' he said.

She nodded at the ground.

'They're still asleep,' he said.

She looked at him; he was looking at the two men.

'They might as well sleep away,' he said. 'We're not going any-where today.'

They were up in the eaves of the house. There was a small window in one wall; it was open and a bird was flying in and out in beautiful arcs, swimming like a fish through the air. He watched it while he drank the tea. She stood there pretending to watch, too.

'What's the name for that bird?' he said.

Her tongue felt thick and useless in her mouth.

'I only know the word for it in the Irish,' he said. 'Fáinleog.'

'It's a swallow,' she said. 'My father says that they swallow the air as they fly.'

He didn't answer.

'Tá fhios agam caint as Gaeilge,' she said. I can speak Irish.

Her mother didn't like her to. Speak English, Hannah, she said always. Who'll want you, speaking Irish like an old one?

He stood up but he didn't look at her. He walked over to the window and put an arm on either side of it and leaned out, and looked at the purple mountains beyond.

Without waiting to think, she said, quickly, and in English, 'Is it terrible?'

She felt so embarrassed that she nearly turned and ran down the stairs.

She thought he would not answer. Then he said, quietly, without turning around, 'It's bad enough, all right.'

There was a stir in the room. They turned to look, and one of the men, the big one, was sitting up.

'How was the night?' he said, looking at Hannah with undisguised interest.

'Grand,' answered O'Riada shortly, walking away across the room. 'All quiet.'

44

The big man groaned theatrically, and stood up, stretching his arms out.

'Oh god, oh god,' he said. 'Is there any bit of food?'

'I brought the breakfast,' said Hannah.

'Oh, god bless you,' he said, winking at her.

He took a hunk of the bread from the basket and shoved it in his mouth, looking at Hannah all the time.

'You've made the acquaintance, I see, of our commander-in-chief,' he said, eventually. 'Is he full of the chat? Are you full of the chat, O'Riada?'

Hannah went down on her knees and started to take the things out of the basket.

'It's a fine day,' said O'Riada. 'It will be a clear night. We'll head out tonight.'

Hannah looked up at the big man. His big face had collapsed a little.

'Right, so. The leg is still killing me but whatever you think best. But would we be well advised to take it easy here for one more day? It's all quiet,' he said, and his voice was wheedling now, 'and the rest will be doing Tiernan the power of good. The nerves are shot to feck with him. Is he able at all do you think to head out tonight? Would we be the wise men to keep the heads down for another day?'

'We go tonight,' said O'Riada.

He didn't look at them. He took his shining gun out of his belt and started to clean it with the end of his shirt. There was no expression on his face.

'You and Brennan go on.'

It was the third man. He was sitting up against the wall; Hannah didn't know how long he had been awake, and listening.

'I'll head out on my own,' he said. He sounded angry, like he was already halfway through an argument he was losing. 'I'd only slow you down. If I started shouting and roaring again, and us in the pass, I could bring the whole fecking British Army down on us.'

'He's right,' said Brennan.

'No,' said O'Riada. 'He's not. And no one's asking you what you think. You're to do what you're told and that's all you're to think about.' He turned to Tiernan. 'You'll be grand after that sleep you had last night. You're coming with us.'

Brennan threw his hands up in the air.

'Ah, sure, I'm after forgetting that the country boyos have to stick together. Didn't the two of you run around the schoolyard with no shoes on and not a word of English between you? All stick together now, boys! O, a cuaisle a cuaisle! All together now for a bullet in the head when Tiernan starts his crowing again tonight.'

There was a terrible silence in the room. Hannah felt the heat rise up in her face. Without even wanting to she looked at O'Riada, and he, sensing the movement, looked across the room at her. His eyes were all pupil, black and flat. He can't see me, she thought. His eyes are too black with anger to see. There is danger here, she thought, and I am afraid. She stood up and turned away from the men and started to walk towards the stairs. Her throat felt tight. It was hard to swallow, and it was hard to see properly; the edges of the room seemed blurred to her.

'I'm only saying it for Tiernan,' Brennan was saying sulkily. 'I'm as ready as the next man. If it wasn't for the old leg—'

Hannah heard him sit down heavily on the ground, as if he'd been pushed.

'You'll have that gun polished away,' Brennan was continuing brazenly, but his voice sounded tight. 'I'd say 'tis the cleanest gun in West Cork. The Big Fella himself doesn't have a cleaner gun.'

He gave a sharp, defiant laugh at his own joke.

'Isn't that right, miss?' he shouted after Hannah, almost desperately. 'Doesn't he have a lovely shiny gun? Lovely black curls and a shiny gun, fighting and dying for old Ireland.'

Hannah turned.

Brennan was sitting on the ground and O'Riada was standing above him. He was holding his gun to the back of Brennan's head, and on Brennan's face was a look of such fear and shame that she almost cried out in pity.

'This is the last time I tell you this,' said O'Riada. 'We don't leave a man behind. We don't even leave our dead behind. Do you hear what I'm saying to you? You've been trouble since we started out and I'll have no more trouble from you.'

He hit Brennan across the back of his head with the gun. Brennan crouched down, away from the blow, and put his hands up to shield himself from further, expected, blows. It is not the first time he has been hit, she thought.

'I hear you,' he said to the ground.

'Do you? Do you?' said O'Riada, and he raised his gun again and clicked it, lightly, softly.

'He hears you,' said Tiernan.

He was on his feet, standing behind O'Riada.

'Give me the gun.'

He put his hand on O'Riada's shoulder.

'A chara,' said Tiernan. 'My friend. No.'

O'Riada dropped his hand to his side. His shoulders were rising and falling as if he had run a race.

Tiernan put his hand out and O'Riada handed him the gun.

No one seemed to breathe for a moment, then Tiernan turned to her as if he'd just remembered that she was there.

'Go on out of it, miss,' he said. 'Go away.'

She walked backwards, falling shamefully, and through the open attic door she went, and down the ladder into Mary's room and then started down the narrow attic stairs, flying like a bird through the air, her hands pushing out against the walls pressing in on her, down the wider stairs past her sleeping family, into the kitchen. Her father was standing in front of the low fire with his hands out to it.

She went to the sink so she had her back to him. She was ashamed of her burning face.

'You gave them the breakfast?' he said.

'I did,' she said, trying to make her voice flat. She put her hands in the empty sink, looking for something to do, to hold on to. Her heart was beating so fast that she had to fight to stop herself from putting her hand on her chest to steady it.

It was hard to speak, but the silence hung heavy now she'd stopped speaking. She didn't want to worry him with the silence, so she added, 'They'll leave tonight, they said.'

'No,' he said. 'Surely they'll stay for a couple of days. It's too much them coming and going in the one day.'

She nodded. She didn't know. She knew nothing, she realized suddenly. The weight of what she didn't know, what she didn't understand, was too much to take in.

'He's only young, O'Riada,' said her father. 'He's not more than twenty-two. But they say there's few men better than him. They say Michael Collins himself holds him in high regard.'

She turned around.

'Won't they want him even more so, Dadda?' she said. 'If he's well known, if Michael Collins speaks well of him, won't the Tans be mad after him?'

She sounded like a child, she thought. I'm no better than Eily, or Mary hiding in her bed.

'I'll go up and talk to them now,' he said. 'I'll be back down before Denis comes.'

He picked up the Webley that he'd put on the table and held it out to her, flat on the palm of his hand.

'I didn't want to give you this last night in front of Mammy,' he said. 'You'll have to take it now, Hannah. You know how to use it – sure, I never saw anyone learn how to handle a gun faster.' He tried to smile at her. 'I have one and you take this one. Hide it somewhere you can get to fast. Tell no one.'

She walked over to him and took the gun. It was cold and heavy in her hand.

'We'll be all right, girl,' he said to her.

There was nothing to say. You're wrong, Dadda, she thought.

I know that much now, anyway. I know we won't be all right, at all.

She tightened her grip around the gun, rubbing her thumb against it, and watched her father as he walked up the stairs, towards the attic.

VII

I NEED LUCOZADE AND CRISPS, she thought to herself as soon as she got into John O'Connor's car. And a Valium. And then a cigarette. She gave him a small formal smile and settled herself into the seat and clipped on the seat belt. When he turned to put on his seat belt she hoicked up the waistband of her leather trousers over her stomach and adjusted her top. She'd put the cashmere wrap on the back seat; she would drape herself in that when they arrived at the house. She didn't want to run the risk of forgetting to hold the hated stomach in when she was distracted.

He'd insisted on driving her. She had wanted to follow him in her own car but he wouldn't have it, so here she was, trapped. The car was almost unbearably warm, and it smelled, she noted with alarm, of very strong air freshener – there were three terrible little pine trees hanging in a cluster from the mirror.

I won't be sick again – that part, at least, was over, she thought. She used the word 'sick' now like an English person, even in her head, to herself. 'I am sick,' she had said once to a grand English friend and they had looked at her with alarm: to be sick was to vomit. One was ill, and sometimes, regrettably, one was sick. Dogs vomited. Americans threw up. She felt ill now, but she wouldn't be sick, and so she amused herself for a moment imagining having to vomit in this car and the panic and ensuing awfulness. John O'Connor was the kind of man who loved his car: he had walked into the dining room jingling his car keys on his small finger, with the little BMW disc glinting in the light. She looked at him. Imagine him thinking she'd be impressed by his car. A car! He knew nothing of her. He was operating so far from the reality of her world that he might as well have been waving at her from the other side of a thick glass wall. She was impressed by almost nothing, nothing, that money could buy. She had been surrounded by money for so long now that she was cold to it. She looked across at him. You think you're the big man, with your shiny car and your shiny shoes and me sitting here nice and quiet with my seat belt on, she thought. You haven't got a clue. She felt quite suddenly a shot of something like happiness run through her. I've earned my freedom from people like John O'Connor, she thought. At least I've managed that.

She wound down the window and the damp cool air wrapped itself around her head. She closed her eyes for a moment. She might have to be sick after all.

He turned on the ignition.

'Now, so,' he said.

She said nothing, but he didn't seem to mind; he didn't need her to speak. He turned the car onto the street and waved at someone on the footpath.

'Howya, Joe,' he shouted through the closed window.

She watched him. He was a big man – his thighs were straining against his too-tight trousers, and he had huge hands, like shovels. The life was bursting out of him.

'You're from the town, John?' she asked.

She saw in the half-second it took him to reply that he was surprised at her asking a question. He doesn't approve, she thought. He wants to be the one asking the questions this early on.

'I am,' he said. 'Born and bred. Sure, I went up to the city there to college, I did Arts —' History and Irish, she thought to herself — 'but when I finished I came back here and went into the business with my father, the timing was right.'

He'd been wearing a suit since he was twenty-four and sure of his welcome at every turn; his father's son, handsome, easy in his manner, the quick word always to hand. She thought of the people she knew who had learned to turn their faces away from the world and who were bent down and into themselves, broken by having to leave a whole life behind and start another life somewhere else. It was perilous to leave your own place behind — she understood that, now. How much easier it was to stay under the skies that had made you, to stick to a predestined course, not to have to cleave yourself from the life you should have had.

'Are you long gone from home?' he said.

'I left after college,' she said. 'As soon as I could.'

'Straight to London?'

'Before London I went to America,' she said, and because it comforted her to hear the word, and all it meant, she said, again, 'America. I was only there a few years and then I moved to London. For work.'

It seemed incomprehensible to her now that she had once been a person who had moved continents because of work; it felt like she was speaking about a different person, entirely. She knew that she had once been vibrant and bright, someone of some import at the beginning of her career, someone to be reckoned with, even. She'd peaked too early, a friend had told her once. They had been trying to be unkind, but they had been wrong, she'd thought at the time; the trouble was that she had never peaked at all.

'And the family's still here?' John said.

'They are.'

'Dorothy said that on the phone.'

Dorothy had phoned him. Well.

'The house we're going to was my grandparents'.'

'That's right.'

He, unlike Dorothy, was unaffected by this information. He doesn't like me much, she thought. I'm not twenty-three anymore, and he's probably five years younger than me and I'm overweight and my clothes are wrong. The women here dressed carefully in open-toed high-heeled pumps and wrap dresses and good coats and wore lots of make-up and little gold earrings and had lovely shiny hair. None of them were stuffed into too-tight leather leggings or wore very big sunglasses in November or had hair that was meant to look a bit undone but probably just looked mad. She remembered being twenty-three and men looking at her face like it held the answer to a question they had to answer. When she was twenty-three she could throw drinks at people in pubs and slap someone during an argument and say something true and cruel and clever and it was all, always, all right; her beauty had been like a key that opened all the little locked doors in people's minds, click click click, and let her in, and out.

She looked out the window. They had left the town and were heading towards the mountains.

'How long will it take us?'

'Not long, about an hour,' he said.

She turned around.

'An hour?'

'We'll be there before you know it. The road is grand until we get up into the hills.'

'They were very isolated in that house,' she said. 'They were a long way from the town.'

'They were, I suppose,' he said. 'But they'd have had the local community – the other farmers, the dairy, the national school – near enough. The people at that time never left their place. They were lucky if they made it to the city once in their lifetime. They would have come to the town once a year, maybe, for the mart, or at Christmas. Sure, they never went anywhere unless it was to go to America, and they never came back from there.'

'It was hard for them,' she said.

'Ah, it was harder and it was easier,' he said, waving his hand. She laughed and, encouraged, he repeated, 'Harder and easier.'

'You're interested in the place because of your family?' he said, after a minute. He was better disposed to her now, she thought.

'I am,' she said. 'I suppose. They were there during the 1920s and the War of Independence and all of that. And before, even.'

'Ah, yeah,' said John, with a laugh. 'That land was O'Donovan land when the people were still running cattle through the woods.'

He was laughing at her. She'd been gone long enough now for him to feel comfortable laughing at her like she was an outsider.

'They're well known, the O'Donovans,' he said. 'You know, I suppose, of Hannah O'Donovan, and what happened with the Black and Tans and your man O'Riada and all that?'

'I do,' she said. 'My grandmother used to say that the farm was lost to them because of what happened at that time, and she was always sorry about that, she always said that things would have turned out differently for the family if we'd been able to stay where we belonged. Things went wrong once they moved to the city.'

'It happened to a lot of people,' said John. 'Once they had to leave the land, they were lost themselves, really. They weren't a people made for the city.'

'No,' she said.

She looked at the land moving past her in a slow green spool and the great white sky beyond it and put her hand up to the car window.

'In London you can't see the horizon,' she said suddenly.

Her voice sounded too high to her.

'London,' he said. 'None of my people ever had to go to London.'

'No horizon!' she said. 'And I'm getting old now, John, I'm nearly forty. Too old for London.'

He looked over at her. There was something in his eyes that she couldn't read.

'So you've come back here,' he said.

'Which is funny,' she said, 'if you think about it. Because I ran out of the place.'

She had said too much. She wasn't used to saying so much. She put the back of her hand against her open mouth as if she would hold her face together. Her chin was jerking a bit: ever since the first miscarriage there was a nerve that pulled at the side of her mouth and make her chin jump when she was tired, or anxious.

'Ah, sure,' he said. 'It all changes once you're headed for the big four-oh.'

'That's it,' she said. She remembered her friend Mary from school saying that. Her parents were from the country. It sounded right, so she repeated herself. 'That's it, sure.'

'Is your husband Irish, too?'

'No, he's English,' she said.

'And do you have any children?'

She could tell from the casual way he said it that it wasn't easy for him to ask. He'd asked, though; he wanted to know. Everyone always wanted to know.

'No,' she said. 'Not yet.'

I've had four miscarriages, John, she wanted to say, and then a stillbirth a few months ago, so no, none yet.

'Do you have any?' she said.

'Three,' he said. 'We're mad. Three. Two would have been enough for me but the wife wanted three.'

'I'd say you have your hands full,' she said, grimly. 'But it must be great fun.'

'Define fun,' he said, forgetting himself, and she laughed, then, properly, and he laughed back in response.

She looked at him, considering.

'Will we stop for a cigarette?'

They had only been driving for half an hour, but she wanted to get out of this car suddenly. And she wanted to give him a bit of a shock. The women he knew would have given up smoking after college. No one in his circle would smoke. It wasn't of his class. Women who worked in supermarkets smoked. For someone like her to smoke – it made her nearly unIrish. She's been too long in England, he would think, and he'd almost feel sorry for her.

He stopped the car by the side of the road.

'Work away,' he said.

She got out of the car. They were in open country now. It was hilly land, and rough, and the few trees there were ash and rowan, a few old crooked hawthorn, twisted from the wind. She remembered driving through the countryside as a child and asking her father where all the trees were.

'The English took them,' he said, and she had felt sad for the poor trees, imagining them being pulled up from the land by the roots and it hurting them, and then being put on ships and taken to England, and all the time them crying for Ireland and their cold bare roots white and sore in the air.

She took out a cigarette. She didn't want it, but she lit it and took a long drag and then let her hand drop to her side, the smoke rising out and up into the air. She definitely felt sick now. The wind was stabbing at her and the sun was breaking through the scudding clouds, hurting her head.

She looked out at the land. It wasn't pretty like the English countryside, but it was beautiful enough to break your heart. Everything in this country would make you heartsick, she thought, taking another, deeper drag of the cigarette. You were only able for it, really, if your heart had already been broken. So she was all right, then, she thought, exhaling, slowly, up into the sky. She was broken enough now, finally, to be able to come home.

VIII

S HE WAS COLD, THOUGH the range was hot and there was
already warmth in the day outside, but she was cold in her bones
and her hands felt damp and cool and too smooth to the touch. She
had put on her apron and put the gun in its big front pocket. It was
heavy. There was something wrong about how heavy it was. It pulled
the apron down and made the ties around her neck dig into her
skin, but she couldn't think where else to put it; her mind wouldn't
let her think. She stirred the porridge with one hand and rested the
other on top of the gun. The metal was warm, now. It had taken
the warmth from her.

It had been early in the morning when the Tans had come, and
a sweet, still day it had been, the first good day of spring and not
a sign of trouble until they heard the boots in the yard. There had
been five of them but when they first came into the house it had felt
like they were a great crowd and them all shouting and pushing and
making a terrible noise. The one who was in charge had pushed her
father against the table while he was shouting the questions at him
and he'd stumbled, had nearly fallen down on his knees, and when
she went to help him he'd shouted at her too but he hadn't touched

her; he had told her to get outside with the children, get in the yard, missy. They'd looked all over the house, laughing and calling to each other as they went from room to room. One of them had fallen over Liam's little wooden chair with its seat of rushes and the others had laughed at him and he'd kicked it to pieces then in his anger. They had thrown the boys' schoolbooks on the floor so that the spines were broken, and emptied out all the presses and threw the clothes out of the windows and all the white things had floated like leaves down onto the dirty yard, and Mary had run around trying to catch them as they fell, her face turned up to the windows and her eyes wide and terrible-looking.

Before they left one of them had hit her father in the side of the head with the end of his gun. She'd heard him, days later, talking to Johnny Mac about it.

'They picked the wrong head, by god. They'd need more than a rifle end to put a dent in this, I tell you,' and they had laughed, and she had burned with the anger and the shame of it all and turned and walked away before they could see her.

The memory of that day was too fresh in her head, still, so even though the porridge wasn't nearly ready she put the spoon down on the stove and went out into the yard. Mary was filling the bucket from the pump. She was singing very quietly to herself.

'When you've finished that, Mary, will you come in?' she said.

She'd enough of Mary hiding outside for an hour in the morning while she faced her mother. Mary straightened up. She looked confused. She was fifteen years old, only four years younger than her, a big, quiet girl from the mountains in Kerry. When she'd first arrived, before they'd tired of it, the boys used to make fun of her accent, just loudly enough for her to hear. Oh, Mary is a grand girl. Mary would carry a churn for you. Eily had laughed at her frizzy halo of hair and her white, plain face and her clothes.

'She doesn't own a thing, I'd say, that came from a shop. I'd say she's never even been inside a shop. Sure, they wouldn't let her in,' she'd said once and her mother had said, 'Eily, stop,' but with a laugh.

'I want to take the horse out early, Mary. Will you help me with the breakfast?' she said. She turned before Mary could answer her and went back into the kitchen.

Her brothers were sitting at the table. Liam's face had been washed and his hair had been brushed down flat on his head and he was wearing his good jumper.

'You're all ready for school,' she said, making herself smile approval at him though it was hard to talk and nod and smile.

'Eoin brushed my hair,' he said. 'It hurt me. Where's Dadda?'

She brought the bread over to the table and started to slice it.

'He's busy now,' she said.

'With the men who came last night?' asked Liam.

He had lovely eyes, green like her father's, and the black circle in the middle was ringed with brown. All the rest of them had her mother's too-pale blue. He had a small freckled nose and ears that stuck out like handles on a jug. She took hold of one of his ears and pulled on it softly.

'Don't mind that,' she said. 'Eat your breakfast.'

She looked at Eoin and Ciaran. They were watching her. They were both still, silent, and their faces were drawn tight and pale. She shook her head at them, no.

Eily came in and sat down. She arranged her dress over her knees, pat, pat, and smoothed down her hair. Then she poured herself the tea and drank it, looking off into the distance like she was absorbed in some lovely but sad thought. You think we're all watching you, all the time, thought Hannah. That's why you fix your face like that, with your lips open a bit and the eyes down. You think you look gorgeous. You look like a gomeen.

Mary was at the range now.

'I'm going out on Pangur,' said Hannah. 'Tell Mammy when she comes down.'

'What about the breakfast?' said Eily, and she turned herself slowly in her chair to look at her as she spoke. 'Where's the porridge?'

'You know what to do,' said Hannah.

'And them upstairs?'

'That's done already,' she said.

She started to take her apron off and stopped. She'd eaten nothing since yesterday and slept only fitfully. She picked up a piece of bread and folded it over and shoved it into her mouth and took a drink of milk; the bread stuck for a minute in her throat and she had to sputter some of the milk out. She was aware of Eily watching her. Without looking at her, she walked out of the kitchen and into the yard; once she was outside she wiped her mouth with the back of her hand and then her hand on her apron.

'Come here a minute, will you.'

Eoin was behind her. He put his hand on her arm. She shook it off.

'I've to get the horse.'

'I'll come with you.'

They walked across the yard and under the stone arch. The horse

63

had its head over the stable half-door; he gave a soft neigh when he saw them.

'Fan noiméad,' she called to him. Wait.

She went into the tack room. She took the apron off and hung it on a peg. She put the bridle over her shoulder and the saddle across her arm.

She went to the horse and put her hand on his nose, and then laid her head against his warm cheek. The horse, waiting for her to speak, slowed his breathing.

'Hello, my friend,' she said.

'What are they like?' said Eoin.

She stood up, stroking the horse's nose.

'There's three of them,' she said. 'They're young.'

'Did they say anything?'

'No. They're leaving tonight.'

'They'll need help getting from here to the pass. Some of the lads from the team said they'd take them. I'd take them.' She could hear the eagerness in his voice.

'Wouldn't they be delighted,' she said, 'to know that they're to have a crowd of amadáns with hurleys leading them through the fields? Wouldn't they sleep easy knowing that?'

He didn't answer and she turned to look at him; he had dropped his head with embarrassment. He had always been easily hurt, and she was sorry, suddenly, and then, terribly, she felt hot shameful tears come into her eyes.

'Daddy said we're to stay away from them,' she said. 'They'll find their own way. It's not our business once they're gone from here.'

'Hannah,' he cried. 'It's our business all right. Who else are they doing it for but us and our kind?'

'I know,' she said. 'I know that. But you're fourteen. You're in school. And you've to watch the other two. They've no sense. You have to take Liam to school now and make sure he doesn't gab all over the place, and Ciaran, too. Daddy will look after things. We each have our own bit to do. You do your bit.'

'What are you doing?' he said, sulkily.

'What I'm told to,' she said.

'Jesus, that's the first time I've heard you say that,' he said.

She pretended to aim a kick at him, and he gave a hop out of the way.

'Go on now,' she said, with affection.

She opened the stable door and went inside. She put the bridle on the horse, and then the saddle. She walked him out, clicking to him.

'Hold him a minute,' she said to Eoin, handing him the reins.

She went back into the tack room, and went to the apron on the peg and took out the gun. She held it flat against her forehead for a moment. Think, she told herself. Think faster, think better. She was wearing a cardigan and a thin cotton dress to her knees and her old boots over her bare legs. She opened the top two buttons on her dress, and put the gun down inside her undershirt. It lay between her breasts against the band of her brassiere. She buttoned up her dress and the cardigan and looked down at herself. The gun was too big: her chest was uneven and bevelled, ridiculous-looking. She ran her hand over herself and then shifted the gun so it sat under one of her breasts. It was uncomfortable, but it looked better, she thought; she shook herself a bit, and the gun barely moved. Then she turned around and walked out of the stable, slowly, looking down at herself.

Eoin was facing the horse with one rein in each hand. He was holding the reins too short and pulling the bit down.

'Don't hold him like that,' she said. 'You know it hurts his mouth.'

'He's an impatient fecker,' said Eoin. 'I'm trying to distract him. Aren't you an impatient fecker?'

'Come here to me,' she said to the horse.

She took the reins from Eoin and stood to the horse's side, facing his tail. She put the foot nearest his flank in the stirrup and the horse began to dance across the cobblestones, away from her, so in one smooth movement she threw herself across his back and lifted her leg over and into the other stirrup. She gathered up the reins through the air and then pulled up her dress so it was bunched between her thighs, exposing the length of her legs hanging down.

Eoin walked over to her and put his hand on the horse's neck. He didn't look up at her.

'What am I to say if anyone asks me if we have news?'

The horse was dancing now, backwards and forwards.

'You're to say nothing,' she said. 'Say we've heard nothing.'

He looked up at her, and then he looked beyond her, over her shoulder and up at the window in the attic; some movement had caught his eye. She turned the horse around in a small circle and looked up. She could see nothing, but she knew he was up there, watching her. She had to stop herself raising her hand in a hello. She turned the horse around again, and looked at Eoin.

'I'm going up to the long field, and beyond. I'm going to see that it's all quiet.'

66

'Ah, Jesus, Hannah,' said Eoin with sudden desperation. 'And if it's not? Did Daddy tell you to go as far as the long field?'

'I'll be back soon,' she said. 'He needs the run anyway.'

She put her legs to the horse's side.

'Come on,' she said. It came out in nearly a shout and the horse threw his head back in surprise.

They left the yard in a great clatter, and her with her hand across her heart, holding on.

I X

S HE'D HAD THE SAME dream again last night, she realized.
You can't tell anyone your dreams, no one wants to hear them.
They're only interesting to you. Simon had told her that a long
time ago.

She wondered what John the estate agent would do if she said to
him, 'I had a baby who died, John. And ever since she died I keep
having the same dream. I dream I'm on a small boat with the baby
and we're on a very hot still sea and the baby is getting burned
because I have no suncream and she's not dressed properly, I don't
have a sunhat for her and there's no cover on the boat. And we're
drifting away from a big boat and my father is on that boat and I'm
calling out to him to help us but he doesn't hear me, he just keeps
drifting away, and eventually I shout out so loudly that I wake myself
up, and that's how the dream ends. I have other dreams, and some
of them are terrible, but this is the one I have most often. What do
you think it all means, John? My father is dead. What am I doing
calling for him? My husband doesn't want to talk about it, he can't
bear to talk to me about anything really, and I've no real friends, I
don't have even one good friend I can talk to but I feel I can talk

to you and I'm curious to hear what you think, John, I really am.'

They'd turned off the road now and were driving down a lane with grass growing along the middle of it. The ditches on either side were too high to see over. It was like descending into a sea of green water: the air was green, the sky overhead was green; the car was swimming through the greenness. John had hardly spoken since she'd got back into the car, stinking of cigarette smoke, but he tapped the dashboard now with one finger and pointed ahead.

'Here we are,' he said. 'You've your own private entrance off the main road, grand and private.'

She nodded. She had been about to say something about no one being able to hear you scream here but she let it go, which was a tiny victory for John that he didn't even know about.

They came to the end of the lane and turned into a yard. John switched off the engine and they both sat in silence for a minute, looking at the house.

'Well, now,' he said, and it came out as a question that hung in the air.

She said nothing. The house was a grey stone farmhouse. It had small windows, a low front door. The glass in most of the windows was broken. There was grass growing between the stones in the yard.

She got out of the car and walked towards the house. John followed her. She stood looking at it. Neither of them said anything for a long time.

'My grandmother, Rose, used to say that her mother ran a beautiful house,' she said, eventually. 'She used to make her own brown bread every day; she remembered the smell of it. The family had a maid at one time, and a business in the town.'

'Oh, they did, they were a well-respected people,' said John.

She could feel him watching her.

She walked up to the house. She touched the pale stone, pat pat pat.

'They shot them out here, didn't they? In the yard.'

'That's what they say,' he said. He was looking up at the roof, the walls, his face twisted against the thin sun.

'I'm looking for the bullet holes,' he said, without turning to look at her. 'My father told me you can still see the bullet holes in the wall.'

'Let's go in,' she said.

'Right,' he said, quickly, lightly.

He went to the door and pushed at it. It gave a little.

'It's not locked,' he said. 'Only stuck.'

He gave it a hard shove with his shoulder. The door gave way, and he stepped inside.

She followed him into the kitchen. It was a long, narrow room with a low ceiling. She thought of her Georgian townhouse in London and its soaring ceilings – it was a different world here, small and mean and dark. The people here would have had to walk around nearly bent over, only half able to see things, scrambling about, almost, looking down, always. It would have done something to their minds, surely, she thought, to never have been able to look up, to be forced to look down like that all the time; it must have shaped how they saw the world. She felt a sudden, desperate, familiar stab of anger. Such darkness they had had to fight against, she thought, a darkness put upon them.

John was walking around the kitchen. There was a range along one wall, and some blackened pots still on the grate. There was a table in the middle of the room, with broken chairs set against it, crookedly, and a glass-fronted cupboard with a few cups and plates on its shelves. In the corner of the room was a stack of old newspapers. There was a clock on the wall, its hands stopped at six.

'The furniture is still here,' she said. She felt unsteady, uneasy. This was not what she had expected, at all. 'They left it all behind them.'

'It was sold for the land,' said John. 'The farmer who bought the place from the family had no interest in the house, my father said. He didn't walk inside the door in all the years he had it, they say.'

He looked around the kitchen. 'The family left a lot behind them all right,' he said. 'I suppose they were going to the city and they thought, what do we want it for? They'd have had a sale and what didn't sell they just left. Maybe they thought they'd buy all new things in the city.'

But it's as if they just walked out of here yesterday, she thought. This isn't right. What did they take with them? The clothes on their backs. The Singer sewing machine, the good crockery with the red and blue pattern and the gold rim that she remembered from her grandmother's little house in the city. Photographs. Things they could carry, she realized. Things they could take with them in a hurry.

It was dark in the kitchen – not dark like the night, but grey, like a late dusk, and full of shadows. The air was warm and heavy and smelled of damp. There was thick dust on every surface. She put her hand on the table and when she lifted it up her handprint was perfectly formed on it. It was difficult, suddenly, to breathe. Her handprint looked terribly wrong on the table. She had disturbed the air in the room. She had left a mark.

John had gone through to another room, and she went after him. She could not be left alone here.

'There's a little living room here,' he called back to her, already moving on.

She looked into the room. It smelled like the cold, wet Sunday afternoons of her childhood. There was a chair by the window, empty shelves on the walls.

John had gone up the stairs already.

'The bedrooms,' he shouted down. She could hear him throwing open doors.

Two of the rooms and the landing had been papered in a rose print that had been bleached by the sun to white in places; in the corners, where it touched the ceiling, it was curling off the walls. The air was different up here. It's softer, she thought. Lighter. And it's fizzing with something strange.

She went into the smallest of the rooms. There was a single metal bed frame against one wall, but no other furniture. She stood in front of the fireplace and put her hand out to touch a rose on the wall. John came in behind her and in two steps was at the window, his huge frame blocking the light; he was filling up the room, dominating it. She felt the change in the air almost like a physical thing on her skin. Get out, she nearly said. You shouldn't be in here. She wouldn't have wanted you in here. She wouldn't have liked you. She knew that suddenly, with certainty, and then felt cold and afraid that she should know such a thing. Her heart gave a painful flip in her chest.

'This might have been Hannah's room,' she said.

She was surprised at how difficult it was to say her name. The sound of it fell into the silence of the room like a stone falling down an empty well.

'Ha?' he said. 'Oh, at one stage, maybe.'

He was already going out of the room, bowing his head low under the door frame.

'There's one more room above,' he said. 'The maid's room. And above that there's the attic.'

They went up the stairs. They became narrower with every step. John had to ascend them sideways. He had cobwebs in his hair and his dark jacket was dusted white from the walls now.

'Maid's room,' he said, opening the door at the top of the stairs. He sounded impatient.

He went in front of her. It was a narrow, dark room with a sloping roof.

'The attic's above,' he said. 'There's a secret door in the ceiling.'

There was a ladder lying on the floor, against the wall. He stood it up. It had two missing rungs. He shook the ladder, annoyed.

'Will we risk it?' she said, trying to sound cheerful, trying to jolly him along like they were having an adventure together. She was uncomfortable with this unhappy John.

'Right,' he said. He looked up at the ceiling. 'There it is over there,' he said. 'My father told me where to look.'

It was hard to see it. If you didn't know where to look, it would be nearly impossible to spot.

'They did a good job with that,' she said.

'They did,' he said, putting the ladder against the wall and standing on the lower rungs, testing them out. 'They had to. Anyone they had to hide they'd have hidden them up there. It's been there since the days they were hiding priests, I'd say. And the rest of the time it would have been used for the men to sleep in during the harvest or the like.' He gave a wave, an expansive et cetera, and then, with a deliberate sigh, started up the ladder. 'Hold it for me.'

As she held it, she watched him go up. He was too heavy – he would break it, surely. And he looked ridiculous climbing up in his tight suit and his pointy shoes. He looked like he was in the wrong place, completely. He got to the top and pushed at the door. It was stuck, and he had to shove at it with all his strength. The ladder wobbled.

'Hold the ladder,' he shouted, alarmed. She was going to start laughing, she thought, and she had to bite her lip to stop herself. Her chin began to crease with the effort of not laughing.

'Jesus,' he said, in disgust, and looked down at his dusty suit, and then up at the door. He gathered himself together and gave it a great grunting push and the door swung open. He put a hand on either side of the opening and heaved himself up. She could hear him upstairs, walking around.

'Will I come up?' she called.

She heard him coming back. He leaned down through the opening.

'Come on,' he said. He held on to the top of the ladder and she came up slowly, testing each rung before she put her foot on it.

'We need a new ladder,' she said.

'That's the least of your problems,' he said.

She stopped and looked up at him.

'You know what I mean,' he said, trying to keep the annoyance out of his voice. 'Come on.'

She got to the top of the ladder. He put his hand out for hers and pulled her up.

The attic was long and had a high roof. There was a window high up in the wall at the end of the room. The air smelled strangely sweet.

'It's nice,' she said.

'It's a good space,' he said, mollified. 'You could convert it. Attic conversions are all the rage.' He hit the wall closest to him with the flat of his hand.

She went over to the window and looked out. She could see the yard below, and, beyond, the fields running up to a wooded hill. She felt tired, now. She wished she could lie down on the old pile of blankets on the ground and sleep in the sweet, warm air.

'We'd better go out and see the land,' he said.

He was looking at his watch, for show. I'm a busy man, the gesture said. I can't spend all day hanging around empty attics.

'All right,' she said. They went down the ladder, him first, backwards, then her.

They went out of the room and down the stairs, John taking them two at a time. She stopped, and waited, and once she'd heard him go through the kitchen and out the back door she went back into the smallest bedroom. The air in the room was unsettled. This house is full of people, she thought, all the people who've passed through here. The air is thick with the trace of them. They never left, properly. Too much happened here and they're tied to this place, and they're still here, like the baby is still here – they can't get away.

At that thought she went out of the room, and started down the stairs. There was something in the bedroom pulling at her, pulling her back. She was afraid, she realized. She wanted nothing more now than to get out of this house and into the fresh air.

The stairs were narrow and steep and she had to put out both hands against the walls to steady herself as she went. Her breath was coming fast, in and out through her mouth. I will cry out, she thought, if I don't get out of here quickly. She began to run, and just as she thought, I'll fall if I'm not careful, her feet were going from under her and she fell down two steps and landed on her knees. The pain and the shock made her shout out, 'Ahh,' and that frightened her too, that she had made such a noise. She stood up, breathing hard, and said, out loud, 'Shit,' and then, louder again, 'Shit.' She was nearly crying now.

She put one hand against the wall and the other hand out in front of her and she made it down the stairs, shaking and hardly able to see. The door at the bottom was closed. This house is all small shut doors, she thought, suddenly furious, and she took hold of the door handle and pulled at it viciously. It was loose in the door and rattled when she shook it and she could not get the door to open. I'm turning the handle wrong, she said to herself, that's all it is, but the more she tried, the more the door seemed to stick and she was sweating now, her hair was stuck to the back of her neck, and she had the narrow dark stairs behind her and there were things coming down them at her, reaching for her. There was something whispering hotly in her ear and she began to kick at the door, but she couldn't shout, she couldn't make the sounds come out of her mouth. All she could do was pull at the handle and kick the door and there was a warm darkness, surely, behind her that was beginning to press against her and just as she thought she would fall down the door swung away from her, open.

John stood on the other side. He started to say something but she pushed past him and through the kitchen, blindly. She went out through the open kitchen door and into the yard. She put her face up to the sky and tried to breathe.

'Are you all right?'

She made herself open her eyes and look at him; she could tell from the way he was looking at her that she didn't look all right, at all. She nodded at him and waved her hand to signal I'm fine, because she couldn't speak yet. She put her hands on her hips and tried to give a laugh.

'I got stuck, John,' she said. 'That door – '

She had to put her hand up to her mouth; she couldn't say any more.

He said nothing. She turned and walked across the yard away from him. She went under a stone arch that was dark and smooth and curved above her like a little bridge. Beyond was another, bigger yard.

'What's all this?' She said it loudly and with a confidence she didn't feel.

'They'd have kept the animals here,' he said, coming up behind her. 'There's a couple of old stables, and the rest of it.' He paused. 'The whole place needs work, of course. The house, as you saw . . .'

He stopped and began to jingle the change in his pockets and rock on his heels, backwards, forwards.

She went into an outbuilding, seeing nothing at first in the darkness.

'There's still stuff here,' she said, after a moment. 'An old saddle and things.'

She walked out and looked around the yard at the rusted farm tools.

'They'd no more need of it all,' he said.

'It's sad,' she said. All the world is sad, and me drowning in it.

He was quiet for a minute; she didn't expect him to answer.

'It is, I suppose,' he said, suddenly, with feeling.

Poor John, she thought. I'm infecting him. Everyone who spends time with me becomes sad, in the end, because the sadness leaches out of me and puts its little damp, bone-smooth hands on the people around me. You're terrible to be with now, Ellen, Simon had said. You're sad, all the time. I feel like I'm dragging you after me through life. You're not the person you were. Everything is black for you now.

'The price of it is good,' she said, to cheer John up.

'Oh, it is,' he said, sounding startled. 'For thirty acres, and the house and the outbuildings. And you can lease the land to the local farmer, you'd have a bit of income there, and it wouldn't cost that much to do the house up.'

She could feel him looking at her out of the side of his eye.

'Hmm,' she said.

'Will we go on and see the land?' he said.

She looked up at the sky like she was thinking, but she wasn't thinking about anything – her mind was empty, and anyway, she'd made up her mind before she'd left London. She was going to buy the farm, without even telling Simon. She wanted it. And she liked buying things. She bought things all the time: it made her feel connected. It made her feel like something was happening.

'No, there's no need,' she said.

Don't do anything until you've spoken to me, Simon had said. You're just going to look at it.

'I'm very interested,' she said. Her heart was beating a bit faster. She couldn't stop herself from saying what she said next.

'I'm going to go for it.'

He looked at her.

She felt excited. It was an almost sexual excitement. It was good to feel something that made her feel alive, finally.

He was looking at her properly, for the first time, like she had just suddenly become visible to him. Now you see me, she thought. Now I'm interesting.

'I'll phone the office and tell them we have an offer,' he said. 'What's your offer?'

She had to stop herself from laughing: she felt giddy, light-headed.

'Oh, asking price,' she said. 'Asking price.'

'Well now,' he said. He was unsmiling, watchful. 'We'll get things going straight away so; I suppose you'd like to get things going while you're here?'

'We might as well,' she said.

John said, 'Right,' and took his phone out and turned his back to her and began to talk.

Her heart felt a bit flattened suddenly, like someone had just sat down hard on her chest. She listened as John explained that he had asking price on the O'Donovan place; his voice, deliberately casual, was swollen with pride: every *r* was rolled out slowly and lusciously; he was enjoying himself immensely, and taking his time at it. He was interested only in himself, of course, and in presenting himself to others, and in how others saw him: she was invisible again now to him. Things had moved on from that moment where he had seen her, where she had felt herself to be solid, and present. Now she would have to call the bank and make the transfer and then there would be papers to sign, and serious discussions to be had; she would have to tell Simon, it would all have to be explained and justified and decided. The excitement started to leak out of her.

She turned around and began to walk back towards the car. John was laughing on the phone; he didn't notice her go.

SHE ORDERED A BRANDY at the hotel bar – it seemed like the kind of thing to do after agreeing to buy a house. She held the glass up to the light: the brandy really was the most beautiful colour. She took a small drink. It burned, and she imagined the liquid running down her throat like a hot flame and painting her all golden on the inside. The bar was empty – it was the middle of the afternoon – apart from two old men at a table by the fire. They were having tea and sandwiches. They were both beautifully dressed in fine soft tweed jackets, and their downy white heads were bent low, together, as they talked very quietly, each laughing with pleasure occasionally at something the other had said. The sight of them made her feel safe and sure. These were people who had managed life well. She would be a person like this, one day. Now she was a person who could be plunged into despair by hearing the wrong word: 'greyhound', for example, or 'mobile home', or – shudder – 'velour'. She was out in the world, really, without the right kind of skin. She took another drink and felt her face heat up and something inside her flickered, and ON! it came – the old remembered feeling of being suddenly and dangerously alive and recklessly able that only came from alcohol.

She picked up her phone and dialled Simon's number.

'Hello, Bunny,' he said. He sounded tired, as if even the prospect of talking to her was a tiring one.

'Hello,' she said. Her voice always came out half broken and cross and thin-sounding when she spoke to him. She didn't know how to speak to him in a normal voice anymore. 'I saw the house.'

'And?'

She could hear him moving around and imagined him in his office, sliding from one side of the room to the next in his expensive chair, various screens winking at him from his desks.

'I liked it.'

'Right,' he said, slowly.

She wished she could have a cigarette.

'I made an offer there and then, and the agent put it to the owner, and he's accepted it.'

There was a deadly silence.

'What kind of offer?'

'Asking price offer. I didn't think there was any point messing about for a few thousand euros, going backwards and forwards. I couldn't be bothered.'

'Bunny!' he shouted.

'Don't shout at me, Simon,' she said. 'I'll just hang up.'

'I'm not shouting at you,' he said, still shouting. 'But if I was shouting – I mean, I thought we'd talked about this. I thought we said you wouldn't do anything until you spoke to me.'

'Simon,' she said. 'I saw it. I liked it. I want it. You've seen it online. What more is there to talk about?'

She had called the bank already, and told them to prepare the funds for the transfer. They would call Simon today, she knew, to get his permission. She'd complained to him about that once, about him being the main account holder on everything, back when she still cared about such things, and he'd laughed at her as if she'd asked why the sun came up in the morning and had said that he was the main account holder because it was all his money, and then he'd seen the expression on her face, and had said, with amusement, 'Poor little girl, poor little Bunny,' and had tried to kiss her.

'So you wouldn't like my input,' he said.

She didn't answer, and he started talking. She was sick of listening to Simon talk. He spoke in long sentences full of words like 'agenda' and 'appropriate' and 'due consideration' and when her turn to speak came she never managed to say what she meant – she usually just disagreed with something he'd said in the last half of his last sentence and that meant another long, terrible reply. Sometimes when she was listening to Simon speak she had to stop herself from banging her head against the wall with the frustration of it all. He was impossible to talk to. He was impossible to listen to.

She took the phone away from her ear and held it up in the air, facing away from her, and with the other hand she took a big drink of the brandy. One of the old men looked over at her and then he smiled, kindly, at her; she smiled back and rolled her eyes dramatically at the phone. He gave her a broader smile and then gave a comical shake of his shoulders, like he was trying to shake something off them, and she laughed and put the phone back to her ear.

'What?' Simon was saying. 'Can you hear me? I'm coming over. I'll be there tomorrow.'

She sat up.

'You can't,' she said. 'What about your work?'

'I can work there,' he said.

'There's no wifi,' she said.

'What, in the whole country?'

'I don't know about the whole country, Simon, I just know that there's very little in this town. You'd have to go to the top of the local mountain to get a decent signal.' She was breathing a bit fast now. Simon turning up wasn't part of the plan.

'I'll text you my flight details,' he said, and this time he hung up on her.

'YOU'RE ON THE BRANDY, I see.'

John was leaning towards and over her. Her face was level with his groin. She could smell his too-strong scent. He had a pile of papers under his arm, ready for her to sign.

'I'll join you if you don't mind,' he said. It wasn't a question: he had already turned towards the bar.

They would wipe her out, these men. They wouldn't leave her room to breathe and she would have to make herself so little and so quiet to fit into the space they left behind them that she would have to get smaller and smaller all the time and eventually – soon – she would just disappear with a small damp pop, like a bubble.

She watched John as he walked away from her. He had a fat bottom – how had she not seen it before, when he was on the ladder? – and it cheered her to see that and made her feel quite in control, suddenly. He turned around when he got to the bar and began an elaborate dumb show of tipping his thumb towards his mouth and pointing at her, mouthing, 'Do you want another drink?' and then giving her an encouraging thumbs up. She raised her empty glass and nodded, giving him a small, cool smile. You think you can handle me, John, she thought. You think you're miles ahead of me.

Let's see.

X

S HE SAW THEM COMING along the lane. There were two lorries. She had covered no great distance since she'd left the house, though the horse was desperate to run: she wanted to keep away from the centre of the fields and next to the ditches and she couldn't let him go on the rough ground. The day was heavy with the insolent heat and the horse was black now from the sweat. She was fighting to hold him, and worried he would break, and with the work of it she had nearly forgotten why she was out there when she saw the first lorry.

She was sure they hadn't seen her: she was at the curve at the top of the hill by the big oaks, hidden from view. She tried to hold the horse to get a good look but he wouldn't stand. She wasn't sure how many men there were: there were at least eight in each of the lorries. Even from this distance she could see the rifles glinting in the sun.

She felt, immediately, very calm. She felt as if everything was slowing down. She felt the thrum of the horse's blood beneath her run slow. She saw a bird whirling in the sky above her and his gyrations became beautifully languid. She felt herself grow small and the world grow huge around her as it hummed its secret song to her.

The horse stood still.

She shortened the reins. She didn't know how long she had been watching the lorries – it felt like a very long time. She didn't know how long it would take them to get to the house. But the road wound around the hill, awkwardly, and the lorries would have to follow it up and down. The line to the house, across the fields, was straight. She turned the horse too tightly and stood up out of the stirrups and leaned forwards. He, understanding the signal, and not expecting it, rose up and stood for a moment suspended on his hind legs, as if he could not move. His front legs pawed helplessly at the air. Would he fall backwards? She loosened the reins and put her heels low and bent down to his ear.

'Come on,' she said, and she started inside to hear the tightness in her voice.

The horse leapt forwards. She could barely hold him. She would fall, surely. She grabbed on to his mane; her legs, out of the stirrups, flapped uselessly by his sides. He headed for the middle of the field. He will not stop, she thought. He will cross the field, and he will try to jump the ditch, though it is six feet tall and nearly as wide.

She could not make him head for the gap in the ditch. She gathered herself into a ball and lay against his mane. He cleared the ditch, barely, and stumbled as he landed. She pulled him up. He was shaking from the shock; there was white foam on the bit. She put her feet back in the stirrups and kicked him as hard as she could on the girth and shortened the reins so that his chin was almost against his chest. A shudder ran through his body, and then he collected himself, gathering himself up, and began to gallop again but he was listening to her now: he tucked his head in and took the bit and let her guide him down the fields, down the hill, past the dark wood where the river ran thickly. She couldn't see the lane. She didn't know where the lorries were. But she could see the house in the distance, standing, quietly.

She rode into the orchard in front of the house. She got off the horse and threw the reins over his head. She thought he would run, but he stood there, shuddering, watching her. She turned her back on him and tried to run but her legs were weak and she moved like a crab towards the yard, nearly crying out with frustration.

There were no lorries. She moved across the yard and went into the house. Her mother was sitting in the kitchen, and her brothers and Eily, too: was it possible she had been gone so little time that they were still here, in the old world, like people frozen in a painting?

Eoin stood up when he saw her, nearly knocking over his chair.

'There are two lorries coming,' she said.

Eily began to scream. Her white face opened up and the scream came out like a long thin white ribbon.

Hannah walked over to her. She wanted to hit her – she was surprised at how strong the desire to strike her hard across the face was. Instead she took hold of her upper arm and squeezed it, tight.

'Shut up,' she said. She didn't look at her mother.

'Where's Daddy?' she said to Eoin.

'He's still up there,' he said. His face was dark red and blotchy; he looked like he was about to cry.

'Take them out to the fields,' she said to Eoin. 'You know where to go.'

She ran to the bottom of the stairs and looked up: such narrow stairs. She could feel the tightness of them wind around her. She turned around; they were all running out of the kitchen. Eoin was carrying Liam. He gave her a look – there were no words, really, for such a look. She turned back to the stairs and ran up, fell up, pulled herself up on her hands.

She could hear the voices above the door. She went up the ladder and banged on it.

Her father opened it and pulled her up.

'There's two lorries coming,' she said to him.

His face collapsed; it was as if the flesh had fallen away from the bones behind it. He was become, instantly, an old man.

'Ah, god,' he said, and put his hand to his head and staggered a bit, backwards.

O'Riada was standing behind her father.

'When did you see them?' he asked.

'Fifteen minutes ago,' she said. 'I was out on the horse, over by the hill.'

'How many?'

'I couldn't see. Maybe eight on each lorry.'

Brennan turned away and walked towards his pack. Tiernan fell down onto his haunches and put his hands in his hair.

She looked at O'Riada.

'Go on,' he said to her. 'Get out.'

'I've a gun,' she said. 'I know how to shoot it.'

Some emotion flashed across his face; she couldn't read it.

'No,' he said. 'There's too many of them.'

He was standing very still, silent, completely alert. She understood that he was deciding what to do, and yet she wanted to cry out to

88

him, I am afraid, I don't know what you want me to do, what are we to do? Tell me what to do.

'Can we get out anywhere?' Brennan said to her. He had his rifle and pack over his shoulder and his gun in his hand, ready to go.

She had thought about this before they came.

'You can get out that window onto the roof.'

'Come on,' said Brennan, turning away from them at a run, already halfway across the room.

'Jesus, if they come up here they'll know,' cried Tiernan. 'And what about the family then? Brennan?'

Brennan had stopped and put his hand up, wait. He was listening for something.

'I hear them coming now. They're on the lane. Come on, lads,' he said.

'I'll go down to them,' said Hannah. 'They might know nothing. Maybe it's just a chance they're here. They've come before, for nothing. Go out on the roof.'

She was speaking directly to O'Riada.

Her father dropped his head.

'Ah, Hannah, no.'

I love you, Dadda, she thought. And I'm grateful you always loved me so well. There's nothing else to be done now.

O'Riada was watching her. He can tell what I'm thinking, she thought, but I can't see beyond his black eyes. She put her hand down her dress and pulled out the Webley and held it out to him.

'Take it,' she said. 'It will be worse for me if they find it.'

She turned to her father.

'Where's yours, Daddy?'

'In the barn.' He sounded ashamed.

O'Riada took the gun from her and put it in his belt.

'We'll go up on the roof,' he said. 'We'll wait and see.'

He turned to the others.

'Now,' he said.

She shoved the breakfast things onto the tray as best she could, nearly falling as she went. She put some of the cups and the bread that was left in the pockets of her dress. The air smelled of cigarette smoke.

He was walking away from her now. Would he not turn to look back at her?

'The rest of them are gone out to the fields. Come on, Daddy.'

She went to the door.

'Good luck,' he said.

She turned and he saw that he was standing there, watching her. She nodded at him.

She went down the ladder first, then her father handed her down the tray and everything on it rattling and shaking terribly, and he followed her, the old blankets under his arm, nearly falling as he went. They started down the stairs, their breath coming fast and steady like a child's. Ah, I can hear the noises from the roof, she thought, and she felt like screaming then and wished she could put one hand over her mouth. If they hear those noises, we are done for. They will find them and we are done for.

She kicked at a bedroom door as they passed it and her father opened the door and threw the blankets on the bed. They went into the kitchen and she emptied the tray into the sink, cups and plates and tray and all, but it looked wrong – They will see that, she thought – so she took the tray out and put in on the shelf. She put on her apron. The air in the kitchen was still warm and heavy with the weight of memory of the people who'd just been there. The table was set for breakfast; the little sugan chair was upturned on the ground. She was standing it up when the door opened.

'Morning, morning, morning,' one of them shouted to the room. He was the officer – she knew it from his coat. As he was shouting he was waving his arm around and the other men were pushing in behind him. They filled the kitchen. Some of them went into the front room, more of them up the stairs, and yet the kitchen was still full with them.

'You know why we're here. If they're here, we'll find them and if we find them, it's bad news for you, isn't it?'

He was standing directly in front of her now and his breath was hot on her cheek. He took hold of her chin in his hand; his fingernails were cutting into her skin. He was looking at her mouth. For a mad moment she thought he might kiss her; she had never before been this close to a strange man and surely it must mean he would kiss her. She tried to turn her face away, and he started to squeeze her jaw tighter and tighter and then he gave her a great shove and she fell back against the range, hitting her head hard against it. Where was her father? She turned and saw him fall: he had been hit and was still being hit and now another of the men was kicking him in the back, in the stomach, in the head while the other one continued to hit him; they went at it, solidly, like men digging a hole.

The officer ran his pistol along the table – swoosh – and knocked everything to the ground in a great crash. He started to move in circles around the room, taking big, slow steps and waving the gun in the air with elegant swoops.

'You know who we are looking for.'

'We do,' Hannah said.

He stopped and turned and looked at her. He had small little eyes, too close together.

'The whole place knows who you're looking for. Look away. They're gone over the pass.'

He was on her.

'And how do you know that, now, you bitch?'

He grabbed hold of her hair.

'Everyone knows.' She wouldn't cry from the pain and the fright. 'Wouldn't they have gone straight from Skibbereen to the pass? They wouldn't stop.'

He was still holding her hair with one hand and he pulled her to her feet like that and with his free hand he hit her with his closed fist across the face. He's broken the bone, she thought, almost abstractedly, he has broken my jaw.

'Everyone knows,' he repeated. 'What does he know?'

With his pistol he pointed at her father on the ground.

'He knows nothing,' she said. 'All we know is that they're over the pass.'

He let go of her and walked over to her father. The two soldiers stood back; they were red from the exertion. One of them wiped the sweat off his face. Her father was lying perfectly still, like he was asleep. The officer pointed the pistol at the back of his head and spoke to her.

'Where's the rest of them? It's not just you two here.'

'They're gone to school. My mother took the milk to the dairy with the maid.'

She was watching her father. She wouldn't look at the officer.

He leaned towards her a little.

'Come here.' He said it in a whisper.

She moved towards him and he put his hand on her arm, quite gently, and began to tap at her with one finger. When he spoke it was in rhythm with the tapping.

'I'll kill him,' he said. 'So you'd better start talking.'

'Hannah.'

She didn't turn. She kept her eyes on her father. If she stopped looking at him, they would kill him. She was keeping him alive by looking at him.

One of the men started shouting, 'Heh heh heh up up up,' and they were all swelling towards the kitchen door then in a great roar.

Hannah turned around. It was Denis. The light of the day was very bright behind him and he was all dark in the light. She couldn't see his face.

The officer started to poke at him with the end of his pistol like he was a soft thing, a rag doll of a person. Denis took off his cap and put his hands up very slowly.

'Easy now, easy,' he said, quietly. He put his head down low.

'Who the fuck are you?'

'I work here. I work on the farm with Seanie every day.'

'He's the workman,' said Hannah. It was hard to get the words out. 'He helps my father around the place. He's here for work.'

'Get in here,' said the officer.

He grabbed Denis by the shoulder, and pulled him into the kitchen and stood him against the wall, and he stood back and watched then as a soldier tore away his braces and pulled off his old waistcoat and pulled open his shirt, tearing it down so it hung by his waist. He stood half naked. His head was bowed. She felt so ashamed for him that it was nearly impossible to watch.

'He has nothing,' said the soldier, turning to the officer. He put his rifle against his soft white belly. 'He's just an old Mick. He smells of cowshit like the rest of them.'

Denis lifted up his head then and she looked across the room at him and he looked at her, very calmly and steadily, and there was no fear in his face, but she saw great rage there, and a perfect hatred too; his face was pulled tight from the emotion, and it felt almost obscene to be seeing him, Denis, like this. She could not reconcile this Denis with the Denis she had known her whole life. This is what they have done to us, she thought. They have blackened our hearts and made us strangers to each other.

The soldiers were coming down the stairs. They were laughing. Some of them were smoking.

They have not found them, she thought, wildly. We are saved. She lifted her hand to put it to her mouth to stop the shout that was coming out, then she saw that Denis was watching her. Do not move, his face said. Do nothing that will make them look at you. If they look at you, they will understand. Do not breathe. Do not stir.

Very slowly, she put her hand back down by her side.

'There's nothing,' one of the soldiers said to the officer. He looked down at her father. 'What are we doing with this one?'

The officer turned towards the kitchen door. The morning sun was filling the kitchen now. For a moment they were all still, and there was no sound. He didn't turn around to answer.

'Take him out and finish him off,' he said.

Denis put his hands down.

'Ah, now,' he said. 'Aren't I after just seeing Sergeant Barker and didn't he tell me this place wouldn't be touched.'

The officer walked over to him.

'Did I tell you to talk?' he shouted.

'You didn't, you didn't, but I'm only passing on information. You've the wrong house here and it might mean trouble for you. It's many the year I've been working here and I've been friends with Tommy Barker all that time, I'm well known to him and all down the barracks, and Seanie O'Donovan is well known to him too. I'm only, now –' he put his head to one side and screwed up his face in a comical twist; he was at once a wizened wheedling old man and the voice was the singing lilt of the peasant begging favour – 'passing on the information. What ye boys do is up to ye. I'm only saying.'

There was a silence.

'You're a lying Mick.'

'It would be a big lie, easily found out,' said Denis. 'Wouldn't I be the foolish fellow now to be telling such a lie.'

The officer leaned back from him. Denis gave him a half-smile and nodded his head slowly like he was nodding it to a secret tune that was playing in his head.

'Sure, the foolish fellow, and no mistake.'

One of the soldiers put his rifle back on his shoulder. Another one dropped his cigarette to the ground and put his heel on it. Something in the room had shifted. The officer looked half over his shoulder. He was breathing hard.

'Come on,' he shouted then, and he waved his rifle out the door. He turned back to Denis.

'Me and Tommy Barker is going to have a little talk today,' he said. He tapped Denis on the shoulder, softly, with the head of the rifle. 'I'll see you later.'

'You know where I am,' said Denis.

And then they were gone.

She ran to her father. There was blood on the ground underneath his head. His eye was a throbbing black unseeing globe, streaming terrible liquid. His ear was a little red flower of pulped flesh. She sat down behind him with her legs stiff straight out in front of her, like a rag doll, and moved forwards so that her legs were on either side of him and she was able to lift his ruined head and put it on her lap. He made no sound.

Denis crouched down next to her. He had the pot of water off the fire and a clean rag soaked with the water. He was breathing too fast, like he had been running. Then he started to wash her father's face.

Neither of them said anything.

She could see them as if from a great distance. She was in the sky looking down and this had all been happening forever and would never end, never end. She and her father and Denis would be on this floor forever, feeling nothing, with hearts like little pale cold stones. She did not dare to think of anything but this moment, with them all here, forever.

And then, her father made a noise.

'Jesus, you're a tough man,' said Denis triumphantly. 'Isn't he a tough man, Hannah? They did their worst and by god, he's going still.'

Denis half stood up and put his hands on his knees and regarded her father, considering.

'We'll sit you up,' he said.

He waved at her, and she shuffled to the side out of the way. He put his arms under her father's arms and pulled him along the floor to the wall and sat him against it. His head hung forwards and Denis put his hand to his forehead and guided his head back so it rested against the wall. He took a small bottle out of his pocket and made her father's mouth into the shape of a little funnel and poured in the clear liquid. Some went in. Some ran down his chin. Her father sputtered and coughed a bit and tried to turn his head away.

'Now we're in business, boy,' cried Denis.

He put the wet rag in her father's hand and made the hand into a ball and lifted it to his eye.

'Keep it against your eye, Seanie, do you hear me?'

Her father made a sound.

'Do you have any more clean bits of rags?' he said to Hannah.

She stood up. She had to put her hand against the wall to steady herself. Her hands were covered in blood. The blood had soaked through her apron and dress and her thighs were warm and wet.

'Go on, Hannah,' said Denis.

She got an old sheet from the cupboard by the stairs and began to rip it into strips.

'Where are they?' said Denis. He was still in front of her father, holding on to his shoulders to keep him upright.

'They went out on the roof.'

He made a soft hissing noise.

'They were the lucky boys that the attic wasn't found. How those gomeens missed the attic I'll never know.'

'It has a secret door,' she said, quietly.

'I know,' he said. 'Still and all.' He looked over at her. 'Is your face all right?'

Her face was burning with the pain. I am on fire, she wanted to shout. She was afraid to touch her jaw. She nodded, and then she started to half cry and she had to turn away to hide herself: Denis hadn't seen her cry since she was a child. When she was a child he had been kind to her, always – once she'd fallen from a tree she shouldn't have been climbing and had torn open her leg and her mother had shouted at her and sent her to bed with no dinner, but the day after Denis had brought her a little wooden fox that had fitted perfectly into the palm of her hand. He had carved it for her from hawthorn, the fairy wood. It was bad luck to bring hawthorn into the house but she could have it, he'd said, because she was one of the fairy people, so the bad luck couldn't touch her.

'Am I, Denis?' she'd said, looking at the little fox in her hand. 'Am I one of the fairy people?' and he'd told her that she was a siofra, that the fairies had taken her mother's real baby and put her, Hannah, in her place, and she'd felt sorry then for her mother who must be sad without her real baby and maybe that was why, she thought, her mother was so often angry and loud with her and said to her all the time, Go away, Hannah, I'm tired; she was tired, she thought, from lying awake all night thinking about her real baby caught in the fairy world with the bad fairies.

When she was older she saw that Denis had told her the story to make her feel better about being a child who liked to be up in the trees and watch how the birds flew in the sky, but she'd believed it when he'd told her, and she believed it for a long time after.

She walked towards him and handed him the rags.

'The rest of them are out in the fields,' she said, to say something.

'Will you go out and get them now, Hannah,' said Denis. 'We'll need Eoin to help us lift your father to the bed.'

She nodded and walked to the door. Beyond all was brilliant with golden light. She stepped out, into the new world.

XI

FOR SUCH A BIG man John had a small penis. She wasn't surprised. It bent to one side, though, and curved like a banana
– that surprised her. He opened his mouth too wide when he
kissed and didn't move his jaw and left his small blunt tongue to
do all the work – stab stab stab it went, too fast. He was drunk,
of course – they had been in the bar for hours – but she knew that
he wouldn't make a better job of it sober. He had sharp fingernails
and they felt rough on the soft skin of her breasts as he kneaded
them under her clothes.

He'd started kissing her as soon as they got into the bedroom. She
was glad when it started. I've broken things now, she thought. I've
done something I shouldn't have done, and I'm glad of it. Whatever
was left unbroken, I'm breaking. She got on the bed and he started
rubbing her breasts and moaning a bit and then he put his finger in
her mouth and began to move it around. It tasted of cigarettes. She
guessed she was to suck it. She felt herself begin to gag, so she moved
her head to one side so he had to take it out and then she pushed
herself back up the bed. He got off the bed then and opened his belt
and took off his trousers and stood before her in his shirt and black

socks and white underpants. She said nothing. Then he pulled down his underpants and walked towards her with his erect banana penis.

She got up off the bed. She felt quite sober, suddenly.

'Where are you going?' he said.

She gave a small tinkling laugh.

'I think that's enough now, John,' she said.

He lurched towards her with his mouth open, like a snake's. He was tall, and wide, and he smelled strongly of something too sweet. He swayed over her and she stepped backwards; he stepped after her like they were engaged in some mad, formal waltz. He took her hand and put it on his penis. She let go.

'Come on,' he said, in a low voice.

She had her back against the wall now and he was nuzzling her neck and putting his hand up under her shirt again. She felt a second of panic. She put one hand flat against his chest and pushed him.

'That's enough,' she said. She made the words come out with an upper class British accent. Her British accent was almost perfect if she didn't have to say too much, and if she spoke very crossly. 'That's quite enough.'

He stumbled backwards a bit.

She waited. If he came at her again, she might take off her shoe and hit him with the stiletto heel. On the nose.

He waved a hand in the air.

'Feck it,' he said.

He turned around, looking for his clothes. He bent over to pick up his pants and his big bottom glowed white in the dusk. She had to turn her head away. She picked up his trousers and handed them to him. He sat on the bed and pulled on his clothes. He didn't speak.

'My husband is coming tomorrow,' she said.

She had told him that in the bar. She had told him about Simon, at length. She felt sick now at the things she had told him.

He looked at her. He stood up, putting his hands in his pockets to rearrange himself. He gave the pockets a shake. He seemed fortified by the familiar jingle.

'Well, I'm looking forward to meeting him,' he said.

She opened the door and he walked out without looking at her. She closed it behind him and took out her cigarettes and put one, unlit, into her mouth, and then pretended to smoke it, very slowly.

Her mind was splintering now; her mind was becoming a rabid dog that chased her thoughts; it was beginning to dissolve, jaggedly, around the edges. And her breath was starting to come too fast: each breath was coming off the end of the last one.

She dropped the cigarette and lay down on the bed because she felt sick and dizzy but it was a mistake to lie down, she saw, immediately, it made everything worse. Her mind was gone away from her, beyond her control. She felt like she was driving too fast through the darkness and her thoughts were the other cars coming at her out of the fog; she couldn't see the cars until the very last minute when the headlights bore blindingly down upon her and she had to swerve out of the way, but the swerving itself put her in danger and she felt sick, sick and dizzy, from trying to swerve and not lose control and she was lost, now, in the darkness and – Oh, I'm so tired from it all, tired from the struggle and not able, even, to give the struggle up. I can't even give up. I can't get away from myself.

She became aware that she was making sounds, as if she were in pain. The pain, the struggle – that was the real thing. That was what ran beneath her surface. When she got dressed, when she ate, when she spoke to someone or read a magazine or lay in bed, there was, always, this struggle. It was becoming more difficult, all the time, to contain it, to hide what was real. It was breaking through. Soon there would only be the struggle left.

THEY HAD FOUND OUT at the twenty-week scan that the baby's brain wasn't developing properly. She had a condition that was incompatible with life, the doctor said, so she would die soon after she was born, minutes after, probably. Probably. There was, of course, the tiniest of chances that she would defy her fate and live longer. One could never say. These things were always, by their very nature, uncertain.

We should abort, Simon had said. There is no hope. We shouldn't have to go through the whole pregnancy, the labour, for nothing. But she had refused. They had, by this stage, been through the miscarriages, and then the four rounds of IVF, with no success at all. She could not give up on this baby, she had decided, who was alive inside her, who was growing, who might be the one baby in ten thousand who defied the odds, and survived. I have always been lucky, she had thought, I have always been different, and if I believe enough in me, in the baby, then I can make this all right. If I want this enough, I can make it happen.

Do I not have a say? Simon had said to her when she had told him that she was going to keep the baby and she had answered him, No. It is my body, she had said, and I am in control of what happens in it and to it, I decide.

She had been wrong about that, she had realized, when it was all over: she was not in control of her body, at all. She was in control of nothing. She had gone against Simon for nothing. She had gambled, and she had lost. She had lost the baby, she had lost Simon, she had lost herself, really. She was not lucky after all, it had transpired. She was not different, or special. She was a fool, Simon had told her one terrible night after the baby had been born, and died, and he was right, she saw: she was the worst kind of fool and more than that, she was not to be trusted – she could no longer trust herself, because she had made the wrong choice, the worst possible choice, for them all. She had destroyed them with her vanity, her deluded self-belief.

It had been absolutely silent in the room when the baby was delivered; the silence had been as sharp as glass. One of the nurses had wept, but soundlessly. She had felt that she should cry, but she didn't. She couldn't, and she didn't try to. She was honest in that, at least, she had thought afterwards. They had let her hold the baby right after she was born and she was warm, but already you could feel the coldness begin to run through her as her life ebbed away. That's your little life, now, she'd said to herself, that's it, and then she'd made herself say it out loud so that the baby would hear her. She hadn't been able to keep the distress out of her voice, and she'd been ashamed of that: she had let it be seen how much she suffered, which was a private thing, not to be admitted even to herself. Whenever she thought of those words now – and sometimes she deliberately said them in her head to hurt herself – she felt a blackness run through her like a heavy, cloying oil.

The baby's eyes were closed tight as she held her, and her fists were rolled up into little balls, like she was trying to hold on to something. She looked like she was asleep, Simon had said afterwards, didn't she look like she was sleeping peacefully? But he was wrong. She didn't. She didn't look like she was sleeping, at all.

SHE MUST GET UP. She would drown, lying down. She sat up, very slowly, and when that was done she swung her legs around and put her feet on the ground. 'Now,' she said, out loud. She was drunk, and she hadn't eaten anything since breakfast, and in being able to tell herself that, she knew that the worst of it was over. She stood up and went to the window.

The town was going home for its tea. There was a gang of teenagers in tracksuits outside the fish and chip shop opposite the hotel. There was one car stopped at the traffic lights. The darkness was coming in fast from the hills. It was a small, dull place, and this was the biggest town in the region. This was a veritable Manhattan around here.

She felt a sudden vicious surge of bitterness. These were an inward-looking people here, suspicious and mean-minded most of them, content enough to live out their days under the drizzle. Anyone with a bit of gumption got out. It was hard to be proud to be from here. It was hard to be proud to be Irish and it was getting harder all the time. She had been at a grand wedding once in London and she was made to dance with one of the groomsmen and he had said, of the bride, 'I didn't realize she was Irish Irish,' and he had cocked his head at a gaggle of the bride's relations getting drunk at the bar. 'I thought she was Irish like you,' and he had meant, she knew, Anglo-Irish.

She had only laughed in response. She had let him believe what he wanted. She had let him imagine hunt balls and a big old house needing a new roof. Afterwards, in the taxi to the nightclub, he had put his hand on her knee and she had removed it, without a word. It was an entirely civilized exchange.

Later that night she had seen him kissing one of the bride's Irish Irish cousins with great gusto. At breakfast the day after he had boasted to the table that she had been mad for it. She had said nothing. They had all laughed, and she was complicit in her silence.

And now she was back here buying a bit of Ireland with her British husband's money. What would Hannah O'Donovan think of all of it? For the longest time now she hadn't wanted to be Irish. She had never wanted to be British. And what was she now? She kept looking out the window. She didn't know. She didn't know the answer, anymore, to any of the important questions, at all.

XII

SHE WAS STILL, IN the centre, and everything was happening about her, very smoothly, very quickly, and with no trouble. It was as if they all knew exactly what part they had to play in things. Everyone knew exactly what to do, except her.

She was standing with her back against the kitchen wall – if she moved away she would fall over. The blood on her hands was drying dark. There was blood under her fingernails. The blood on her dress had soaked through to her thighs. One month she had not changed the hated pad in time and it had soaked it through – the blood had run down her legs. She had been at school when it had happened. She couldn't tell the master, and she had no friend she could confide in. At the break she had stayed at her desk, the blood coming out in little terrifying pumps, and when home time had come, finally, she had waited until she was the last one to leave. The blood had soaked through her stockings and her underskirt and her dress – when she put her hand up to her dress it came away wet with blood – but it was not noticed, ever: the dress was of a heavy dark material and she had soaked it in a bucket in her bedroom until it was clean. But the shame of it, and the fright, had stayed with her, and she felt the shame now, all over again, and the panic, and the fear. She should wash her hands, at least, she thought, but that would be to move from the wall. She made herself look away from her hands. Look up, Hannah, she said to herself. Wake yourself up.

The kitchen was a strange world now, full of men: O'Riada and Brennan and Tiernan, and Denis had let Seanie Mac and Joe Fitzgerald in with only a nod as a greeting. And Tim Delaney and Johnny Cronin – they had arrived together. She had been at school with Johnny Cronin and once at a dance he had asked her if she wanted a lemonade and had only laughed good-naturedly when she had answered, out of fright, no, Johnny Cronin, not from you.

She watched as Denis introduced the men to O'Riada. They had lined up in a row and when it was their turn Denis said their full name and the place they were from and they stepped forwards in silence; O'Riada only nodded at them, or put his hand on their arm or shoulder in greeting – he didn't speak. Only Denis spoke, and he was listened to: he was a person of some significance in this world, she saw.

Her head was full with a noise that was like the sound of crackling paper. She couldn't hear properly, she couldn't think properly, though the introductions were over and the kitchen was nearly perfectly quiet now; the men made only a murmur as they picked over the weapons on the table and hung the shining rows of bullets over their shoulders and tied belts and pulled on their caps.

'Hannah?'

She stood up as straight as she could, startled. She had been about to fall down, she realized, and O'Riada had his hand on her shoulder and was standing her back up against the wall.

'Your face looks bad,' he said. 'You'd want to put something on it.'

She put her hand up to her cheek.

'It's all right,' she said. It was difficult to speak, because her lips were split and already swollen. She touched her finger to them, amazed at their awful size.

'You did a fine job,' said O'Riada. 'No one could have done better.'

She nodded and touched her lips, slowly, distractedly. They were hard with dried blood, she told herself, as if she were telling someone else about someone else's body, entirely.

'We're going after them now, Hannah,' he said. 'For what they did to your father. For what they did to you.'

'But they're in the lorries.' She didn't understand – would they run after them? They wouldn't catch them on foot.

O'Riada didn't answer her.

'They've armoured lorries,' she said, more loudly. 'Is it mad you are?'

Some of the men turned to look at her; the room quietened. O'Riada stepped back from her, into the middle of the room. When he spoke, it was to her, directly, but he was addressing them all, she saw, and she could feel the others go still to listen to him.

'We've to stop them before they get to the barracks,' he said. 'We'll get them at the narrow bend by the bridge. There'll be a tree down there for us. We'll cut across the fields.' He turned to the room. 'Not a bother on us boys, ha?'

'Not a bother,' Johnny Cronin called back, with a laugh.

'It will be fast,' O'Riada said to her. 'They're not expecting it. It won't be difficult.'

He swung his arm above his head in a great swoop; it was an unexpectedly dramatic, nearly practised, gesture.

'And don't they deserve the lesson?'

'They do, they do,' the men murmured shyly, watching each other discreetly to see how to respond.

'Don't they deserve the lesson, boys?' He was shouting now. 'That man up there is left blind. We've enough of it, don't we, boys? We've been running from this lot for long enough. Here is where we meet them. It's now time, as the farmer says, to lower the blade and make the final cut. Today's the day we send a message out. We've enough of it. They're going to hear that message loud from us today.'

The men, as if they were one, gave a great shout of an answer, a cheer that made a shiver run through her. The room was filled then with the swell of voices, and with a stir of activity. The men began to press towards the door. She saw that Eoin meant to go with them.

She went to him, pushing past Denis, past Johnny Cronin.

'No, Eoin.' She tried to hold on to him but he shook her off roughly.

'Stop, Hannah,' he cried, turning away from her, and she heard the anger, and embarrassment, in his voice.

She turned to find O'Riada; to get to him she had to push through against the wave of men trying to get out the door. He was standing, still, in the middle of the kitchen. She made herself look into his face. Her heart had fallen down deep in her stomach, and throbbed there, dully.

'He's only fourteen. He can't go.'

'He's well able,' he said. He wouldn't meet her eye; he looked above her head, watching the men file out. 'He can hold a gun, can't he?'

'I can hold a gun,' she said, and she hit herself in the chest with her fist. 'Me. I'm a better shot than him. I'll go instead. Take me.'

'You won't be fast enough across the fields,' he said, quietly, and she understood, suddenly, from the way that he said it, from the way that he was looking at her, that she was of interest to him, that she was, perhaps, something to him.

'Don't take him.'

She said it very quietly so that he had to lean in to her to hear her. She could almost feel his face against hers. She could feel the warmth coming off him. She could smell him.

'Leave him come,' he said. 'He'll be all right. I'll look out for him.'

She understood that it had cost him to promise it. He leaned back from her and took the Webley out of his belt. He was looking at her very carefully, like he was trying to understand something.

'Someone here has to watch this place. Do you understand me?'

She put her hand out for her gun, and took it from him.

'I do,' she said. She put the gun across her chest. 'Will you come back?'

'We will,' he said. 'This will be the safest place after. We'll come back for the night.'

He moved towards her again – she stood, frozen – and he put his cheek almost against her cheek, slowly, gently. She could hear him breathing. She could feel him smelling her hair. He began to say something when Brennan shouted out, 'Are you finished with your romancing yet?'

He was nearly out the door; he had turned back to watch them and his big face was cracked open with a good-natured smile.

'We've business to be doing this morning, chief, no time for the courting.'

The men gave a whoop and a laugh.

They're like men going out to play the long poc for the day, she thought. The terrible tension she had felt in the attic that morning was gone, and in its place, in action, there was almost joviality.

When she turned back, O'Riada had turned away from her, and was moving towards the door.

'Come on,' he said to the men, and then, they were gone.

SHE WENT UP TO the bedroom. Her father's face was black against the white pillow.

'They're gone,' she said, to the room, to herself.

'They're gone after them,' said her mother, in a dull voice.

'They are,' she said. 'Eoin went with them.'

Her mother was huddled over the bed like an old woman. She didn't answer.

'You should have stopped him,' said Eily.

She was sitting in a chair in the corner. Her face was white and pinched.

'I couldn't,' said Hannah. 'He wanted to go. No one could have stopped him.'

'You didn't even try, I suppose,' said Eily. 'I'm surprised you didn't send Liam after him. I'm surprised you didn't try to make Mammy go.'

'You're mad,' said Hannah.

Eily began to laugh, a high-pitched, forced laugh.

'I'm the mad one? That's very good. I'm the mad one.' She stood up and walked up to Hannah. She was as tall as her, but thinner; she had a long, thin face and her long blonde hair was like a shroud about her.

'If it wasn't for you . . .' She stopped. Her face was working; Hannah knew that she was considering whether to go on. 'All those nights the two of you sat up talking, night after night talking and planning and, oh, if only you hadn't started all this, we could have gone on about our business and been none the wiser –' she was crying now and it was difficult to make out what she was saying – 'none the wiser. They wouldn't have come near us. We were asking for trouble.'

'It had nothing to do with me,' Hannah said, in astonishment and great rage. 'Daddy believes what he's always believed.'

'You've never been happy.' Eily was spitting at her now, almost. 'You've never been settled. You unsettled Daddy. You let him believe he could change things. You encouraged him. Why didn't you stop him, Hannah? You were the only one he would have listened to.' She moved closer to Hannah. 'You have ruined us,' she said, almost in a whisper. 'We are all finished, because of you.'

Eily raised up her hand to her. Would she strike her? Hannah thought of her broken face, her lip, and she had to stop herself from putting her hand up to protect herself. If Eily dared to strike her, she would knock her to the ground, she thought, and she would enjoy it. She would put her hands around that skinny white throat and she would shake her until Eily begged her to stop and even then she wouldn't stop.

'Eily,' she said.

At the sound of her voice Eily put her hand down and stepped back from her.

'You know I'm right,' she said. 'Mammy knows I'm right.'

Hannah put her hand out to her mother, in desperation.

'Mammy. Tell her it's not my fault.'

She felt as she did when she was a child, and Eily would cheat at a game and there was no way to make her admit to the cheat.

Her mother put her hand up to block her face.

'Ohhh,' she said, in a long moan.

'Mammy,' she said, mad with the injustice of it. 'You know it's not my fault. Tell her.'

Her mother wouldn't look at her.

'It's between the two of you now, the two of you. I don't know.'

'Oh Mammy,' she shouted, in disgust. Her mother would not side with her. She had known this, always.

'We're finished now. Do you understand that?' Eily had stepped forwards again; her face was too close to hers, and she could smell her too-sweet breath. 'Whatever happens, we'll always be known as supporting them.'

'What's wrong with being known for that?' Hannah cried. 'We do.' It seemed to her that Eily must be stupid.

'I don't!' It was a great shout. 'No one asked me if I did! I don't give a feck about it! Who cares about stupid old Ireland? I don't!'

Her mother was crying openly now, and groaning and swaying.

'Why can't we just leave things as they are? If we didn't fight them they'd leave us in peace. Half of the country goes to London anyway. There's no difference between us. It's all only an idea, the whole stupid war.'

She was crying hard now, and she fell back in her chair and put her head in her hands.

Hannah walked over to her.

'Look up at me,' she said.

Eily covered her eyes with her hands.

'You look up at me now,' she said, and her voice sounded so dangerous that Eily stopped crying and looked up at her, sniffling. She heard her mother turn on the bed to watch her.

'Look at my face. Look at my hands. That's Daddy's blood on my hands. Do you see it? Do you see what they've done to us?'

She put her hands in front of Eily's face. She tried to turn her face away and Hannah caught her by the shoulders and pinned her back against the chair and then rubbed, savagely, her hands all over her face. Her face was small and as fragile as a child's; she could feel its little bones compress and crack like greenwood under the force of her hands. It would be easy to break the bones in her face, she thought. She could crush her little face, if she wanted.

The shock of what she was doing made her feel like a gate had been opened inside her. She was flooded with fright and with the thrill of it. She couldn't stop; it wasn't enough. She grabbed Eily and pulled her to her feet. She was astonished by the strength in her hands. Eily's shoulders were thin and sharp like a little bird's wings, and when she shook her it seemed like she would break, almost. She shook her so that her head flew backwards and forwards on the little stem of her neck. She felt outside herself now. Without thinking she stopped shaking her and with all the force she had left in her body she threw her across the room. Eily hit the wall and let herself slide onto the floor into a little crumple.

Her mother was still sitting on the bed like a frozen thing. She had her hands to her mouth but made no sound. Her eyes were huge and red, like they had been burned into her head. Hannah couldn't look at her. As soon as she let Eily go she felt sundered by the shame. To have let them see how much she felt, to have not been able to manage her fear and anger and hatred – she wanted to weep, like Eily.

'You're no better,' she said to her mother, with her back to her. 'What good are you?'

Her father made a sound then. Hannah understood from the sound that he wanted her to stop. She went to him and took his hand. O'Riada had said that he was blind in the eye; he was right, she saw.

Without looking up from him she spoke to her mother.

'Get out,' she said, quietly.

'Don't you speak to me like that,' her mother said, but Hannah lifted up her head and looked at her and into the look she put hatred and despair and disgust and her mother turned her face away from her and Hannah saw that she was crying, silently. I have broken free now, she thought. Nothing, now, will be the same.

Her mother got up from the bed. To go out the door she had to pass by her; as she went by she gathered her shawl and her skirts against her so as not to even brush against her. She doesn't want to touch me, thought Hannah. She doesn't want to look at me.

Out of the corner of her eye she could see Eily getting up. There was no blood on Eily's white face. Though she had rubbed and rubbed, it hadn't come off her hands. It was still all on her. Her mother was standing in the doorway, waiting for Eily, and watching Hannah, warily, like she was a stranger.

'Get on out of it,' she said to Eily. 'We need clean warm water for Daddy. Send Mary.'

She turned back to her father. She put her hand on his head and pushed the wet hair back from his forehead.

'The men are gone after them, Dadda,' she said. 'They'll get them.'

She put her head down on the pillow so that her face was in the curve of his neck.

'We'll get them for you.'

He made a small sound.

'We've started now, Daddy,' she said. 'And we'll keep going until we're finished.'

XIII

SHE WENT INTO THE bathroom and tried to look critically at herself in the mirror. She didn't look good. Simon had known her for ten years and he would know that she was hungover. Would he know that she had kissed someone? She put her face up to the mirror and made a kissing face, pouting her lips, and then touching them very gently to the glass. She looked at her mouth, and bit her lip, testing it out. She took her lipstick out of her bag and very carefully, very slowly, put it on. She considered herself. She looked worse now. Her lips looked swollen and unnatural and the lipstick was too dark in colour. She began to rub at the lipstick with a towel but it went onto the skin around her lips and she had to try to fix that, then, with foundation, and then powder, but that only made the rest of her face look pale and underdone in comparison, so she had to put even more make-up on to try to even it all out and by the time she'd finished she looked like she'd been made up by an overenthusiastic and possibly demented child. 'God almighty,' she said out loud to her reflection, and she turned away from the mirror, raging with frustration.

She had determined not to think about the events of the previous evening, at all. When she met John O'Connor again she would pretend that nothing, at all, had happened. Nothing. And what had happened, really? Nothing. There was nothing to be concerned about. She told herself that over and over, but she didn't believe it – she couldn't even convince herself. Really, she felt sick to her stomach when she thought of what she'd done. It was, almost, unbelievable.

She went into the bedroom. She was considering having a cigarette out of the window when she heard a car door bang outside on the street. She went over to the window. Simon.

From behind the curtain, she watched him get out of the taxi. Only Simon would get a three-hour taxi from the airport. He was a tall, well-built man and he was beautifully dressed and he had lovely luggage, and golden hair that shone even in the wet grey light. Everything about him spoke of prosperity. She remembered when her sister's son had been little and she had been playing with his feet and singing the nursery rhyme, 'This little piggy went to market, this little piggy stayed at home, this little piggy had brown bread and butter—' and Simon, who had been listening, had laughed out loud at her. 'Brown bread and butter? We say roast beef,' and so she had changed it, thereafter, to roast beef. His people had been raised on roast beef. Public school and roast beef. You think you're better than everyone else, she had said to him once, and he had answered, honestly, I don't, but I don't think anyone else is better than me, either.

He was standing across the road from the hotel, looking up at it. She moved behind the curtain. She had known to expect him at midday, but it was shocking to see him here, so out of context. It was almost too much to absorb. She turned and looked again: he wasn't on the street now; he had come into the hotel.

There was a knock at the door.

It took her a moment to disentangle herself from the curtain. She went to the door and touched her lips and sucked her stomach in and straightened herself up: Simon hated it when she slouched. There was another knock on the door. She opened it.

'Hello, Bunny,' he said.

He kissed her on each cheek. He smelled of expensive lemony scent. He took these things seriously – not for Simon the offerings of the duty-free. He sourced scents from small ancient apothecaries in places like Capri.

'Hello, Simon,' she said. It came out wrong: she sounded coquettish.

He looked at her.

'Can I come in?' he said.

She gave a little laugh and opened the door wider and stepped to one side.

He came in, bumping against her with his luggage. He had two bags and he hit against her with the edge of the one hanging over his shoulder. She rubbed her hip, where the bag had hit her; it had hurt. Simon didn't notice. He wasn't the kind of person who noticed things like that, and if you pointed it out to him, he would either get cross or say sorry, sarcastically.

'You have a lot of luggage,' she said.

'I brought my running stuff,' he said. 'And all those bloody supplements. And the two Macs. And . . . the rest of it.'

He put his bags on the bed and looked around the room. He went to the window and looked out and gave a sigh.

'It's raining,' he said. 'Raining as usual in diddly diddly land.'

She didn't answer. He turned and put his coat across a chair and his bags on the bed and unzipped them, taking his phones out of his pockets and various sockets out of his bag and starting to plug them in. The room, suddenly, felt very small.

She was standing in the middle of the room now. He hadn't looked at her. Sometimes, she thought, whole days passed and he didn't look at her.

'How do I look?' She was sorry as soon as the question was out.

He looked over at her, narrowing his eyes a bit.

'OK. Tired. Your face looks a bit . . .'

'Bloated.'

'Well, you said it, not me, so don't start having a go at me. Have you been eating bread?'

'No,' she sighed. I've been drinking and smoking. And I might have had an allergic reaction to John O'Connor's tongue.

'Do you want to go down for lunch?' she said. If they stayed here, he would want to have sex.

'What? I don't know. What's the food like?' He was looking at his phone.

'Fine,' she said. 'Organic. Locally sourced.'

He was busy with the phone.

'I found out that the owners of the hotel are my cousins.'

He didn't answer. He always waited to answer her. It was like a game they played – he waited to answer, she held herself back from repeating what she had just said.

'Well,' he said, after a bit, once it was clear that she wouldn't say more. 'That's not that surprising, is it? Isn't everyone here your cousin?'

'I'm just saying,' she said in irritation. 'I'm just telling you.'

He put down the phone.

'Oh poor Bunny,' he said. 'Do you want a cuddle?' He made a kissing sound and came to her and squeezed her tight. 'Mmm,' he said. 'Squishy Bunny.'

She wriggled away.

'Let's go for lunch,' she said.

'OK,' he said. 'One minute.'

He unzipped a bag and took out a bulging bath bag and went to the bathroom.

She sat on the bed, and waited.

When he emerged he was buffed, shining.

'Right,' he said, and then his phone began to ring. 'One minute.'

She stood up.

'I'll meet you down there,' she said.

He looked annoyed.

'No, wait for me. I'll be one minute.'

She sat on the bed and listened to him talk. The minutes passed. Eventually, she stood up again.

'Simon,' she said.

He raised one finger to her, wait. She sat back down on the bed. Her chest was tight with agitation. It was hard to think properly; her thoughts were narrowing themselves down into little mean avenues. Soon, she would say something in anger and there would be an argument. You make me a person I don't like, she thought. You've made me someone I'm not in control of.

She stood up again and picked up her bag and walked to the door. She put her hand on the handle and looked at him; he was watching her as he spoke. When he saw that she would go, he ended the call.

'Ellen,' he said. 'Don't push my buttons. I only needed five minutes.'

She didn't answer.

His phone beeped and he looked at it.

'I have so much to do. I'll get nothing done while I'm here.'

'I told you not to come. There was no reason for you to come.'

'I have come,' he said, drawing himself up tall, 'to support you. Don't you want my support?'

In the early days, she had been mad about him. If they were out somewhere together and he left the room, she didn't relax until he came back; she would keep one eye on the door, waiting for him. It had always been an edgy, uncomfortable thing. She had never felt at ease. 'But does he get you?' Caroline had asked her. Caroline had been confused by the relationship from the start. She hadn't answered but in her head she had said, to herself, He doesn't, and I don't care, and I'll pay the price, because I want him. He's the opposite of everything I am, and I want him. Now she was uncomfortable around him. She could have laughed out loud at the irony of it all.

'Let's go,' she said, and she went out of the room.

DOROTHY WAS IN THE dining room. When she saw them at the door she came towards them, waving, her huge breasts bouncing together as one formidable shelf.

'Hello, hello.'

She felt quite sick suddenly with panic. Dorothy had seen her with John O'Connor in the bar. She had spoken to them – she would have seen how drunk she was. Had she seen them go to her room?

'Good morning, Dorothy,' she said.

She sounded like the Queen; she could feel Simon looking at her sideways.

'This is my husband. Simon. Simon, this is the Dorothy I was telling you all about. We are related.'

Ellen gave them both a kind of crooked, snarling smile.

Dorothy ignored her. She took hold of Simon's elbow and guided him across the room. She had to follow them. Dorothy was murmuring to him, and laughing. What was she saying? She was gesturing, floridly, at a table now, pulling out the chair, helping him sit down. She waved a white napkin over her shoulder and spread it on his lap; she was practically stroking his arm. She's flirting with him, she realized then. She's a flirt.

She sat down opposite him.

'Thank you, Dorothy,' she said, without smiling.

'You're very welcome,' said Dorothy, but directly to Simon, and then turned smartly, giving her heel a little kick out behind her, and made for the kitchen.

She saw him come to my room, she thought. She knows.

'You have a fan,' she said.

He was looking around the room. He looked back at her, blankly, and didn't answer.

'I had to jog to keep up with you,' she said. 'You should have waited for me. I had to walk across the room alone.'

'Oh, for god's sake,' he said.

She didn't want to have an argument, here, now. She had to pull herself together.

'What did you think of Dorothy?'

Was it possible that she had whispered something to him as she'd led him across the room?

'Who?'

'Dorothy,' she said loudly, annoyed enough now to not care about hiding it. 'The woman who showed you to the table.'

'Oh. She's mad.'

She gave a small laugh, and he picked up the menu.

'I'll have the poached eggs. What can they do to poached eggs? Not much, not much.' He gave a bit of a wriggle: he was happy that she had laughed at what he had said.

'And a black coffee. And then we can go and see this house as soon as we've finished. Right?'

'Right,' she said.

Simon was a person who burned through time. She had never seen him sit down to read a newspaper, or watch TV in the evening. And yet there was never enough time for anything. The more he did, the less time he had for anything.

'We'll see it now and then we can decide, today. It might be a push to fly back tonight. That's the disadvantage of being out here in diddly land. You're hours from the airport. It's not going to be a weekend place, is it?'

She said nothing. It was easier to say nothing.

'Phone the agent, then,' he said.

'I don't want to phone the agent,' she said. 'The agent showed me the house already. I've made an offer, the offer's been accepted.

If you want, we can go to look at it on our own, I know where it is.'

'Ellen,' he said. 'Call the agent. The offer you made . . .' He was looking at her, assessing her mood. 'Look. I want to see the house before we make any serious offers. I'm not seeing it with you and then going to see it again with the agent. Waste of time. I want to talk to the agent today.' He pointed to her phone on the table.

There was nothing to be done. She felt very tired, suddenly. The whole plan she'd had of coming to Ireland and buying the house and changing things, sending things off in a different direction, seemed impossible, suddenly. She felt the old, familiar numbness begin to settle on her. She picked up her phone and called John O'Connor's office. John would be happy to show it to them today, said the girl on the phone. He would meet them in the hotel in half an hour. Mr O'Connor, his father, would be coming with him. She hung up, her face set.

'He's coming,' she said. 'The guy I met yesterday. And his father is coming too.'

'The father is coming,' said Simon. 'They know we're serious.'

They know we're serious, Simon, she thought, because I've said I'll buy the house. They believe me. I've signed documents. I've given them bank details.

'Yes, you're right,' she said, and gave him a little smile. 'Clever Simon.'

He liked it when she agreed with him. He gave her a proper smile and she smiled back and she thought, I should just pretend he knows more than me, all the time. I should just smile and pretend my way through the whole thing, and then everything would be fine.

*

THEY WERE STILL EATING when John O'Connor and his father arrived. She could see Dorothy, standing guard at the door, pointing them out in the dining room.

They came to the table.

Ellen stood up.

'John,' she said. He was looking beyond her shoulder. He would not look at her face. 'This is my husband, Simon.'

Simon half stood up to shake hands with him, then sat back down and picked up his cup of coffee. She knew what he was doing. He would make them wait for him.

'I'm Charles O'Connor,' said John's father. He shook hands with both of them. 'God, you're still eating. I'm sorry,' he said, not sounding sorry at all. 'We'll join you.'

He is old, thought Ellen. He is eighty, perhaps. Why is he here? Why is he still working? He looked like his son but there was something finer about him, something more decent. She liked the way he looked straight at her with open interest. He saw her. She wasn't invisible to him. He reminded her of her father, a little. But every old Irish man I meet reminds me of my father, she told herself. It means nothing.

He turned and pulled two chairs from the table next to them and sat down.

'Sit down, John,' he said, pointing to the chair, not looking at him.

'We need to be getting on,' said John.

'Finish your coffee,' said Charles to Simon, with a smile. 'We have all day.' He turned to look at his son, calmly considering him. 'John is in a hurry,' he said. 'I'm retired officially, of course, but I still like to call into the office every day to keep an eye on things and every day I say to John, take your time to talk to people, take your time to learn. He's still learning! Always in a hurry, aren't you, John?'

John said nothing. He sat down heavily on the small dining chair. He is too heavy for it, thought Ellen, it will collapse beneath him. Please let it collapse beneath him.

She put her head on one side and looked at him straight on.

He still had not looked at her. She could feel the anger coming off him like heat.

'I was just telling Simon, John, that I met you yesterday.'

There was a voice in her head saying, *Stop*, but it was a small voice, easily quietened. She waited.

'That's right,' he said, eventually, when he saw that she would not say more until he responded. He shifted in the chair, pulling his tight trousers up on his thighs. 'I wasn't sure I'd be hearing from you today.'

'Really, John?' She gave a little mannered frown. 'Why's that?'

John reddened.

'I thought you might have changed your mind overnight.'

'Oh no,' she said. She looked at Charles and gave a little silver laugh. 'Sure, why would I change my mind? I only saw the house yesterday. My mind is made up.'

She pointed at John.

'He's a bit hungover this morning maybe, Charles. He was in flying form last night in the bar.'

She leaned back. She gave Simon a flicker of a look; his face was expressionless.

'Jesus,' muttered John, loudly enough for them all to hear.

'John,' said Charles, standing up. 'I'll go on with these people on my own. You can go back to the office.'

'I'm happy enough to come.' He tried to say it jokily but it came out almost as a plea.

'No,' said his father, his voice going up on the *o* in frustration. 'No, no,' he said, more calmly, collecting himself. 'No need. I'll see you later on.' He turned to Ellen and Simon. 'John has to hold the fort here,' he said, with a managed smile. 'He's very busy in the office.'

John stood up. He had a newspaper in his hand and he was clenching, unclenching his fist around it.

He nodded at Simon. Simon regarded him, coolly.

'I'll see you all later, so.'

He didn't look at her, or at his father, before he left.

There was silence, for a moment.

'I'm done,' said Simon, pushing his chair back.

Charles looked at her half-eaten plate of food. She pushed it away from her.

'Right so,' said Charles, standing up. 'Off we go.'

THEY GOT INTO HIS car; she didn't even try to argue that they should take hers. Simon sat in the front. She could tell that he liked Charles O'Connor and was determined to charm him, and this meant talking to him incessantly and acting like she wasn't even in the car. She didn't mind. She sat in the back and lay her head against the cool window and watched the mountains go by. The window smelled familiar, like the car windows of her childhood: it was the same mix of rain and rubber and the dry air in the car. She thought of all the hours she'd spent in the car as a child, looking out the window at the great world beyond, impatient for the time when she could join it. She sat up to make the memory go away. The rain had lifted now and the sky was run with purple. She looked up; Charles O'Connor was watching her in the mirror.

'It will be a lovely evening,' he said to her.

'It will,' she said. She turned to look out the window again. 'Did you know the O'Donovans, Charles?'

'Oh, I did,' he said. 'I knew your grandmother, Rose, when we were children, and I remember your great-grandmother, Eily, even. She was a stern woman, I recall.'

Simon laughed a false laugh, har har.

'No, but now, she was a great businesswoman in her day they say, and she ran that place brilliantly while she had it – the farm, the shop in the town that was her brother's, I believe. I heard that things went wrong for them when they moved to the city, which is a pity. They were fine people.'

THEY'D GONE TO THE city – 'We were run out of it,' her grand-mother Rose used to cry, 'run out of our own place!' – and had started up a coal business; she'd seen photos of her great-grandmother Eily standing next to a broken-down-looking horse hitched to a cartful of coal. But the coal dust got into her great-grandfather's lungs and he'd died within a couple of years.

'I found him dead in the dahlias,' her grandmother used to tell her, screwing up her face comically: Ellen remembered that, the strange gap between what her grandmother was saying and how she was saying it, and trying, as a very small child, to make sense of it. She'd gone into the garden, she said, to call him in for his dinner and had found him lying face up on the grass, his eyes still open, one hand stretched out towards the flowers. 'Daddy, I said, but I knew he was dead, I didn't even wait for an answer. I just turned around and into the kitchen to tell my mother. Sure, he was dead once he left the land. We were only waiting for it to happen.'

The coal business had to be sold then, and it was sold for nothing, because they'd made nothing from it. They had only debts. The small house they'd bought had to be sold too, and Eily and her child moved into a rented room in the centre of the city. Eily went to work as a cook in a local hotel and her child ran wild all day long with the children from the lanes.

'And my mother would stand me in the tin bath every night,' she remembered her grandmother saying, 'and scrub the dirt off me and curse the neighbours' children and the lanes they'd come from. "We are from better stock," my mother used to tell me, "you remember that, and only for things going wrong for us we'd be on the farm still and your father walking his fields every evening. Only for we lost the land, we'd have been all right."'

'IT'S A LONG TIME ago,' said Simon. 'All of this.'

'Well, of course, they were before my time,' Charles said. 'They were of my parents' generation, Eily, and the sister, Hannah, of course. It was your grandmother Rose I knew and I barely knew her; she used to come down for the summer holidays when we were children. But I know the stories. She was a remarkable person, and only nineteen at the time it all happened. They were different times then.'

'Eily?' Ellen said, confused. She had never heard anything of any interest said about a nineteen-year-old Eily. Eily, in fact, seemed to her to be an entirely unremarkable figure.

'No,' he said. 'Oh, Eily – no. I'm after confusing you. It's Hannah I'm talking about.'

'Oh, well, I'm interested in Hannah,' she said, brightly. 'I'd love to know more about her.'

She felt something shift in Charles, very slightly. He turned to the side to look out to the hills. She watched him holding himself in, deciding whether to continue.

'It's not my place to say it,' he said, 'but as you say, it's all a long time ago, I suppose, and what's the harm now . . .' His voice trailed off.

'What's that, Charles?' said Simon, leaning towards him. Simon had a sharp ear for an indiscretion.

'Well,' said Charles, and he gave a jiggle of pure pleasure in anticipation. 'When I was growing up it was always said that Hannah had a baby out of wedlock, and that's why she had to go to America. The whole town knew, really, that Hannah had a baby but it was never said out loud, of course. It was only whispered at the back of the church on a Sunday morning.'

He turned around and looked at Ellen with the open, hopeful expression of a child.

She didn't answer for a minute. She couldn't think of a normal-sounding thing to say.

'So,' Simon was saying. He is enjoying himself now, she thought. 'What became of this illegitimate child? Do we know who the father was?'

'The father,' said Charles, 'was the leader of the Volunteer regiment in these parts, a fellow by the name of O'Riada, who distinguished himself in high office afterwards. The child – I don't know what became of the child.'

'Well,' said Simon.

'Well now,' said Charles.

Simon turned around in his seat to face her.

'What do you think of this development?' he said. 'Illegitimacy. IRA blood in the family. Who knows what else?'

She looked at him straight on, saying nothing.

'All these years, Charles,' said Simon, still looking at Ellen, 'I've been hearing about the great Hannah O'Donovan who fought off the Black and Tans with a stick or the like and saved the family and now we learn this. It puts her in a different light, rather, I think.'

'Stop, Simon,' she said, in a low voice. I do not care, she thought, if Hannah had ten illegitimate children. I care that Simon thinks I would care, and that he uses this to be unkind to me, to humiliate me in front of a stranger.

She tried to take a breath but it would not come. 'Charles, will you stop the car a minute, please? I'd like to get out for a breath of air. I'm a bit carsick, I think.'

Charles pulled over slowly onto the side of the road.

She got out of the car, leaving the door open behind her, and crossed the narrow pale road. The land fell sharply away from the road, dipping down into valleys and dark woods. I would go down

133

there, she thought, and lie beneath those dark trees and leave this emptied-out world forever if I could.

Charles got out of the car. He crossed the road and came towards Ellen.

'I've upset you, I think,' he said. 'I shouldn't have said anything. My wife tells me all the time not to say anything to anyone because I always say too much and I always get it wrong. And sure, who knows the truth anyway. Who knows. I'm wrong, I'd say, I'm wrong. I'm only an old fool.'

He looked so distressed that Ellen gave him a half-smile and a nod. She wanted him not to be upset, just like she had wanted the nurses and the doctors in the delivery room that terrible day not to be upset; she wanted everything to be calm, and still, and manageable.

'It's all right, Charles,' she said. 'Like Simon said, it was a long time ago.'

Her voice sounded strange to her, like it was a recording of her voice.

'A long time ago,' he said, gratefully. 'And whatever happened, we don't know, we don't know at all why people did what they did. Sure, Hannah went to America and no one knows what happened to her afterwards. She never came back and she had no more contact with the family. So who knows what the truth is, at all.'

He looked at her, pleadingly, and when she didn't speak he said, 'It's your mother you should talk to. She'll know, surely. Or Dorothy in the hotel. She's our expert, she did a course in local history up at the university; she curated a show even at the museum there a few years ago about the War of Independence and all that.'

'I don't speak to my mother,' she said. 'I haven't spoken to her for years. And I doubt that I'm going to start talking to Dorothy about this. This is a private family matter.'

She went past Charles and got back into the car, and put her seat belt on. Her face was red with embarrassment from having spoken with such open anger. She was so unused to saying what she felt that she had frightened herself.

Charles got into the car and turned on the engine. No one said anything. Ellen kept staring straight ahead. She wasn't going to make it easier for them by saying something, she decided. Eventually, Simon gave a sigh.

'Have you recovered?' he said. When she didn't answer she saw him look at her in the car's rear-view mirror. 'Do you still want the house?' he said, then, and then he gave a laugh to cover the hope in his question.

She looked away from him, out at the land and the sky. I don't care what he thinks, she thought, and I don't care if he knows it, I don't care who knows it. I'm not pretending anymore.

'Shut up, Simon,' she said. 'Will you just shut up.' She put her shaking hand across her mouth. 'Sorry, Charles,' she said.

He lifted his hand up in supplication.

'Don't mind me. I'm only sorry for the upset I've caused.'

They drove the rest of the way to the house in silence.

THEY PULLED UP IN front of the house and it looked even smaller, and greyer, and more run-down than she had remembered. They got out of the car. Simon stood looking at the house, the yard, the falling-down outbuildings with his hands on his hips.

'Right,' he said, slowly.

He's seeing for the first time where I really come from, she thought. He's seeing the desperate smallness and shoddiness of it all and maybe he's remembering the stories I told him when we first met about how I came from the land, how my people had a house in the country and he realizes now that it was built on a lie, that I knew what he believed to be a lie and I let him believe it anyway, that I helped him to believe it. He sees what I am now, really, for the first time.

'It needs work,' said Charles.

'It needs gutting,' said Simon sharply, and then he added, 'I'd say,' remembering that he was trying to be nice. He began to walk around the yard, taking pictures on his phone.

'I always say live with a place first,' said Charles. 'And then make some changes after the first year. That's my advice and it's good advice. Take your time.'

'Hmm,' said Simon, marching on.

She walked out of the yard and climbed over a small falling-down stone wall into an old orchard. She walked through that and into the field beyond. The air was heavy with the damp. The grass wrapped itself around her legs; it was difficult to walk. She stumbled on a hidden tussock and fell onto all fours. She could smell the wet earth – if she could only lie down here, and put her face to the ground and fade away into. Her phone started to ring. She stood up, with difficulty, and answered it.

'Where are you?'

She wanted to throw the phone into the field.

'I'm in the fields.'

'That's very annoying,' he said. 'You should stay with me so we can go around together. It's not productive if you go off on your own. It's a waste of time.'

'Right,' she said.

'So come back.'

'Right,' she shouted. She hung up, and kept walking.

She walked until she came to the top of a hill. To her left, there was an old wood. Below her, in its small valley, was the house. She could see Simon standing in front of it, talking to Charles. He was waving his phone around in irritation. She saw Charles point up at her, and Simon turned and looked in her direction, and then started walking towards her, up the hill.

She sat down on the wet ground and watched him coming. He wasn't wearing the right kind of shoes for this: the wet grass would ruin the suede. And his trousers.

He was panting slightly by the time he got to her.

'Well?' he said. 'I thought you were coming back.'

'Well, I changed my mind,' she said, pertly. She put her elbows on her knees and her chin on one hand and looked up at him. 'You'll ruin those shoes.'

He stood in front of her.

'Look,' he said, 'I don't know what I have to do to make you happy. Whatever I do, it's not enough. You want the house, so we come to see the house. Here we are. And you're still not happy.' He turned away from her and said, to the fields, 'I give up.'

She wanted to run around the fields pulling her clothes off. She could no longer stay in this tight little box, explaining herself to Simon.

'I want to buy it,' she said to his back.

'And what about this Hannah O'Donovan thing?' he said.

'I don't care,' she said. 'I want the house.'

He kept looking down the hill at the house. There was something about the way he was standing that made her feel almost sorry for him.

'And will you be happy then?'

'I don't know,' she said. 'We'll see, won't we?'

She stood up, and walked past him and started back towards the house. After a minute, Simon followed her.

XIV

'I'VE EXPERIENCE OF SHEEP.'

Hannah was standing with Mary at the end of the bed. They were looking at her father. They had pulled back the sheet covering him and taken off his braces and his pants and his waistcoat and unbuttoned his shirt. There was blood on his underpants. His body was crackling and flaming with black, blooming welts.

'Do you have experience of people?' She tried to keep her voice as flat as possible.

'Sure, I suppose it's the same thing, nearly,' said Mary, too cheerfully. 'I used to bring the sheep down from the mountains after the winter and some of them would be half eaten by dogs or the maggots and I'd fix them up no trouble. I'd do the lambing for you no trouble.'

Hannah looked at her. She tried to take a deep breath but it only went as far as the back of her throat.

'Can you help me here, Mary?'

She didn't answer. She is simple, after all, Hannah thought in desperation. Why doesn't she answer?

'The boots did their damage,' said Mary suddenly, with something like interest.

His stomach was covered with the marks of the hobnails; there were prints of the horseshoe-shaped heels all down his thigh, where they had stamped on him.

'And they've broken the ribs on him,' she said. 'We'll bind them up to give him a bit of relief. They've broken the feet and the fingers. We'll splint the hands as best we can. They might have broken his back but there's no way of knowing. We'll take a door off the hinges and lay him on it, it would be better for him than the soft bed.' She stopped and walked over to him and put her face down close to his. 'We can stitch the cuts in the face.' She looked up at her. 'And I'll make a poultice. I used to make a good one for the sheep; it will draw things out and dry up the cuts faster.' She sighed. 'I don't know what to do about the eye. I've seen sheep lose the eye and it didn't look as bad as this.'

It was the longest speech Hannah had heard her make. All she could do was nod at her, yes.

Mary stood up.

'That's all now. We could give him a drink of hot whiskey when we do the stitches. We've nothing else.'

Ciaran helped them take the door down. They lay it on the floor by the bed and though he was a great weight, together the three of them managed to get him off the bed and onto it. Mary knelt on the floor next to him and worked quietly and efficiently and with unexpected gentleness. It was over quickly, the cleaning and the binding. Before the stitching they half sat him up on Ciaran and poured the hot whiskey down his throat. He tried to give a smile and make a sound when he smelled the drink – he's trying to make a joke of it, Hannah realized, and she thought then for a moment that she would have to leave the room. She felt Mary watching her.

'You'd better have a drink, too,' she said to Hannah.

Hannah didn't look at her.

'Go on,' said Mary. 'The stitching will be as bad as you can imagine.'

She took the cup and swallowed.

'Take more,' said Mary.

'What about you?' she said. She wouldn't be told what to do by Mary.

'I'm grand,' she said, turning away from her.

The drink was hot in her throat. It was hot in the room though they had opened the window, and the white curtain blew very slowly in the hot breeze. The room smelled of blood and whiskey now; the smells were caught on the heavy, hot air like fish in a net. When the needle went in the first time the pulling sound it made hung on the air too, and each time the needle went in and out after that it traced over and back over that first sound and after a while it was as if the air itself was being stitched into a terrible kind of skin. The room was full of the sound of the stitching and the smells and it was becoming difficult to breathe; she could see what she felt on Ciaran's face when they looked at each other across her father's body and she thought, He'll never forget this, and he's a child, still, he's only a child.

She held her father's hand. He tried to call out the first time the needle was pulled out but after that he was silent, and she didn't watch, but the listening was worse, she thought, that dry tearing sound was worse than watching.

Mary was sweating: her face was red from the effort of it.

'There we go,' she said, eventually, and she sat back with her legs out in front of her. She sounded defeated.

Hannah looked at her father. Mary had closed the biggest cuts on his face but the flesh was pressing against the black stitches as if it would break through and his face now was terribly swollen, worse than before, even.

'It's all I can do,' she said. 'The poultice will help.'

Hannah nodded.

'What will we do with the eye, do you think?' asked Mary. She got up onto her knees and leaned towards Hannah's father and put her face too close to his.

Hannah, standing behind her, shook her head.

Mary stood up.

'I'll go down and make the dinner,' said Mary, after a while.

HANNAH STAYED IN THE room all day. After Mary had put the poultice on his face, her father fell into a sleep, and she lay on the floor next to him. She put the gun on the ground next to her, where she could reach it, and it sat, quiet as the night, taking in the sun. She was very tired – she didn't remember ever being quite so tired – and her face hurt terribly and more, all the time; mostly, she could think of nothing beyond the pain. She tried to follow the light on the ceiling as it moved around in a slow circle, a small little sun clock, trapped in the room; she tried to think of Eoin, to imagine what was happening, but she was hardly conscious of anything beyond her contracted world of heat and light and pain and her at the sharp centre of it, burning away. The hours passed without her being able to follow them. No one came into the room. She heard Liam call out once from somewhere in the house, but otherwise, all was perfectly silent.

Towards the evening Mary came with bread and tea for her. Hannah pretended to be asleep while she was in the room. She could feel Mary standing over her, looking at her, for a long time; it seemed that she would never leave. When finally she did Hannah half sat up against the wall and tried to eat the bread but it was too hard, so she soaked it in the tea and sucked at it. Her mouth tasted of blood – the smell and the taste of it were one thing to her. The blood on her legs had dried hard, and she still had the blood on her hands but it was dark now and when she rubbed her hands together bits of it flaked off and floated into the air and swam there with the motes of lazy light. Everything seemed slow to her. She could feel the blood in her body run slow and smooth. She was dissolving, it seemed. The edges of her were disappearing into the evening. She was being washed away into the bloody light.

The light began to change to evening. Her body was sore from lying and sitting on the hard bare floor for so long, so she crawled onto all fours to the end of the bed and then pulled herself up on its metal end. She went to the corner of the room. There was a cracked mirror on the wall, above the washstand. She made herself look into it, and nearly cried out with shock at what she saw. Her face had planes in it, great levels where shadows could fall and settle. Half of her face was monstrously swollen. Her lips seemed huge, the top one bursting with dark blood. She poured the water from the old enamel jug into the basin and picked up the white towel and washed the worst of the blood off her lips. She bathed her face and very slowly washed her hands. The water in the basin ran rose now, and yet there was still blood in her mouth, blood on her hands. She looked at herself again. Her hair was standing up in odd angles all over her head. She picked up the brush that was on the table. It was soft-bristled and backed with dark green embroidered fabric, part of a set that her mother had given Eily last Christmas. She imagined Eily standing in front of the mirror brushing her long golden hair. She put the brush back down and put her face against the mirror. Her eyes were black and flat and it took her a minute before she realized, my eyes are like his now.

She stood back. There was something happening outside. She stood very still and listened; it was as if the air itself was stirring and opening up in anticipation. She looked at her father: he was unmoving, gently sleeping. She went to the bed and bent down and picked up the gun and, holding it in front of her with both hands, walked to the door. There were heavy footsteps on the stairs. It was Mary. She looked at the gun.

'They're back,' she said, not taking her eyes from the gun.

'All of them?' she said.

'Sure, I didn't look properly,' said Mary, sounding sorry. 'I came straight up to you.'

She let the gun drop down to her side and put her hand on Mary's arm. It was the first time, in all these years, that she had touched her. She wanted to say, Mary, will you help me? I don't know what to do. I don't know what's happening, and I want it to stop, help me. Mary took hold of the hand on her arm and shook it, quite formally, as if she were the priest and she was welcoming her to the Mass on Sunday. She gave a choked laugh then at the ridiculousness of it all: her and Mary, standing on the stairs, shaking hands, and the world around them falling down.

'Will I fix your hair?' said Mary, suddenly, fiercely.

She nodded. She couldn't think, she couldn't speak; she thought, for a moment, that she would cry. She put the gun in her apron pocket. Her hands were sweating, so she wiped them on her dress and then she sat down on the step and Mary stood behind her and smoothed down her hair and then very slowly and without any skill twisted it into a plait down her back. She moved around Hannah to check her work from the front and pushed some strands back from her face and then patted the top of her head like she was a child. Mary was breathing heavily through her mouth with the effort of concentrating so hard. When she'd finished she put her hand out towards Hannah's battered face, as if she would touch it, and clicked her tongue, sadly, and sighed.

Their faces were level. They looked at each other.

'You're lovely now,' Mary said to her, and gave her a mad smile. Hannah didn't move.

'Right, so,' said Mary, standing up. She was nodding and smiling encouragement at her, so she made herself stand up, too, and together, they went down to the kitchen.

EOIN WAS STANDING IN the corner: that was the first thing she saw. Her heart gave a great jump of joy. He looked over at her and tried to give her a smile, but he didn't move away from the wall, and he didn't speak. O'Riada and Tiernan were sitting at the table – Tiernan had his head down low, in his hands. Denis was at the range. O'Riada had looked up at her when she came into the room and kept looking at her, and to get away from the look she went to stand next to Denis. There was someone missing, she knew, but it took a moment to realize who. Brennan.

'We'll have some dinner,' Denis said to her. He was stirring a pot.

She began to take the plates off the dresser and put them on the table.

'How's himself?' asked Denis.

'He's asleep,' she said.

When she went back to the range again he spoke to her very quietly so that the others didn't hear.

'Are you all right yourself?'

'I am,' she said. She turned away from him; she wouldn't cry.

She began to slice the bread at the table. Mary put the plates of food down on the table and the men sat, and without speaking, they all began to eat, apart from Tiernan.

'Eat.' O'Riada pushed the plate in front of him, spilling some of it.

Tiernan picked up the spoon but made no move to eat.

'Eat it,' said O'Riada, in great anger. 'We have to eat,' and Tiernan started to spoon the food into his mouth then.

His shout had left a space in the room for her to ask the question; she made herself ask it without even thinking about it first.

'What happened?'

'Ahh,' said Denis, and then he began to rub his hands up and down his face, up and down as if he would rub it out.

'We lost Brennan,' said Tiernan.

His voice was shaking.

'We had it all done, we thought, all done, but one of them on the ground hadn't been finished off and we didn't realize it until we heard the shot. I was behind the car picking up the guns and I heard the shot and by Jesus, I thought . . .'

He put his hands down flat on the table and then slid them towards him so that he was holding on to the table's edge. Hannah watched his hands open and close, open and close as he spoke.

'I thought someone was shooting at me.' His voice was flat. 'But it was Brennan – the soldier shot Brennan in the face when he was bent over him.' His hands plucked at the table's edge uselessly. 'He shouldn't have fecking gone near him,' he cried suddenly, lifting his head, and his cry was an appeal to them all. 'He was told over and over again to stay back. How many times before was he told to wait for the all-clear before going anywhere near them? He had to go over and have a look. He had to have the look.'

Eoin had put his spoon down. He was crying.

'In the face,' said Tiernan, dully now. 'Blew the face off him. We couldn't do anything. We tried to kind of hold his face together because he was still alive and his arms and legs were shaking and you knew he was roaring but there was no sound coming from him, just a wet kind of noise coming from his throat.' He drew his hand in a kind of veil over his face. 'All the bones in his face . . .' His voice was very quiet. He stopped.

'Jesus,' he said. 'Poor old Brennan. Ha, lads? I never thought it would be Brennan. He was one of those you thought could survive anything. Even after he was shot in the leg, he was all right.'

Tiernan stood up from the table very quickly, pushing his chair back noisily. No one said anything. After a moment he sat down again.

'Where is he?' asked Hannah.

'We hid him in the woods,' said Denis. She could hear the tiredness in his voice, and he looked so sad, so broken by sadness that she felt her heart turn over painfully in her chest. They had carried him all the way to the woods. It was miles to the woods.

'I'll go back later and bury him properly. I'll get a couple of the lads to help me. And I'll try to get the priest to come.' He held his hands up with the palms facing upwards, out flat, in supplication. 'His people are from up the country. We'll get word to them after it's done.'

'What happened to the one who shot him?'

No one answered her. She looked around the table at them. She was trying to understand. She must understand this, clearly.

'Did you get them?' she asked. 'Did you get them all?'

'We did,' said O'Riada. He was speaking directly to her. 'We got them all.'

WHEN THEY HAD FINISHED eating, O'Riada took a packet of cigarettes out of his pocket. They all took one, even Eoin. There was a long period then when no one spoke. The only sound was the crackling of the tobacco.

'What's the plan now, boys?' said Denis, eventually.

'We'll stay a few hours and rest,' said O'Riada. 'And we'll head off in the night.'

Denis stubbed his cigarette out on the plate and stood up. He put his cap back on his head.

'I've to go up the fields and bring the cows in,' he said. 'The poor old cows know nothing. And then I've to go to the woods and see to Brennan.'

'That's nearly the worst part of it,' said Tiernan, almost to himself. 'Digging the hole and then the filling it in after and the old scratching sound the earth makes against the shovel.'

Eoin stood up. It was his habit to go with Denis in the evening to bring in the cows. There was mud on his face. His head was hanging forwards as if it were too heavy for his neck.

'I'll give you a hand,' he said.

Denis put his hand on Eoin's shoulder.

'This man here was great altogether,' he said. 'Divil a fear of him.'

He was holding Eoin by the shoulder now and shaking him, and Eoin was trying to laugh and there was snot running out of his nose and he was rubbing his nose with his sleeve and his eyes were small and closed-looking from the crying. He couldn't speak. Hannah went around the table and stood next to him. She wanted him to stop crying. She was ashamed of him – he would be ashamed of himself later, surely, for this.

O'Riada stood up. He went to Eoin and put out his hand to him.

'It's a hard business,' he said to Eoin, shaking his hand, quite formally. He wanted to put an end to this scene in the kitchen, she could tell. He wanted to move things along. 'Today was a bad day, you won't be forgetting it fast. But it gets easier. The next time will be easier.'

Eoin nodded; he was crying harder now, and it was terrible to watch.

'We'll go now,' said Denis, pushing Eoin towards the door. 'And I'll say goodbye to you, I won't be seeing you again tonight.'

Tiernan stood up slowly then and leaned across the table and shook hands with Denis wordlessly. Denis turned to O'Riada. He didn't look him in the face when he spoke to him – she noticed that, and remembered it later.

'You'll be all right, so?' he said.

'We will,' answered O'Riada.

'I'll get word to your mother that you're all right.'

'Good man,' he said, shortly, dismissively.

'Right,' said Denis. 'We'll be seeing you soon enough. Keep the head down now.'

He went out into the yard, and called back, impatiently, 'Come on, Eoin, will you.'

Eoin had stopped and turned and Hannah saw that he meant to say something to O'Riada.

'Go on, now, go on,' said O'Riada, stopping him. 'You're grand. Go on,' and so Eoin went out after Denis into the yard.

She watched the door close behind them. She was standing next to O'Riada, close enough that if she moved her fingers she could touch him. She wanted to touch him. She wanted to put her head on his shoulder and for him to put his arm around her and for the two of them to walk out of this kitchen on their own and never come back, never come back here, and for it just to be the two of them together out in the world. It was an effort for her to turn away from him and go to the table and start to clear it. Mary had heard the bang of the door and had come out from the scullery. She began to scrub at the table with great energy like she had run out of time and everything had to be finished, now. She felt slow and useless next to her.

'Go on over there,' Mary said to Tiernan, waving him away, and he got up from the table wordlessly and went to stand by the range. He lit another cigarette and smoked it in deep slow drags. His eyes were fixed on the ground and he smoked into his hand like the poor people did, as if he were ashamed of the cigarette and would hide it.

O'Riada went to stand with his back against the wall, and he watched Hannah as she did her work. His watching was an open, brazen thing, and under his black eyes she grew hot. Her hands became useless things – she nearly dropped a dish, but Mary caught it in time. She tried to catch her eye but Mary turned away from her, quite deliberately. I know what's happening here, Mary's turned shoulder seemed to say, we all know what's happening here, and I will have no part in it.

When she had finished the work Hannah said to Mary, 'I've to get the horse.'

He was still in the orchard, with the tack on him. The evening was coming in fast, and he would be waiting for her. He had been waiting for her all day, covered in cold sweat and the bit still in his mouth.

'I'll go up and see to your father so,' said Mary. 'And the boys will have to be fed now.' She didn't look at her. She is angry with me, thought Hannah, or she is embarrassed. Or she is afraid.

She took the apron off over her head and tried to smooth back her hair in the same gesture. She walked over to the door and looked out into the radiant evening. She heard O'Riada shift and then walk towards her. He stopped behind her; she could smell him there. Without turning to look at him she walked out into the yard. She started to walk to the orchard with O'Riada walking close behind her.

She opened the small wooden gate to the orchard and walked in amongst the low, fragrant trees. The horse came towards her, shaking with distress. She took the saddle off and then the bridle and threw them on the ground with as much violence as she could manage. The saddle, which she had always handled like a precious thing – she didn't care if it was spoiled, now. The horse sighed and moved his jaw, testing it out. His back was stained dark with sweat. He put his head on her shoulder, against her head.

'Sorry,' she said. 'I'm sorry.'

She put her hand on his curved jawbone and he breathed in, smelling her.

She could feel O'Riada standing behind her. He put his hand on her shoulder.

'Hannah,' he said.

Her name sounded safe, and wonderful, in his mouth.

He will leave tonight, she thought. He will leave, and I will be left here without him and I will never be able to think of anything in the same way again afterwards. The only thing that I have is this, now, and it's already going.

She put her hand out behind her and he took hold of it. She turned then, and faced him. It was impossible to look at all of his face at once – it was too much. She looked at his beautiful mouth, and then she closed her eyes and leaned towards him, her face lifted up to his.

X V

SOMEONE HAD TOLD HER once that it wasn't possible to love too much, but that it was possible to love in the wrong way. Someone had told her, or she'd heard it in a film – she couldn't remember now. She had loved Simon in the wrong way, she thought, nearly out loud. That was the problem. The love she had for him was bad for her.

She sat up in bed watching him sleep. He was breathing quietly in and out, unperturbed, relaxed. He slept naked, always, and he had spread himself across the bed so that she had to make do with the space that was left over, on the edge. She was what was left over after Simon. There was so much of Simon and he was so sure of himself and so unshakeable; he moved through his days like a ship moving through an icy sea, breaking through the ice before him, unaffected, untouchable. She looked at his handsome face and she felt, suddenly, like poking him very hard in the eye. She leaned over him and blew at him. His eyelids fluttered, barely.

'Simon,' she said, very quietly. She gave him a small shove. He didn't respond.

She got out of the bed and went to the window. The street outside was in darkness. She put her lips against the glass and pressed hard and then stood back to look at the imprint. It was cold in the room: Simon didn't like to sleep with the heating on. She went to her bag and took out her phone. She thought then of a message James had sent her, years ago. *You are love and sex and intelligence and laughter*. She remembered the night he had sent it to her. They were in America, it was summer – she could still, now, smell the sweet air, she could still bring up the feeling of the place, and of that day. They had been together all that wonderful day in the hazy hot sun, and that evening – she had to turn her mind away from the memory of the evening. He had texted her that night when she had gone home and she had been so full of love for him that she could barely read the message. She remembered now how her mind had been full with him, how her body was dissolving from him; she had felt like she was about to tip over into something liquid, that her bones would melt from him. She was losing herself in him, at that time.

And yet she had left him, after the summer, and now she couldn't even remember what he looked like. She couldn't remember his face. He was gone from her, completely, utterly. He had loved her in the right way, and it hadn't satisfied her. She had wanted something wrong. To be with James was a surrender; it was an end. She was a little ruthless, she knew, and a little cold; it made her careless with people, and it made her careless with herself. She had a restless heart, and she had fed it, her little monster heart, and left him, and kept going on, alone, until Simon, through the time she had been with Simon, until now.

To acknowledge that she should have stayed with James was to admit that everything, after him, had been wrong. She had made a great mistake and once it was made she had continued to make mistake after mistake, and now here she was. She looked at Simon lying in the bed. It was too late for her in most of the ways that mattered now; she had burned through happiness and burned through herself and she had thrown away the love she was meant for. She knew that she would never again feel the way she had felt that day in America, when she had been outside of time, beyond herself, set free by love. She would never, again, be free.

She went back to the bed and sat on the edge of it and went through her phone numbers. She still had James's number, though she hadn't spoken to him since the last day of that summer in America. He had finished his studies, she knew; he had taught, and probably taught still, at the university in the small city he came from; he had married a girl he had known since childhood. He had done nothing she hadn't anticipated. She tapped the screen with her nail. She imagined phoning him, and him sitting up in his bed in his house in the suburbs at the sound of the ringing and his wife saying, 'Who's that?' and him looking at his phone and saying, 'No one, no one, go back to sleep.'

She went into the bathroom with the phone. It was just after midnight. She dialled the number, and waited. The phone rang for a long time, but she had expected that. She waited. Then, 'Hello?'

It was the same small, light voice as always.

'Hello,' she said. 'It's Ellen.'

'Oh, Ellen,' said her mother.

'I'm back in Ireland and I thought I'd ring,' she said. She wanted to cry now – hearing her mother's voice was like being slapped in the face.

'Oh well, we're always delighted to hear from you,' said her mother, very carefully.

Who's we? she wanted to shout. You live on your own.

'I haven't heard from you for a long time,' she said.

'Ahh,' said her mother. 'I sent you those emails and you never responded so I said to myself, she's busy, I'll leave her alone.'

'That was two years ago, Mammy,' she said.

'You know the number here,' said her mother, in the same mild, dangerous voice.

'Any news, anyway?' she said, desperately.

'No, no, all the same, no news,' said her mother. 'You haven't spoken to Fiona for a while.'

'I haven't heard from her for a long time,' she said, quietly.

She had phoned Fiona every Friday night, for years. But just after the second miscarriage, two weeks after, only, they had gone back to Ireland for Christmas and Fiona had acted, all that week, like she was annoyed to have them there, like they were too much for her. She'd invited them to her house on the last day of their visit. Come at twelve, she'd said. She had been quite specific about that. But when they'd turned up she had still been in her pyjamas, watching TV. After a while Ellen had said, 'Will I make some lunch?' and Fiona had answered, sounding half surprised, 'Oh do, do,' but had made no move to help her. There was hardly any food in the house, and it was cold, and Ellen was tired and hungry. She'd moved around the strange kitchen, opening and shutting cupboards and not able to find anything she was looking for, and all of it under Simon's cool gaze. Eventually she'd found some pasta and had cooked that; there was no sauce, so she'd grated some old cheddar onto it. Simon drank glass after glass of whiskey – he'd poured it for himself from the only bottle in the kitchen. She had made herself tea. She had wished that she could sit in a comfortable room in front of a fire and have someone look after her, have someone be kind to her; her body was sore and she was aware that she was moving slowly, and not thinking sharply. I'm not right, she remembered thinking to herself, and I need someone to help me, and she'd almost started crying then from the loneliness and the desperation of it all.

In the car on the way back to the hotel she had become nearly blind with the anger.

'Wasn't that unbelievable?' she had appealed to Simon, and he had answered, languidly, 'All of your family are rubbish.'

'But that,' she had said wildly, 'that was terrible.'

'She doesn't know you've just had the miscarriage,' he'd said, not looking at her, looking straight ahead and at the road instead.

He will always defend the other person, she had thought, the person who is not me.

'That's not the point,' she had said, very quietly.

'It was only lunch,' he had answered. 'Get over it.'

She'd gone back to London and she hadn't phoned Fiona again. Fiona had sent her a text after a couple of weeks: *Are you odd?* And then, a few days later: *You're definitely odd.* And then, weeks later: *I'm pregnant. I had terrible morning sickness the week you were home. Ring me when you can.*

She had not replied, and after that she didn't hear from her again.

They had all let her go, easily, and after a while that had become the thing that mattered above all the rest of it. None of them had looked for her. They had let her fade away.

'How is she?' she asked.

'Oh, great,' said her mother. 'The children are lovely, little dotes. She had to go back to work when they were still babies, of course, and that's not easy, but there you go, she had to do it.' She paused. 'Some have to.' She gave a sniff. 'How are things with yourself?' She could hear in her voice that it was difficult for her to ask this.

'Fine,' she said. I can't have a baby, Mammy, she wanted to say. No one knows why. I've been to every doctor in London and still no one knows why. I gave up work so I could concentrate on getting pregnant, that was what I said to people when they asked, but no one asks anymore now, even though I look five months pregnant all the time. And Simon's given up on me, I don't think he loves me anymore and it all gets worse with every day that passes, he likes me less and less all the time. And I had a little girl, Mammy, but she died as she was born, she just slipped away from me like a little fish going back into the water, and I want her back, all I want is to have her back. People say I can keep trying for another baby but I don't want another baby, I want her, I want my baby back.

'Are you here on your own?'

'No,' she said, 'I'm here with Simon. In Lisarna.'

There was a silence.

'We've come to look at the old farm. It's on the market.' She paused, for effect. 'I'm buying it.'

She felt cold saying that, but wonderful – a whoosh of energy ran through her. Now, Mammy, she thought.

'That's great,' said her mother. 'What will you do with it?'

'I don't know,' she said. 'I'll see.'

'How much?'

She felt her heart close up like a small fist.

'More than it was sold for.'

Her mother gave a little false laugh.

'Well, it's nice you're thinking of keeping it in the family, I suppose.' She paused. Ellen waited. 'But they say that place only brought us bad luck. There was always a funny old feeling about it. Sure, we were run out of it in the end.'

'I know that,' said Ellen. She felt unaccountably miserable, suddenly. 'I remember all that. But the land . . .' She stopped. 'I don't know. The land was ours for a long time, wasn't it? And I just thought it might be good to get back what was lost to us.'

She could hear her mother breathing. Why did she say nothing?

'I've talked to people here,' said Ellen. She had not planned on saying this. 'About the family. I want to ask you something. Someone today told me that Hannah, your granny's sister, had a baby by that freedom fighter guy and went to America with the baby.'

'What?' her mother said. '*Hannah?* What are you talking about?'

'The person who told me sounded fairly sure,' said Ellen. 'I'm going to look into it.'

'How are you going to look into it?' said her mother, lightly, mockingly. 'Are you going to talk to the half-cracked cousins we have down there? You'll get great information out of them.'

'I'll figure something out,' she said. 'Don't worry about that.'

She sounded, she knew, like a truculent child, and she was suddenly so angry that it was hard to speak. It had always been like this. She was told nothing. Nothing was ever said. Say nothing, her mother used to say, about everything. Don't be telling everyone your business. Keep your counsel. Don't be making a fool of yourself for anyone.

'Sure, Ellen,' said her mother. 'What does it matter? What are you worried about all of that stuff for?' She gave a sniff. 'Phoning me up in the middle of the night to ask about all this. I don't know.'

She didn't answer. All this time, she had been out in the world, alone, and she felt so lonely then that she nearly said, out loud, *I miss you, Mammy, do you miss me? Did you ever think about me? Why did you let me go?*

Instead, she said, 'I might come up to see you.'

'Oh, you're always very welcome here,' said her mother. 'The house is freezing, though, because I don't turn on the heating. It's too dear. So you'll have to take us as you find us.'

She wouldn't go back to that house, she knew that. She wasn't wanted there. *I was only eighteen when I left*, she wanted to say. *I didn't know what I was doing. I didn't know that if I left you wouldn't want me back.*

'You could come here,' she said. 'We're staying in O'Donovan's Hotel.'

Her mother gave a tinkling laugh. 'Ellen! O'Donovan's Hotel? Is it all right?'

'It's fine,' she said.

'Ah, but Lisarna is miles away, a good three hours away, and that road is terrible. I'd have to drive home in the dark. I wouldn't be able for that now at this stage in my life.'

'You could stay the night,' she said. 'I'll pay.'

Her mother sighed. 'I don't know now, I don't know. I look after

160

the children two days a week and I'm shattered from that. And I couldn't let Fiona down, you see, I couldn't leave her in the lurch.'

'It's Saturday tomorrow,' she said. Her determination was a thing greater than her anger and her hurt now. She would have her mother come, because she didn't want to. 'And the food is very good here. They do great dinners.'

That would do it.

There was a long silence. She waited. Her mother had said once, to Fiona, but in her hearing, 'Ellen always needed a lot of love.' It had been said with a sigh, like that was the explanation for whatever was wrong with her, that she was, really, a great love-sucking empty hole of a person. There wasn't enough love for her, or it wasn't a love of the right kind, had been the meaning behind it, she thought now, putting her head on one side and looking at herself in the mirror. She looked tired all the time now. She looked old.

'I don't know,' said her mother nervously.

'Don't come so,' said Ellen. 'I'll see you the next time I come.'

Her mother sighed. She's imagining her big dinner floating away from her, thought Ellen.

'I could come for midday, I suppose,' said her mother. 'Simon will be there, will he?'

'He will,' she said.

'Right,' said her mother, slowly. 'I'll come. I hope I'll be all right on that road.'

'You will,' said Ellen, grimly.

'I hope so,' she said, with a sigh. 'I'll go now so I can get some sleep. I was sleeping before when you rang me.'

Ellen said nothing.

'So I'll see you tomorrow just before lunch,' her mother said, eventually.

'Right,' she said. 'Bye, Mammy.'

'Bye,' she said, very faintly. She could hear her struggling to put the receiver back on the phone. When she heard the click, she hung up.

She thought of her mother standing in the dark in the cold kitchen, looking at the phone. She would be wearing an old T-shirt and old knickers, and she would have one hand across her chest, holding her breasts down. There would be a slight smell from her, because she wouldn't have washed properly for a while.

She went into the bedroom and to the bed and shook Simon by the shoulder. She pulled his ear. Then she flicked him quite hard on the face.

'Ow.'

'Simon,' she said, very crossly. 'Wake up. I want to tell you something.'

He didn't open his eyes. 'What?'

'My mother is coming tomorrow.'

He opened his eyes then and looked at the ceiling, not at her.

'Did you hear me?' she said.

'I heard you.' He turned to look at her. 'What time is it? And when did you find this out?'

'Now,' she said. 'I phoned her. I asked her about the Hannah O'Donovan thing and she said she didn't know. She's coming, though.' She sat on the bed next to him. 'I told her the food was lovely.'

'That would do it,' he said. 'That woman would go up a mountain for a nice lunch. What time is she coming?'

'Lunchtime,' she said, and they both laughed then. She put her hand out to him. She had always liked Simon more after she'd spoken to someone in her family.

'Why did you phone her?' he said.

'I don't know,' she said. 'Who knows.' She was going to make some kind of joke about it but she found she couldn't. 'She's staying here tomorrow night.'

'Ellen,' he said, sitting up. 'I'm going back on Sunday. We'll finalize everything tomorrow one way or another and I'm going back on Sunday.' He was watching her, very attentively. 'What about you?'

'I might not want to go back on Sunday,' she said.

She took her hand away from him. She was frightened suddenly by how sure he was that he would leave and that she might not leave with him. He had not come to bring her back, she thought, and her heart gave a hard bang in her chest. He had come to help her to buy this house, to progress things for her here. All along she had thought that she was the one with the plan – to buy the house, to try to start something new – but it was not impossible, she realized now, that Simon had a plan of his own that she was not aware of, at all. All this time she had thought that the buying of the house in Ireland was her idea, and that Simon had indulged her in it. Now it seemed very possible that he had encouraged her, all along, because it was what he wanted. He wanted her to buy this house. She felt quite sick – how had she not seen this? Simon was intelligent; not more intelligent than her, she thought, but he was ruthless, and cunning, and she needed to be alert, now, and to start paying attention, because things were taking an unexpected turn, had very likely already taken a turn that she hadn't anticipated, and she was already behind.

'Right,' he said, slowly, as if he were talking to someone very stupid, or dangerous. 'So what will you do?'

'Why, Simon?' she said. 'Why do you need to know now what I'm going to do?'

'I'd just like to know if you have an idea of your plans,' he said. 'For the future.'

'I don't yet,' she said. 'No plans yet.'

'When will you know?' he said.

When she didn't answer he said, quietly, 'Ellen.'

'I don't know,' she cried.

She had to say something to stop him talking. She was afraid that he was about to say something that would change everything. I'm too afraid, she thought. I can't manage this. If Simon leaves me, I am nothing. I have nothing.

'Maybe I'll come back with you on Sunday.'

'Right,' he said, still studying her.

'I'm going to sleep now,' she said. 'I'm very tired.'

She lay down on the bed with her back to him. He was still sitting up straight. They had told each other lies, she thought, about everything, about the big things and the small things, about themselves, about each other, from the day they had met. It was the only way the relationship could have lasted this long. It had all turned, from the beginning, on a lie. She was tired of all the lies now, but without the lies there was nothing. I don't want to be out in the world on my own, she said to herself. I'll keep lying if I have to. I won't let him leave me.

'Go to sleep,' she said to him. 'I can't sleep if you're awake.'

There was no point trying to have an argument with him. Simon would not argue. He did not hold a grudge. If they had a stand-up shouting match, half an hour later, even, he was ready to make up. Even if he was in the right, and had been badly maligned, he was able to smile beatifically and offer forgiveness. The worst of arguments did not touch him, it seemed, did not hurt him. But it was because he cared less than her, or because he felt less that it was easier for him to forgive; it cost him hardly at all, so that even when she won an argument, she lost. He became upset only when he was frustrated in his plans or his desires, and because he was spoiled, had been spoiled all his life, he was frequently frustrated, and angry, and then thought himself to be upset. He was concerned with others, with her, only in how they related to him, how they affected him. He had always been, ultimately, detached from her. She had never been able to bind him to her.

'Goodnight,' he said.

He rolled onto his side, with his back turned to her. After a minute he began to snore softly. She lay next to him listening to him sleep. It was nearly light before she slept.

SHE WOKE AT HALF past eleven the next morning not knowing where she was. She had had a dream about the baby again, and she had been crying in her sleep, she had dreamed that the tears on her face were from the waves in a sea and then she was in the sea, underneath the water and not able to get to the surface, and the water had been a great weight on her and she was pushing up like she was trying to push her way out of a box, and that's how she'd woken, with a shout of fear and her hands up in the air, pushing up. She lay on the bed, blind from the panic. You're all right, she told herself. You'll remember where you are in a minute. You're all right. The room began to fade into view then and her breath steadied. She sat up. She was alone in the room. She looked at her watch: it was half past eleven, and her mother was coming in half an hour.

She picked up her phone and called Simon. She was sweating, nearly breathless still.

'Where are you?' she said, when he answered.

'I'm out for a run,' he said.

She got out of the bed.

'You know my mother is coming at midday, Simon,' she said. 'Why didn't you wake me up? When will you be back?'

'I'll be back soon,' he said. 'Maybe an hour.' He was enjoying himself – she could hear it in his voice.

'Why didn't you wake me up?' she shouted.

'You're awake now,' he said, cheerfully.

'Oh my god,' she shouted. 'Simon.'

'What?' he said, lightly.

She would have to meet her mother on her own. He had abandoned her.

'Thank you so much,' she said, with as much sarcasm as she could muster, 'for all your help,' and then she hung up.

She went into the bathroom and showered, then put on her make-up and got dressed. She put on black jeans and a toffee-coloured jumper that she knew her mother would like, and knotted a little scarf around her neck. Her mother would see that she was fatter, of course. She would see the new lines at her eyes and the thickening waist and the coarser hair. She picked up her handbag and held it in front of her stomach, and looked at herself in the mirror. It was a very expensive handbag, she told herself, and then she gave a very deep sigh. Oh god, she thought. Oh my god.

IT WAS MIDDAY NOW. She went out of the room and started down the stairs, holding her handbag in front of her stomach. Halfway down she saw her mother. She was standing in the lobby. She had the same badly highlighted hair as always, and she was wearing too much blusher. Her shoes were half-shoe and half-trainer and she was wearing dark jeans, her stomach straining against them like a too-ripe fruit that would burst at the touch.

'Oh, oh,' said her mother, turning and seeing her, nodding and smiling and coming towards her. She could feel her bright little eyes running over her.

'Hello,' said Ellen. She wanted to turn and walk away. Two years, Mammy, you turned your back on me for two years and I'll never forgive you for it.

Her mother squeezed her arm, looking at her all the time, like she was hungry for her.

'Did you just get here?' Ellen asked her. Her voice sounded wrong.

'I did,' she said. Ellen waited for her to say more. 'The drive wasn't too bad,' she said, eventually. 'Two hours.'

Ellen said nothing. There is nothing to say, she thought.

'You're looking well,' said her mother.

'Ah,' she said with a cry, and turned away from her sharply. Her eyes started to burn with shameful tears. I will not weep, she told herself. She hadn't cried in front of her mother since she was a child and she wasn't going to start now. The dining room was in front of her with its rows of tidy white tables – she started to walk towards it, purposefully, without a word. After a moment, her mother followed her.

She walked to a table by the window and sat down. The tears had gone, but she felt shaken at having been so close to crying; she felt now like she couldn't trust herself. She had started to rub her thumb against her fingers on both hands, too fast; to stop she made herself put her hands together on her lap, under the table. Her mother was slower than her – she had always been a slow walker – and by the time she got to the table Ellen was ready for her, nearly. She watched her take off her jacket. Underneath it she was wearing a cream-coloured polo-neck; there were make-up marks on the neck and it was too tight across her chest.

'This is nice,' her mother said, looking around. She sat down. 'Lovely wallpaper,' she said. 'And lovely warm fire. It's nice to be in a warm room.'

Her mother looked at her quickly to check her reaction. She's nervous of me, thought Ellen, and isn't that a terrible, sad thing? Isn't that enough to make you want to give up, nearly? She's always been nervous of me, and that's one of the reasons why she's never really liked me.

Ellen looked away from her, and saw Simon: he was standing at the edge of the room with his hands on his hips, looking for her. He was wearing running clothes. Her mother followed her eye across the room to him.

'Is he wearing tights?' she asked, and gave a little nervous laugh.

She didn't answer – he was at the table, now.

'Hello, Imelda,' he said, and leaned down and kissed her mother on the cheek. 'It's been a while,' he said, quite coolly.

His face was dark red and he was breathing heavily. He had sweated through his clothes: they were coloured dark in patches. Her mother put her hand on her bosom.

'Oh, hello, Simon,' she said, breathlessly, her fingers fluttering. 'Yes, it's been a while, it has.'

Ellen felt a great loathing for Simon rise up in her as she watched him. His lateness was a calculated thing. He chose when to be late, so that when he turned up it was as if he had managed something against the odds, and should be praised for it. She thought of all the times he had boarded planes, late, breathless, waving at the other passengers like he expected applause for making it at all. She had a fork in her hand and had to resist the urge to stab him very hard in the thigh.

'He's been running,' said Ellen, giving Simon a hard stare.

'From what?' said her mother, and started to laugh at her own joke.

'No, no, Imelda, I just went out for a run around the town. I nearly got lost. I thought I'd never find my way back.'

He winked at her mother to make sure she was complicit in the joke, to make sure she laughed at it. He despised her mother, she knew, but he was adept at using her for his own ends, and she was the willing participant in the game: it suited her well enough to be his respondent. They both knew their roles, and played them faithfully. So her mother laughed (too hysterically, though, because she was long out of practice) and Simon sat down heavily and pushed his chair back and spread his legs wide, as wide as he could, she thought. He put his phones on the table, their faces winking with messages and alerts.

'Aren't you great to do it?' marvelled her mother. 'The running.'

'Ohhh,' said Simon, grandly, vaguely, which meant, yes. He pushed his wet floppy hair back from his face. 'Would you like something to eat, Imelda? Or is it too early for you?'

'Oh, no, no,' said her mother. 'I could manage something. Ellen said the food here is marvellous.'

Ellen said nothing.

'I'll have some lunch too, Imelda,' said Simon. He picked up the menu. 'What about you?' he asked Ellen, without looking at her. 'She's only just up, Imelda, so it might be breakfast she wants.'

'Oh, well,' said her mother. She gave a tinkling laugh and leaned back in her chair and raised her eyebrows at him. 'It's fine for some.' She leaned in towards Simon. 'She was always lazy out,' she ventured.

Simon laughed.

'Always loved the bed,' she said with a little sniff, looking back at the menu. 'Good job she doesn't have to get up early for work.'

She would not be drawn into this. She knew their game. They attacked her, together. They didn't have the courage to do it on their own.

'I'm going to have a glass of wine,' Ellen said.

Her mother gave her shoulders a little shake, like a chill had run through her. She didn't approve of the drink, as she called it.

'Do,' she said, tightly, without lifting her eyes from the menu.

'I will,' Ellen said, looking straight at her, challenging her. Then she called a waitress over with a wave of her arm.

'Mammy, what are you going to have?' she said.

Her mother put her fingertips to her lips, tap tap tap.

'Ahh, I'll have the roast chicken, I think,' she said, very quietly.

She fluttered her fingers at Ellen. She wanted Ellen to order for her. She didn't like to order for herself – she couldn't manage it. She didn't have the social skills for it.

'The roast chicken, please,' said Ellen to the waitress. Her voice sounded hard and flat, even to herself.

'And extra potatoes, I think, extra potatoes,' her mother said, waving at her.

'Extra potatoes, is it?' said the waitress, turning to her mother. 'Mashed?'

'Ah, yeah, yeah, mashed,' her mother said in desperation: she was trying to catch Ellen's eye; she would not meet the eye of the waitress.

'Mashed,' said Ellen, to the waitress. 'And I'll have a small green salad and a large glass of white wine. Any kind of wine. Very chilled.'

She looked out the window while Simon ordered, watching her reflection quietly watch her. She had been right, at eighteen, to go. She'd always known that; she'd known it with certainty at eighteen. She'd had to go to survive. What she hadn't known was how hard it would be to stay gone. But she wanted to go now, again, out of this room, and to keep on going until she was free from these people, finally.

THE FOOD CAME. SHE drank her wine, silently, too quickly, and then ordered another glass, and a plate of chips. Her mother and Simon were talking but it was as if they were far away from her: the words went by her like little birds flying by. I am floating away too, she thought, I, too am dissolving.

Her mother ate more slowly than anyone she had ever known,

in tiny mouthfuls, and her great pleasure in the food was a sensual thing that had always disgusted and repelled her. She watched her now as she lifted the fork to her mouth and tipped the food in; a line of gravy ran down her chin and she caught it with her finger and then licked her finger, almost languorously. She thought she would have to make some excuse to leave the table; she had finished her wine now and her mother was still only halfway through the chicken.

Instead, she said, 'Did you think any more about the Eily and Hannah thing?'

Her mother looked at her. She remembered that look: it had had the power once to stop her like a blow to the head. Her mother put down her knife and fork, slowly.

'What about it? There's nothing to think about.' She turned to Simon. 'She'll be obsessed now with this, Simon.'

Simon regarded her mother without expression. He was deliberately unsettling her, she knew, by first encouraging and then discouraging intimacy. He did it to her, too – it was a game to him, a game he was good at.

'Sure, what do we care what happened nearly a hundred years ago?' said her mother, angrily, but looking away from them to the room.

Ellen could tell that she was trying to ignore Simon's deliberate coldness, but it had shaken her, it had knocked some of the brazenness out of her words.

She sniffed. That was one of the things about her: she had a permanent sniff. Blow your nose, Mammy, they used to cry at her, and suddenly she could see them all in the living room in the evening sitting around the fire and laughing and shouting at each other, and her heart gave a painful flip in her chest at all that she'd lost, all that was gone forever.

'Mammy, Hannah had a child, maybe,' she said. 'She went to America with the child.'

'I know nothing about a child. Who told you that? I'd be very surprised if there was a child, Simon. Sure, Hannah had no husband, she went to America on her own, they say.'

'Well, Imelda,' said Simon, beginning to laugh.

'The agent here told us, he told Simon and me,' said Ellen urgently. 'Simon,' she cried, 'stop laughing. Didn't he tell us that? He knew what he was talking about and it was true what he said, you could see that it was true.'

'What agent?' said her mother. 'Why are you talking to agents about this? I don't understand.'

'Charles O'Connor,' she said, impatiently. 'He showed us the farm.'

'I don't understand why you're talking to Charles O'Connor about our personal business,' said her mother. Her face was flushed. 'That old fool. That man is in his eighties. What business does he have—'

Ellen cut her off.

'Hannah was involved with Padraic O'Riada,' she said. She had to get this clear. She wouldn't let her mother slip out of this. 'We all know that. I've always known that. It must have been him. He must have been the father.'

'We don't know that, at all. That could all be a rumour,' said her mother. 'O'Riada was one of them freedom fighter fellas in the old IRA in the 1920s, Simon. He's well known. He's in all the history books.' She stopped. 'That IRA, of course, would have been a different organization altogether to the organization today,' she said. 'The family was never involved in anything like that, at all. Of course, in the 1920s the whole country was up in arms but there was never any question of that kind of thing in the family, at all.'

She looked down at her chicken. The gravy was congealing slightly; she frowned at it and picked up her knife and fork.

'But what happened to Hannah and the child?' Ellen said. She would not be diverted from this.

Her mother looked away from her, and as she moved her face changed – a look came over her that Ellen did not recognize.

'I used to go and stay with my grandmother Eily when I was a child,' she said. It hurts her to talk of this, thought Ellen. It costs her. It is a long time, perhaps, since she's let herself think of this. 'I remember her still. She lived in that small dark house and she always looked wrong in it, I used to think – she always looked like she belonged somewhere else. She used to tell me stories of her life on the farm and she was always talking about Hannah, she always used to say that she was brave like someone in a story, that—'

She stopped. She seemed suddenly flustered. She put her knife and fork down and began to pick at the edge of the tablecloth.

'Of course, Eily suffered because she never knew what happened to Hannah and she waited for her for all those years, and Hannah never came back and her parents went to their graves not knowing what had become of their daughter. And Eily waited and waited and never gave up hope; she waited her whole life for Hannah, and never even had word of her in the end, never knew if she lived or died or was happy or sad or any tiny thing, at all. My mother said that when Eily was dying the last thing she said to her was, "Rose,

Hannah will be coming back soon, you must be ready for her when she comes back." Imagine that! All those years, waiting, waiting.' She stopped. She put her hands up to her face as if to block out the light.

'I don't know why you want to bring all of this back up, Ellen. All these old stories. They were very difficult times and everyone did their best and if Hannah did have a baby—'

'Mammy,' said Ellen.

Her mother put her hands down in her lap. She was completely white in the face, as if she'd had a great shock.

'You knew all along,' said Ellen, amazed.

'I knew nothing,' said her mother, her face tight with anger. She was speaking now in a vicious whisper. 'Or nothing for sure. If Hannah did have this baby – well, it happened a lot in families that babies were born and not spoken of, or hidden. It wasn't uncommon. I suppose I always thought that something must have happened to make Hannah leave like that, to stop her coming back, but I know nothing for sure. Nothing. You should leave it be, Ellen. Leave the past alone.'

'I think it's very odd, is all I'm saying,' said Ellen, 'that someone could be made to disappear like that. It's like she was just written out of things. She just stopped existing. And the baby, too. I mean, what happened to the baby?'

'Hannah went to America and that was that at the time,' said her mother, to Simon. She had turned her face away from Ellen. 'No internet then!' she said, trying to give a laugh. 'No Skype!'

'There's something odd, somewhere,' said Ellen. 'It doesn't add up.'

'This whole thing,' said her mother, turning back to her and speaking very coolly and slowly, 'is a load of old rubbish.' She leaned across the table. 'Hannah went to America, baby or no baby. Hannah never came back. That's all we know, that's all we need to know. It's a big thing to be saying, never mind thinking, that she had a baby by O'Riada. Hannah left, she was never heard from again. Full stop. They're all dead now, all those people, all the ones who knew what happened. And Charles O'Connor – he was always an old gossip. What does he know? Who did he know? No one, no one who mattered. An estate agent. From the town. He knows nothing about us, about our people.'

'But what happened to Hannah?' said Ellen. 'Why doesn't anyone know what happened to Hannah?'

She felt unaccountably desperate; she was nearly shouting.

Her mother looked at her across the table. Her face was absolutely cold; her pale blue eyes were flashing, dangerously.

'Who cares,' she said flatly, with a small, controlled shrug.

No one had looked for her, thought Ellen, because of the child, or because of what she'd done in the war, and the disgrace of it. They had let her go, they had let her story dissolve into nothing. They had made her into a ghost. All these ghosts, she thought sadly, and me one of them, me no more than a ghost now, too.

'I care, Mammy,' she said, her voice rising. Her distress was beginning to feed on itself, and grow. 'I care. It's too easy just to let people go, and forget about them.' She looked at her mother and Simon. 'Isn't it?' she said, desperate now, but no one answered her, and the silence was an answer in itself.

She turned away, ashamed. She had embarrassed herself in front of her mother and Simon. She had said too much, she had shown too much emotion. She could feel them looking at her and then looking at each other. She moved in her chair to look out the window and her own reflection looked back at her, but it looked different – it didn't look like her own face. There was something else written over it. There was something else there.

I'm here, she said, in her mind, to the face in the window.

I'm here, and I see you.

XVI

THE NEXT MORNING SHE lay on her narrow cool bed and tried to make sense of what had happened, but she found she couldn't. She couldn't fix it all in place; her mind kept swerving away from the memory of it. She felt like she did when she was out on the horse and he shied from the cluster of high trees on the hill; he was afraid of the noise the wind made in those trees, and could not be made to go near them. She would get him halfway up the field and then he would hear that sound of the wind that was like a river running through the tops of the trees and he would dance away down the hill, and nothing she could do would make him turn. The horse could not be made to go closer, and she could not make herself look, in her mind, at what she had done with O'Riada.

So she tried to think about things from the end, backwards, from when they had finally pulled apart from each other. They had sat up and, without looking at each other, they had fixed their clothes – he had helped her with her dress; he had tried to do up its buttons with his rough, clumsy fingers – and then, without speaking, they had lain back down on their backs in the long grass between the low trees, holding hands, in silence, for a long time, and listened to the quiet world around them getting ready for the night.

She could recall the feeling of the evening – she could summon that up easily enough. The evening air had been blue about them – the light of the day was gone when they lay down but it would be hours yet before darkness came, and they were suspended, marvellously, in the perfect evening light. When she was lying on her back she had put her hand out and drawn it through the thick light and then looked at it; she would not have been surprised if it had changed colour, if it had absorbed some of the colour from the evening. After what they had done, the state of all things had changed for her. Everything had assumed a new importance; the light had felt almost like a solid thing. The grass and the small insects that lived in it were wonders. The trees above them were weighted with gold. It was a glorious green world thrumming with life; if she listened carefully, she would hear the grass grow, she thought. All that surrounded her was weighted with glory.

She was near, now, to thinking of how it had begun. It had started when he had kissed the swollen side of her face, very gently, and then he had kissed her closed eyes and her forehead and then her black lips. They had kissed each other and though it had hurt her, they had kept kissing and kissing and it was so wonderful that they had both laughed with delight, and then they had stopped and looked at each other and that was the crucial moment, right there – she saw that now. If she were telling it all as a story, she would make clear that that was the moment things tilted in a different direction. Something was agreed between them, something was understood, in that moment. They'd started to kiss again and then they had fallen down onto the grass and pulled their clothes apart and lain on top of each other.

She could not think of what had followed. Lying now on the pillow, she had to turn her face to the side and put her hands over her eyes to try to push away the memory of the noises they had made, the noise of their bodies together, and the smells, and the sweetness of his skin under her tongue. Her mouth hurt terribly and her face hurt from where she had been hit and the dried blood on her legs was mixed now, she thought, with new blood, and at the thought of that she had to get up from the bed and go to the window and open it. She leaned out the window and breathed in the sweet morning air and tried to steady her breath.

She didn't know how long they had lain in the grass, in silence, afterwards. A long time, she thought – she remembered that it had been a shock when he had finally spoken. What they had done would leave her, eventually, she thought, but she would live off what they had said to each other for years.

'They'll be looking for you in the house,' he'd said.

'They won't,' she had answered. 'I often take the horse out in the evening.'

He'd leaned towards her and kissed her again and then he'd pulled away from her and sat up. He had his legs bent up and was sat with his arms stretched out on his knees, and he stayed there looking at her, his face still and unsmiling and his black eyes steady on her.

'When will you go?' she'd said to him when she couldn't take his watching her anymore: she felt like he was studying her for an answer she didn't have.

'Tonight,' he'd said. 'We have to get into Kerry now.'

There was no question of her going with him: she knew that, and yet part of her was waiting for him to ask her if she'd consider it, at least. He could not stay here. I will go with you, she'd wanted to say. Just ask me.

'We have to make a plan,' he'd said then. 'For us to meet again.'

We. He had, at least, said we, meaning him and her, and he wanted to meet again, and he'd moved closer to her so that they were sitting together, hip to hip. He had put his head down and gently butted her on the arm with his forehead and then left his head against her arm, breathing her in. She could feel his warm breath go in and out against the sleeve of her dress.

She had been looking across the orchard at the fields beyond the trees and the thought had come to her with great, frightening clarity: He will go, and I'll be left behind, for I can't get out of here, I can't get beyond these fields. There's nowhere out there for me. I have no money and not enough education and there's no one out in the world to help me. I have no aunt in England, I have no cousins up in Dublin that I can go to. I'm intended for this small world only.

'You won't be able to come back here,' she had said, 'and I can't go anywhere. None of my people have ever left here.'

'I'm from the townland of Baile Mhúirne,' he had said then, and he had lifted his head away from her arm as he started to speak. 'My mother and my sisters are there still, on the farm. My father was killed last year.'

She waited.

'The Tans came just before the day broke. There was a light on in the house because a cow had calved and the family were all after getting up to tend to her. The Tans surrounded the house, front door and back door, and sure, he hadn't a chance.'

'Were they looking for you?' she'd said.

'They were looking for me and they were looking for my father. We'd burned the courthouse in Dunavale to the ground the night before so they were on the rampage. But the only night I'd slept at home that year was Christmas night so they had to make do with my father.'

She thought she should touch him to comfort him – put her hand on his hand, perhaps, or on his arm; that was the right thing to do, surely – but she was too shy to do it. She had never seen affection between her parents. She didn't know how to behave. Standing in her small bedroom, afterwards, she marvelled at her cowardice: she had been too shy to touch him, even after everything they had done.

'They tied him to the back of one of the lorries and dragged him through the country, that's how they did it. When they cut him loose he was still alive so they left him to die by the side of the road. The old woman who lived in the cottage on the crossroads ran out to him and gave him a drink of water and said a prayer over him so he wasn't on his own when he died, he had that at least.'

He lifted up his hands in front of his face and balled them into fists and put his wrists together like they were tied. Then he shook his hands at her, gently, slowly.

'I've been living with my life in my fists every day and every night of the week since then.'

'You haven't been home to your own place since?' she said.

'I've lived out on the land,' he said, 'like a wild dog. Out in the cold and the wet and walking all night and sleeping in the day in a ditch.'

He gestured towards the fields, at the world beyond.

'Things are changing, things are turning in our direction. But they'll get worse before they get better and we have to be ready for that. What your people did before you is neither here nor there now. The people before us had no chance. They were beaten down, treated like animals. Worse than animals.' He gave a short laugh. 'They like their horses and their dogs. They wouldn't treat their horses and their dogs like they've treated us.'

He turned to her.

'We are a nothing people to them,' he'd said. 'A nothing people.'

'What will become of us?' she'd asked, in a whisper, and she'd looked away when she'd said that, afraid of his answer. What will become of me after tonight? she'd meant, and he knew it.

He'd looked at her, and sighed. She could see that he was disappointed by her question, and that had frightened her. He was clever, and he was impatient: she understood that much already.

'I'll go to Kerry and wait for things to quieten down and then I'll send word,' he'd said. She is concerned with the domestic, the small details of life – she knew that he was thinking this, and almost despising her for it. 'And we'll go on from there. It will be a long time before we can make some kind of plan, but the time will come, if we do things right.'

He was saying nothing, she realized, nothing that meant anything, but she suddenly hadn't wanted him to say more. She was cold – the evening had turned cold without her noticing, and the dew was coming down fast – and she was very tired, and she'd started to shake in her thin cotton dress. To do something, to stop the shaking, she'd started to pull at the wet grass with both hands, dragging great fistfuls of it up.

He'd squatted down in front of her then and taken hold of her hands and shaken them out and picked the grass off them; she'd let the grass fall onto her lap. He put his hands out flat and she lay her hands against his. She was surprised at how soft, and fleshy, his palms were. She thought of how soft and sweet his skin had tasted before and how his mouth had fitted with hers and the wonderful, melting joy of it. She'd lifted her face to his and he kissed her again and they kissed and kissed and over again until she'd pulled away to look at him and then he'd kissed her again like he was hungry for her.

'I'll come back for you, Hannah,' he had said suddenly, when they had stopped kissing.

He had hesitated then and she saw that he was about to say more, and to stop him she had put her hand to his mouth. Anything he says now is not true, she had said to herself, though in this moment he means what he says – she had suddenly seen that quite clearly. There is danger, perhaps, here, she thought, without even knowing where the thought came from. I must take care.

He had pulled back, pulling her hand away from his mouth, and had looked at her, questioningly at first, and she had looked back at him, smiling, and then he had given her a slow smile in return. He is more interested now than before, she had thought. This is how one must behave with him, as if playing at a game. A blackbird had flown low through the trees in front of them then and cried its falling, warning cry and they had both started. It was night, nearly. She heard the horse shake himself – the cold of the evening was beginning to settle on him.

She'd stood up. She had put her hand out to him and he had looked at her, assessing her, and then he had smiled and taken her hand and let himself be pulled to his feet.

She'd stood back from him.

'You'd better go in,' she'd said. 'I'll see to the horse and then I'll follow you in. Will you sleep?'

'No.' She saw him making the decision as he said it. 'The more we have of the night ahead of us the better.'

'I'll be in now,' she'd said, and nodded at the house as if to say, Go on.

He'd given her a half-smile and then he'd put his hand out and squeezed her shoulder. She'd wondered if he had suspected something, if he had known what she was thinking. He did not, she decided; he was too sure of her, and at the same time he did not know her, at all.

She'd watched him walk away. He was broad across the back, and slightly bow-legged. She'd felt a great wave of desire rise up in her as she'd watched him and delight then in the desire and in the way it made her feel like she had been set free. She had felt her heart soar inside her – it had soared up, like a bird flying high up into the far-away ceiling of a cathedral. The desire made her feel like she was a stranger to herself, and there was relief in that, and a wild, frightening, freedom, too.

She'd waited until he had his hand on the handle of the door of the house, and then she had gone to the horse, calling to him, quietly and urgently, in the darkening light.

*

SHE CLOSED THE WINDOW against the morning air and went back to the bed and sat on the edge of it with her bare white feet on the floor. She was still dressed – she had lain down on the bed with her clothes on, hours ago. She stood up. She should wash herself, she knew, but she only had cold water and she didn't want to have to stand the shock of it on her body – she was too raw yet for it. Hardly thinking, she took hold of the dress at the neck and tore it open, down to her waist. The buttons at the front popped and scattered across the room. She let the dress fall to her feet and then she stepped out of it. She took off her old white undershirt and threw it on the floor. She unfastened her brassiere and pulled her knickers down. She picked up all the clothes with both her hands and went to the fireplace. Mary had laid the fire, ready to be lit. She put the clothes on top of the pile of kindling and took a match from the box of matches on the mantelpiece and crouched down in front of the grate. She struck the match and put it to the kindling. The wood snapped and split and the fire curled up in little lapping green tongues and the firebugs rose, whistling, into the air.

The dress burned easily; the rest, she saw, would only smoulder and smoke. She turned and went to the wardrobe in the corner and took out her nightdress. She put it over her head and let it fall down to her ankles. Underneath, her naked body felt smooth and perfect and as light as air. Then she lay down on the bed, under the single cotton sheet, and closed her eyes and made herself remember the end of it, after he had gone into the house and she had gone to the horse.

*

THE FIRST TIME SHE'D seen the horse her father had said that he was too big for her. Don't buy a horse you can't mount on your own, he'd said, you'll always have to have someone to help you, but she'd insisted, and he had given in to her with a laugh. She knows her own mind, he'd said to Connie Murphy by way of explanation, and Connie had laughed back, unable to believe his luck – the horse was bad-tempered and too black for luck and he'd feared he'd never sell him. She'd ridden him around the small field in front of them, Connie exaggerating her skill in his high sing-song voice – 'It's up at the Dublin Horse Show she should be' – and her father had smiled crookedly at her, shy from the praise, his eyes nearly closed against the sun as he watched her and his face creased with pride.

She'd thought of that day as she'd walked across the dark orchard to the horse. It seemed to belong to a different life, a simpler, easier life, and she a different person in it. Everything was changed now. The memory of that old life had made her feel small and cold and lost and when she got to the horse she'd taken hold of his mane with both hands and with one hard jump threw herself up and across his back, kicking him in the side as she pushed herself up. It had hurt to sit on the horse – it burned between her legs and her thighs felt heavy and tired – but she'd welcomed the pain: it made her feel alive, it made sense, like the pain of kissing had seemed right. It would have been easier with the bridle and the saddle, but she wouldn't put the bit back in the horse's sore mouth and without the bridle the saddle was useless. She would ride like a tinker. She would ride free, like she wasn't supposed to.

She'd turned her body towards the trees and squeezed her legs against the horse's sides. She was weak – he wouldn't stir for her.

She'd had to kick him hard against his soft belly and he'd grunted in protest but had started to move in the direction she wanted and soon he broke into an easy trot.

The trees against the breathing land had been perfectly still; there was no wind.

There's spirits in those trees, Denis always said, that's why even the birds won't fly through them, and the sound that the wind makes there is the sound of the poor old lost souls crying out for help.

'Go on,' she'd said to the horse.

They'd gone up the hill. When he saw the trees he hesitated, and stopped.

'Go on,' she'd said, urgently, under her breath.

He'd paused to consider, and then he'd walked to the trees, picking up his legs very carefully, like he was walking over glass, his neck curved against his chest in a tight arch. He went in amongst the trees and stood there, shivering gently in the strange cool air.

'Pangur,' she'd said. 'There's my good boy.'

She'd looked down the hill at the house, and waited. After a long while O'Riada and Tiernan had come out with Eoin and she'd ducked down low against the horse's neck, even though she knew they couldn't see her in the darkness, in the trees. They'd shaken hands by the front door and then Tiernan and O'Riada had begun to walk towards the field behind the house, before climbing over the low wall into the field and walking up it; it was a hard hill up and beyond it were more hills and ditches and then the lonely black bog all the way to the mountains. O'Riada walked behind Tiernan, and after a minute, as she knew he would, he'd turned to face in her direction. He was looking for her, or he was saying goodbye, and it was terrible to see him standing there, alone like that: she felt frightened for him, suddenly, and worse, she felt sorry for him, and it was almost impossible not to go to him and hear him say her name again and feel his arms about her. She had to make herself stay where she was, to keep looking at him. He'd put his head down to one side then and in the same movement had lifted his pack further up onto his shoulder and had turned away and walked after Tiernan, then past him, so he was in the lead up the hill, and then he was over it, and gone.

Eoin had stayed watching the spot they'd disappeared into for a long time. He was bent over against the night, with his hands shoved down into his pockets; he could have been an old man, almost, with the hunch on him and the shuffle of a walk he gave. When he'd gone back into the house he'd closed the door slowly behind him, and she'd watched as he'd turned down the lamp in the window.

All was darkness now.

She'd ridden down into the river then, and waded down it to the shallow pool where the trout lived, and she and the horse had stayed by its warm banks all the night long with the big heavy moon hanging low over them in the black sky like a warning.

Afterwards, in the morning, she'd gone back to her small bedroom, and to what lay ahead of her.

XVII

Ellen pulled up in front of the house and turned the engine off.

'Right,' she said to herself, very firmly. It was the voice she used when she was in a shop, trying to return something she'd been wearing for weeks. It was a tone that brooked no argument, and it worked, usually.

'Here we go,' she added, for good measure.

She got out of the car and walked to the door of the house and unlocked it. She went into the kitchen.

The house was quiet and still, as if it were watching her, and waiting to see what she would do.

She took the notebook and pen out of her bag. She had determined that she would go around the house and make notes, lists of things to do, to think about. She would present the list, then, to Simon, and the whole process of buying the house would begin to become more real. She went through the kitchen, opening and closing cupboards and drawers. They had been lined with sheets of newspaper which were stained yellow now. The cupboards themselves were small and poorly made and either too low down or too high up. She picked up her pen. *Replace kitchen units*, she wrote.

The fireplace was small, too, with an ugly tiled back. *New fireplace*, she wrote. And the floor was covered with torn linoleum. Ellen blinked. 'Linoleum' was one of her trigger words, right up there with 'mobile home' and 'tracksuit'. She started to write *New floor* and stopped. She tore out the page from the pad and on the next page wrote simply, *New kitchen*.

She went to the door that led to the stairs. Before she put her hand on the handle she wrote, *Knock down wall and door to stairs, back room*. She took hold of the handle, ready to struggle with it, but it slipped around in her hand and the door swung away from her easily, with a little creak. Ellen looked at it. She had the feeling that something, somewhere, was laughing at her.

She went up the stairs, holding on tight to her notebook and pen. Halfway up the stairs she stopped and wrote, *New stairs*. She would knock down these stairs and put in glass ones, maybe, or maybe she would knock out the whole back wall of the house. It was too small and dark here. She would let in the light.

She went into the small bedroom on the left-hand side of the landing, and went straight to the window and opened it. The cold morning air rushed into the room and she stood breathing it for a moment before she turned to face the room. She felt quite calm, and in control. She had been ridiculous, really, to be so frightened here. She looked about her and clicked the top of the pen several times: it made a satisfying sound. The fireplace could stay, and she would repaper the walls, of course, but with something similar to what was already there. She wouldn't change this room too much. She put her hand on the wall and let it rest there for a moment. She wrote in her notebook, *Small bedroom on first landing OK*.

She lifted her head: there was a car pulling up outside. She went to the window. It was John O'Connor in his BMW.

She turned back to the room. Her face had flushed red and she put her hand up to her cheek to try to cool it. She went to the stairs and looked down, waiting. She listened as the car door was slammed shut. He was coming into the house.

'Anybody home?'

There was a hard, mocking note to his voice. He was standing at the bottom of the stairs now, looking up at her.

'Hi, John,' she said, very coolly, as though she were not at all surprised to see him here, in front of her.

She turned away from him and looked back into the room, her heart banging away in her chest.

He came up the stairs towards her, very slowly. She kept looking into the room.

'I was in O'Donovan's just now and I said to that young waitress one where's our visitor from London and she's gone off to see the old place on her own, she tells me. I heard her telling the mother and the husband at lunchtime, she says. There's no love lost there, she says, you could have cut the atmosphere at lunch with a knife.'

She went further into the room, away from him. He stood in the door frame and put his hands over his head and took hold of the lintel, stretching himself out, swaying slightly backwards and forwards.

'So I says to myself, John, take a look, maybe Ellen's lonely out there, maybe she could do with some company. The husband's a cold old fish, I'd say, and the mother's after leaving her come out here on her own so she can't have that much interest either. Go on out, John, I says to myself, and take a look.'

He stopped swinging and lifted his head up and looked up at her. 'Ha?' he said, gently.

When she didn't reply he laughed to himself and started swinging again, slowly. He hunched his shoulders over so that his back widened and opened out and strained against his jacket, and he let his head hang forwards and down. With one hand he pulled at his tie, loosening the knot.

He swung towards her then, almost playfully.

'You'd want to be careful out here on your own,' he said, softly. 'You'd never know what would happen to you. Dangerous old place. Nothing good ever happened here. They'd bad luck, the lot of them. Your people.'

He rubbed the back of his hand across his nose, roughly.

He was drunk, she realized, and the drink was making him brazen with confidence.

He let go of the door with a final swing and moved towards her.

'You know nothing of my people,' she said.

'I know blood doesn't change,' he said, pertly. 'Luck is luck. Some say they deserved their bad luck but I say, no. They might have killed those Tans and brought a war down on this part of the country and all in it and then after the war they might have switched sides easy as you have it and turned their backs on Michael Collins, but did they deserve to lose the place and end up with a ruined name and all the rest of it? No, I say. None of us are saints now, are we?'

This is about something else, she thought. He knows too much.

'You know an awful lot about my family, John,' she said. 'You're a real historian.'

He was standing facing her, breathing heavily.

'I know that your people were the wrong kind of people,' he said. 'I know that your kind of people were traitors to the rest of us. But what kind of people would you expect a bitch like you to come from? You and your English husband.'

She walked straight up to him.

'I've to go back now, John,' she said. 'Excuse me, please.'

He stood to the side and she started to go past him, but he took a nimble step back so that he was in front of her again, next to the door. He put his arm across the doorway, blocking her.

'Ho ho, now,' he said, playfully, like it was some kind of game they were at. He sounded pleased with himself.

She stopped. He came towards her with his hands in his pockets and pushed his chest and his shoulder against her, pushing her back into the room. She dropped the notebook and pen. She wanted to shout out in indignation, but she'd had such a fright that she found she couldn't, she couldn't make a sound. She had to lean back to not fall over but he leaned in more, pushing against her more, making her stumble.

All the time she looked down, away from him.

'We've unfinished business,' he said.

'You're joking,' she said.

She gave a laugh to show that she found him ridiculous, that she was not afraid.

She tried to move quickly around him, but he just moved to the side and blocked her way. She tried to move to the other side of him and in the same, slow way, he blocked her. She didn't dare to move again. If he stopped her again, she would have to acknowledge what was happening here.

'Ha?' he said to her, taunting her.

All this time he had his hands in his pockets. He didn't need to use his hands, yet.

'Let me pass,' she said, quietly, steadily.

He took his hands out of his pockets then and put them in her hair, against the back of her head. His hands were huge. He will crack my head, she thought, in a panic, and tried to free it by shaking it but he held on and put his face down to hers and started to kiss her, hard. She put her hands up and tried to push him away; she was ashamed to do it, embarrassed, she had to force herself to do it. She pushed at him and he ignored her. She began to think, I can do nothing to stop him.

He was making noises now and moving himself against her. They were moving backwards into the corner of the room, her falling and him holding on to her and propelling her backwards. He kept pushing at her with his chest, with his groin, pushing at her tongue with his tongue, pushing at her head with his hands, and it was all done slowly – he gave the impression, above all else, that he was taking his time. He was in no hurry, it seemed.

She had the wall behind her now. He stopped moving. He took his hands out of her hair. He was standing over her, and she realized that he was breathing very fast, like he had run a race.

He took hold of her shoulders and twisted her so that she nearly cried out and then he pushed her onto the ground. He kneeled above her with a knee on either side of her holding her in place. She didn't speak, but she realized she was making low, gasping noises. He was silent. He pulled off her boots; he was confident, unharried, absorbed, as if he were at some demanding but familiar task. He put one hand down hard on her stomach to push her flat onto the ground and to hold her to the spot, like he was pinning a beetle to paper, and with the other hand he struggled with his fly. He didn't look at her; he was too occupied to even register her, she thought. She was almost incidental to what was happening.

All the time, she was astonished at being touched like this. She had only ever been touched with love. It was so surprising that he should try to claim her like this without speech, without reason, that it was difficult to believe it was happening. Her brain wouldn't let her understand that it was happening. It was impossible to accept. This is not happening, she thought. This cannot be happening.

She moved her head to see what he was doing. He was unzipping his fly, but it was giving him trouble: his hands were shaking now. He lifted his face up for a moment to shove his hair back and she saw that it was twisted, almost unrecognizable, mottled and dark red like he was in pain.

She tried to move backwards, pushing herself on her elbows, kicking with her heels, but he grabbed her ankles with a click of annoyance and pulled her towards him, sliding her along the wooden floor, and she sat up and hit at him with her fists. He gave no sign of feeling her blows. She saw that he'd opened his fly, and that his crooked penis stuck out from his body like a stick. With both hands he pulled her jeans open and lifted her legs in the air and dragged the jeans down to her ankles, shaking her legs like she was a doll – the jeans were tight, and he struggled to get them down, and he was in a hurry now, she saw. He took hold of her black knickers and pulled them down to her knees, then he leaned over her and took her hands and pinned them above her head with both of his.

She looked at the top of his black head as he began to lower himself down towards her. Something shifted in her then. She felt something inside her rise up. There was something in the world, somewhere, turning itself towards her. The house was calling out to her now, calling her name. The wind was pulling at her. Ellen, something said. Get up.

She lifted up her knee and kicked him between his legs with all her strength.

He grunted and fell back a bit like he was deflated, and she had enough space then to lift her knee high towards her face and to propel it forwards and to kick him again, harder, with her heel this time.

He let go of her hands. He fell into a kneeling position with his hands between his legs and his head down. She got up onto her knees and pulled her pants up. He put a hand out to try to grab hold of her so she stood up and hobbled away from him, just out of his reach, but her legs were bound together at her ankles by her jeans and it was impossible to go far. She bent down and took the car keys out of the pocket and then tried to pull up the jeans but they were twisted and too tight to pull up quickly so she sat back down and pulled them, kicked them off, nearly crying with frustration, and all the time watching him trying to straighten himself up and move towards her.

He was up on one knee now, still crouched over with his head down, but he was getting up – that was clear. She thought of stabbing him with the car keys, but she should not, she saw, go close to him – he would grab her by an ankle and pull her back down to the ground and she would be finished then. She had one chance to get to the door before he got up.

She ran along the wall furthest from him and out the door and began to run down the stairs, stumbling, falling over herself. Behind her she could hear John get to his feet. He was on the stairs now, and roaring like a bull, coming down after her. But the stairs were narrow for him and he was struggling: he was coming down them sideways, in his hurry. Without thinking, she jumped down the last five steps. She landed well and was about to go through the door when there was a crash behind her. She kept running, but as she ran she turned to look. He had fallen on the stairs, and fallen badly, onto his face.

She kept going: out through the kitchen, across the yard, towards the car. There was another terrible crash; he was coming through the kitchen now, limping, and knocking things out of his way as he went. His nose was flattened. There was blood all over his face. He was stumbling like he'd been in a fight, a fight he'd lost.

She got into the car and turned on the engine and locked the doors. He ran towards the car and threw himself on it. Without thinking, she drove the car forwards, towards the house. He slid off the bonnet and onto the ground.

'Fuck,' she heard him say.

She reversed the car. He was lying on the ground. She could drive over him, she thought, almost abstractedly, and then decided in the same moment not to. She turned instead towards the BMW and drove into the side of it. There was a tremendous, sickening, crunching wrench and her head snapped forwards and backwards and then she reversed again and turned the car in a tight angle and drove as fast as she could out of the yard. In the rear-view mirror she saw John shout, 'Fuck.'

Fuck you, she didn't shout back. She should have said it, she thought later, she should have shouted it out, but she didn't. She said nothing. She just drove.

She drove down the narrow lane that snaked away from the house. She was shaking so hard, like something from a cartoon, violently, almost comically, that it was nearly impossible to drive. Her teeth were chattering. Her jaw was nearly locked. As she drove she tried to take a cigarette from the pack but she was shaking too much to manage it. In the end she had to empty the cigarettes out onto the passenger's seat and take one from there; the one she picked up was bent, nearly broken, but she lit it anyway and inhaled and exhaled as deeply as she could, and kept going.

She drove back to the hotel and parked in the car park behind it. It was Saturday afternoon, and busy in the town. She sat in the car and smoked and watched the people go about their business. She felt completely outside herself. What had happened in the house seemed as unreal as a dream, and she felt nothing – no anger, no shock. There was just the absence of emotion, of feeling. Only the terrible shaking that would not abate was a sign that anything had happened, at all.

There was a supermarket next to the car park and people were loading their shopping into car boots and calling to their children and shouting hellos to each other or chatting, standing with their heads close together, almost touching each other, in the way that they had here. She could imagine them driving home from the town and unloading the shopping and cooking the tea and settling in to watch the TV for the night and the day after getting up and going to Mass and then the lunch after, and then Monday and the week unspooling after that.

She had never fitted into this life. There was no life, no place that fitted her. When she left a place, and the people there, she felt no loss, no sense of missing. She thought about the people she had left behind with only a detached curiosity until eventually she thought of them no more, and then it was as if they had never existed for her. They faded away, as she had faded from her mother's and her sisters' lives, as they had faded from hers.

I'm a ghost just like you, baby, she thought. I pass through other people's lives like a ghost.

She put her head back on the seat and closed her eyes.

There was a knock on the car window.

She jumped up straight.

Simon was crouched down, looking in the passenger window so that his face was level with hers. He was gesturing at her to open the window.

She opened it. The car was filled with smoke. She had the lit cigarette in her hand. On her lap was a small pile of broken cigarettes that she'd gathered from the passenger seat. There was nothing for it, really, but to wave her cigarette at him in a hello.

He paid no attention to the cigarette.

'You're in your pants,' he said.

She had forgotten that.

'Bunny,' he said. 'What's wrong with you?'

'Why are you here?' she asked. She lifted her cigarette to her mouth but her hand was shaking so much that she had to drop her arm down by her side to hide it.

Simon was looking at her like she was a puzzle he was trying to work out.

'Here, where?' he said. 'In the car park?'

'Yes, Simon,' she said, as airily as she could manage. If only she could take a drag from her cigarette. 'In the car park.'

'I told you that after lunch I was going to go for a drive around the area with your mother. She's going to show me that swimming lake. I said I'd meet her by her car. But you know all this. What's wrong with you?'

She looked across the car park and saw her mother come out of the hotel and stop to look around for Simon.

'Ellen,' said Simon, urgently now. 'What's happened to you? What's happened to the car? The front of it is wrecked.'

But her mother was upon them already. Simon stood up and said, with fake good cheer, 'Imelda. Right. You're ready to go.'

He was trying, she saw, to position himself between her and her mother, but her mother, seeing what he was trying to do, stepped neatly around him. She leaned down and put her face through the window. She took in, instantly, the cigarette, the lack of trousers.

'I went to the house,' said Ellen. She couldn't look at her mother's face. 'I fell in the field and my jeans were saturated so I took them off. I'm frozen.'

That would explain the shaking, she hoped.

'Where are they?' her mother said.

'Where are what?' She was seventeen again, and trapped in the blinding, confounding glare of her mother's suspicion.

'Where are your jeans?'

'In the boot,' she said. She would refuse to open the boot if she asked her.

'What are those marks on your wrists?'

She hadn't even noticed the red marks. They looked like burns.

'I fell, I told you,' she said. She looked away. If she looked at them, she would cry.

Her mother straightened up, very slowly and deliberately.

'Go in and have a lie down,' she said.

'I will,' she said. She put the cigarette out in the ashtray and began to drum her fingers lightly on the steering wheel to show her impatience with all of this. 'Enjoy the drive. I'll see you when you get back.'

They were both standing there, looking at her; they gave no sign of leaving. To get away from them, she would have to get out of the car; she was shaking too much to drive anymore, and anyway, there was nowhere for her to go. But she needed to wrap something around her waist before she could walk into the hotel.

'Do you have a blanket in the car?' She said this to her mother. 'My jeans are too wet to put on.'

'No,' said her mother. She was giving her what she and Fiona used to call the death stare. When they were children they used to imitate the stare by pulling big goggly eyes at each other and saying, 'Noooo,' in a growl until they were in fits of laughter on the floor.

'I'll go in and get a towel,' said Simon.

'Thanks, Simon,' said her mother.

She walked around the car and opened the door and got into the passenger seat. She shut the door with a bang and wound up the window.

'You're smoking again,' she said, looking out at the car park, watching Simon walk away.

'Kind of,' said Ellen.

You're back on safe ground now, Mammy, she thought, pointing out all the things that are wrong with me. You're delighted now that you don't have to make the effort to be nice. And I'm sitting here in my knickers: I can't exactly fight back.

She looked down at her mottled thighs, and thought of crossing her legs to look a bit more nonchalant. There was no point, really. She took a cigarette out of the pack and lit it. There was a tiny flake of tobacco on her lip and she put her finger up to lift it off, very delicately.

'What's wrong with you, Ellen?'

She wouldn't tell her about the baby. That would make it too easy for them both. And anyway, that wasn't the whole thing. There was more to it than that. She could see that, at last.

'There's nothing wrong with me,' she said. Then she added, 'I'm just tired.'

'You're more than tired,' her mother said. 'What happened to you at the house?'

'I fell,' she said. She lifted up her chin and looked at her mother, straight on. She did not have the right to ask her anything, anymore. I've been falling down for a long time, Mammy, she thought, and you knew nothing of it, and it suited you that way.

'Right, right,' said her mother, flapping at her, flapping her away. She sounded hysterical, already. 'Don't tell me anything. Other people . . .' She stopped. 'Other people would gladly talk to the mother they hadn't seen for two years.'

'I'm not other people,' she said tartly. She felt giddy with the bravery of being so brazen. 'Why would I tell you anything?'

Her mother's face was red with emotion.

'Oh, Ellen,' she said, in great anger. 'I don't want to fight with you. I said to Fiona before I came here, I don't want to fight with her, I want everything to be . . .'

She stopped speaking. She turned to look out at the car park, her fingers pressed against her lips.

'You're gone a long time, Ellen,' she said, eventually. 'You went off when you were eighteen, off you went.' She threw her hands open, like she was throwing a bird up into the air.

It was too much to have to bear. She could not take another moment of it. The anger was high up in her throat now, strangling her. She opened the door and got out. People turned to look at her. It wasn't every Saturday, she supposed, that they got to see someone standing in their big black knickers in the middle of the car park.

'Get in,' hissed her mother, viciously, leaning towards her and trying to grab her.

She hopped away from her mother's outstretched hand and then walked, fast, across the car park, leaving the car door open behind her. Her bag and shoes were in the car, and her cigarettes, but she kept walking towards the hotel. She got to the door, and saw Simon coming towards her. He held out a towel to her.

She walked past him like she hadn't seen him. She walked down the dark corridor – terrible carpet! Smell of mushroom soup! – and into the lobby. Dorothy was behind the desk and when she saw Ellen coming towards her she took her reading glasses off to get a better look at her.

'Good afternoon, Dorothy,' she said. 'Could I have my key, please?'

Dorothy handed her the key, without a word.

'Thank you so much, Dorothy,' she said, with as much sarcasm as she could manage.

She walked past her and up the stairs. People were watching her, she knew, so she walked as straight-backed as she could, and she didn't look back.

XVIII

THE MORNING AFTER THE Tans came they sent for the doctor for her father. Eoin took the milk to the dairy on the donkey and cart, as usual – they had to do everything as usual, Denis said – and spoke to Jimmy. He'd get word to him that day, Jimmy promised, but it took nearly two weeks for him to come in the end, because the Tans were everywhere, watching the countryside. Twice the doctor tried to leave Macroom, and both times he had to turn back. By the time he came, it was too late to save the eye.

'He'll lose it all right,' the doctor said. He was leaning over her father's bed and tutting sadly, tsk tsk. 'Even if I'd been able to come straight away, he'd have lost it, maybe. But no one can do anything now, that's for sure.'

He sounded tired, and defeated. Hannah had known him since she was a child, and he was an old man now, she realized suddenly. He's not able for this anymore, she thought, watching him.

Her father lay still and silent, though he could nearly talk now, and move his head from side to side and lift it to drink, and the swelling on his face had eased, a little, though the bruises on his body were darker in colour than ever, and seemed to be getting darker and growing and blooming like unnatural flowers. That was normal enough, the doctor said. He'd had the ribs broken on him, though, and the feet and the fingers too, but his back wasn't broken, and the stitches weren't infected and all in all they had done the best they could and a decent job they'd made of it, but nothing could be done about the eye.

'Will it always look like this, Doctor?' her mother asked.

She was in awe of the doctor and his university education and his polished accent and her voice changed when she spoke to him. She's thinking of things like that even now, in this moment, thought Hannah. That's what's important to her.

'No, no,' said the doctor. 'The swelling will go down after a while, of course. The eye socket itself is broken, so the whole eye looks bulbous, and it's bloody. But after a while we can expect it to turn milky, and the swelling will be gone soon enough, and it won't look too bad. He'll probably choose to wear a patch over it.' He put his hand on her father's shoulder. 'Ha, Seanie? You'll have a patch like an old pirate.'

'Ah, sure,' said her father hoarsely, nodding and trying to laugh up at him.

He was smaller than he had been before the beating – she was sure of that. He had shrunk. Even his great hands, lying flat on top of the blanket, looked smaller, and smoother, and whiter – they didn't look like his hands, at all.

The doctor stood up.

'It could have been worse. I've seen things recently that I won't be forgetting. At least he has one good eye left. At least he's alive.'

'Is it bad, Doctor?' her mother said, putting her hands together like she was about to start into the rosary.

'Bad, bad,' he said. 'They've their backs to the wall now, and they're lashing out at our lads. You can't put your hands in your pockets now when you're out in Mallow town. They'll shoot you on sight if you have your hands in your pockets.' He shook his head in wonder at it all. 'Imagine that. Can you imagine being shot down on the road for having your hands in your pockets?'

'God save us, Doctor,' said her mother. 'Our hearts are only broken from it all.'

'And you've had no word from your recent visitors?' he said.

'Nothing, Doctor,' she said. 'Nothing one way or the other. We don't know if they made it over the pass. We've had no word since they left.'

'As soon as anything happens we'll hear,' said the doctor. 'It's likely they're in a dugout in the mountain somewhere, waiting for their chance to cross. Denis will have word as soon as anything happens.'

Her mother gave a sigh by way of an answer. The doctor turned to his open bag on the chair. He took out a roll of bandage and put it on the bed.

'I've no ointment or anything like it,' he said. 'But we're lucky that Mary knew what she was doing with the poultice – there's no infection. I'll leave that.' He nodded at the bandage roll. 'Keep binding up the ribs like you're doing.' He went back over to the bed and with both his hands took hold of her father's hand. 'I'll call in on you soon again, Seanie,' he said. 'You'll be up and out by the end of the summer, not a bother on you.'

Her father gave a high croak of consent.

'Thank you, Doctor,' said her mother, nearly bowing at him. 'Do you have far to go now?'

'I've to go to see the O'Sullivans back at Skibbereen,' he said. 'The seven of them have the black flu and I've no medicine at all, I've nothing to give them but whiskey and ginger. They won't send the children away, of course.' He shook his head sadly.

'God save them,' said her mother. 'I knew Mary O'Sullivan before she was married. We used to go to the dances together, she was a great girl for the dancing.' She gave a strange, high laugh. 'Do you remember, Seanie? Do you remember Mary O'Leary as she was then, and the dances we used to all go to?' She put her arms across her chest like she was trying to fold into herself and then put one hand up to her mouth. 'It's years now since I saw her,' she said quietly. 'Will you tell her I was asking for her?'

'I will, Noreen,' said the doctor.

'You've a long road ahead of you,' her mother said. Her voice sounded flat now, and empty. 'Will you have some dinner at least before you go?'

'No, no,' he said, and picked up his bag. 'I've to go straight off. Hannah will see me out.'

She went down the stairs with the doctor. At the kitchen door, he turned to her.

'We didn't look at you,' he said. 'The face is all right?'

'It is, Doctor,' she said. 'It's getting better.'

'Are you all right in other ways?' He spoke very quietly now. 'You're very pale. Was anything else done to you?'

She held on to the door very tightly.

'No, Doctor,' she whispered.

He knows, she thought. He knows from the look of me.

'I'll be back in a few weeks,' he said to her. 'You can get me before then if you want. Denis will get me. There'd be no need to say anything to anyone else.'

There's nothing to do, Doctor, she wanted to say. There's nothing you can do now.

'Thank you, Doctor,' she said, still whispering. Her face was burning red. She started to put her hand up to her hot cheek and then put it back down her side. She made herself look straight at him.

'Goodbye, now,' she said. 'Thank you for coming.'

He kept looking at her. He is waiting for me to say something, she thought, or to start crying, or to ask him for help, and I'm not going to do any of those things. She started to close the door, slowly. He nodded at her and turned away, putting on his cap and calling across the yard to Eoin, who was waiting at the gate with the donkey and trap. She closed the door, and went through the kitchen and up the stairs to her bedroom and lay down on her bed with her hands folded across her stomach.

She was waiting. From the night he left, she'd been waiting: for him to come back, or for word of him, and now she was waiting, too, for the bleeding to start. She had a little calendar that she kept under her bed and every morning with a pencil she ticked off the day, and the days passed, and still she waited. Each day now was its own perfect agony: from the rising of the sun in the morning to its setting late at night was an age, an arc of vast eternity. I am in a wilderness of waiting, she thought, and she thought of Jesus in the desert for forty days and though she knew it to be blasphemous, a sin, she compared herself to Jesus and thought, I am lost, too. I, too, wait.

A week after he'd left she began to wake in the night feeling sick.

In the mornings she was light-headed; in the afternoons she was so tired that she sometimes had to lie down to sleep in the stable, or out in the fields in the long grass. Her breasts became swollen and painful to the touch – if someone even brushed against her she would gasp, involuntarily, with the pain. Her body felt tumultuous with energy. It was busy, buzzing with its work. I am occupied, she thought. I am inhabited.

She had first bled when she was twelve. When it had started, she had been afraid to tell her mother. She spent too much time on the old pony and climbing the trees in the fields, she was always told, and now she had injured herself, surely, and it was all her own fault. But the blood did not stop, and the pain was bad and it got worse and after three days she began to think that she would die, perhaps, that the blood would keep running from her until she was only a little white ghost, finally floating away. They would be sorry if she died, she decided, even Eily, and she told her mother, then.

As she was speaking her mother had turned away from her and started to walk out of the room and as she walked she'd said, 'You're a big girl now, Hannah.' She had to run along next to her to hear what she said next: 'Don't tell anyone about this.'

Who would I tell, Mammy, she'd wanted to ask, and why would I tell them? but she said nothing. She followed her mother into her room, silently.

'There,' her mother had said, pulling open the bottom drawer in the chest by the window and nodding at the pads. They were kept under the nightclothes. Hannah had nodded, like she understood, and they had spoken no more of it. She had learned, on her own, what the pads were for, and how to wear them, how to wash them. She took what she needed every month, and what she used was replaced. Nothing else was explained to her. All she had understood, from that first month, was that now her body was another kind of trap she had to learn how to manage.

She bled every month at the same time and for the same number of days, so after a while she knew what to expect, and what to do. Beyond that she knew nothing, she understood nothing. She had seen what the animals did in the fields, she had seen animals born, she'd seen her brothers in the bath when they were little and when she was at school some of the jokes the wilder children told each other made her see that there was much she didn't understand, but yet, when she had started to go to the dances with Eily she had known so little that she would refuse, every week, to dance a slow dance with a boy. She didn't know what would happen if he pressed himself too close to her, or, worse still, if he were to take her outside the dance hall and into the lane and bend her back into the ditch in the dark. When she cycled home from the dance she would see couples lying against the ditch like they had been thrown there, and their laughter would wind its way down the hill after her on the sweet night wind. She would not talk to a boy, even. She was not a girl from the town. She was a girl from a farm, from a respectable family. Her mother had an uncle who was a priest, she would remind herself, and at the thought of that her back would straighten and her chin would go up as she pedalled home through the dark.

She did not bleed, and still without understanding anything she knew, instinctively, what it meant. The days spooled out behind her while she waited. She was riven, consumed with worry. The worry was there with the sickness in the night, and it was there with the tiredness in the day. When she woke every morning she knew that something was wrong before she remembered where she was, even. Every night she would kneel by her narrow white bed and pray, Please, god. Please. But god would not take pity on her, she thought, even as she prayed. That was what the priest told them. God would not take pity on those who had gone against him.

She could not eat, with the worry and the sickness: the food stuck in her throat. She began to grow thin, so thin that her skin was stretched to a pearly, glowing translucence over her ribs. She slept in a fever, and in her dreams O'Riada came for her – he came into the kitchen when they were all sitting at the table and put his hand out for hers and she stood and took his hand wordlessly and they walked out the door together into the sun, with everyone looking at them. She had the same dream over and over, and every time on waking her heart gave the same terrible dull thud and she would think, It was only a dream again. I am still here, waiting, and still he has not come. He has not come, and I have not bled.

She couldn't remember his face, though it had been only weeks since she had seen him. Even in the dream, she couldn't see his face. She could recall his voice, and the way he moved, the essence of him – but she couldn't see his face. Sometimes she almost caught a glimpse of him in some corner of her mind; if she was impatient, then, and greedy, and tried to imagine him fully, the image would vanish, so she learned not to try to look at the image straight on. She accepted, instead, the glimpse of something that was passing even as she saw it. That was all she had, now: a blurred, moving, picture of his face, in profile, as it turned away from her, an idea of the line of his mouth, his nose.

No one noticed, she thought, that she did not eat – if they did, they said nothing. Everything was wrong in the house, now. Everything was changed, and the change in her went unnoticed. Her father could not leave the bed, and so the old daily routines were broken. Denis did not come in the mornings. The kitchen was empty in the evenings. The house seemed huge and everything in it wrong, foreign. Her brothers were free from school for the summer and spent the days in the fields with Denis. They ate in the fields, and came home only when it was dark, to sleep. When they were in the house they spoke in whispers; her mother and Eily did not speak to her, at all. She went to bed, some nights, having spoken only a few words that day. Everything outside her was getting quieter and quieter – the very house itself seemed to be holding its breath – and on the inside a great, noisy tumult was raging that she could not silence. She began to be aware of the workings of her mind. I am thinking this now, she would say to herself. She could longer think without a commentary, she could no longer think in peace. There was a noise in her head, a voice nearly, telling her what she was thinking all the time. I will go mad if this goes on, she said to herself. I am going mad now, maybe.

The weeks passed, and still there was no word from him. Denis knew nothing, said Eoin. They were up the mountain, they were waiting, there was no more news than that.

On the Friday morning of the fourth week she woke at dawn. She could wait no more; it was like the decision had been made for her. She got dressed and sat on her bed and waited until she heard the clock in the kitchen strike seven. Then she went downstairs. Mary was at the range. Her brothers and Eily were still in their beds – it would be an hour before they were up.

'You're up very early,' Mary said to her, turning away from the pots and looking her up and down.

She didn't answer. Into a basket Hannah put a bottle of milk with a screw of paper in the neck, and bread, and two hard-boiled eggs, and a pat of butter and a knife, with Mary watching her all the time. Without a word to her she went out into the yard and to the stable. She took the horse out and got him ready. Her heart was banging in her chest, slowly, steadily.

She set off. Denis was working in the long field by the river; he would have been there since daybreak, she thought. His days often began and ended in darkness now: he was doing her father's share of the work, as well as his own, and the load was heavy on him; the worry was written across his face when he came back into the yard every night. Some nights he was too tired to eat, even, and he fell asleep on his bed with his boots on – she knew that because she had gone, more than once, to his room with the dinner for him and he had been asleep already and it barely nine in the evening.

Soon it would be harvest time and the men would come from all the neighbouring farms and work all day under the high pale sun until the harvest was in. But they would miss her father, and there were many other men, too, who would be absent this year – each year, Denis said, there seemed to be more work to do, and fewer men to do it.

He was at the bottom of the field, mending the fence that ran along the river, with his old black and white dog stretched out beside him in the sun.

The dog heard her first, and lifted up its head, and then Denis turned and stood back from the fence to watch her ride down to him, putting his hand up to shield his eyes against the sharp early sun. It was a long ride down the steep field: the ground was dry and hard and she had to lean back to stop the horse from slipping and tripping forwards. She was sweating through her clothes from the effort, and nearly blind from the cruel sun.

Denis came towards her and took hold of the horse's bridle. She handed him the basket and swung heavily off the horse. Her legs nearly buckled beneath her.

'Oho,' he said, in mock wonderment, looking into the basket. 'Breakfast, by god.' He took the reins over the horse's head and wound them around one hand. The dog grinned a lazy hello at her.

'You're out early,' he said, setting the basket down on the ground.

She didn't answer.

He put his hand on the horse's neck.

'He's looking good,' he said, and he turned away from her, towards the horse. He was making a space for her to speak. 'Ha?' he said, after a minute, to prompt her.

'He is,' she said.

'Sure, he's well looked after,' he said. 'Fear of him.'

He ran his hand down the horse's neck, down his leg and then picked up his hoof, checking it and dropping it and moving his hand back up the leg, along the flanks, feeling the muscle under his flat hand. A shining shiver ran through the horse at his touch.

'He's a gentleman's horse, I always said it,' he said, approvingly.

She had to say it fast, nearly before she could think about it. It was like when she jumped into the cold, deep part of the river: if she didn't do it fast, she wouldn't do it at all.

'Have you had any word from O'Riada?'

He didn't answer her at first. He let go of the reins and started to move around the horse, slowly, hissing to him gently through his closed teeth.

Her heart was beating wildly. He came round to the front of the horse and stood facing her. He took off his cap and wiped his forehead with the back of his hand.

'I heard there last night that they're in a safe house on the mountain.' He shook his head. 'They've been there a few days. They can't move. The Tans won't go up the mountain –' he put his hand up to show the angle of the slope – 'because they'd be exposed on it and they'd be picked off it like rabbits, and our boys can't come down the mountain –' he slanted his hand down – 'or go over it. The Tans are watching, they've men out there day and night. They're waiting for him to make a move.'

'What will he do?' she said.

'I don't know, at all,' he said. 'He can do nothing, sure, apart from sit it out. We can only hope for a bit of luck for him.'

She thought she would weep then, because of how Denis looked, and because of what she had to tell him. Once she told him, she knew, her old life would be sheared away from her, and Denis, and all that he had been to her, lost too.

'I've to get word to him,' she said.

'What word?'

'I have to see him,' she said.

'Ah,' he said, with a strange half-laugh, and when he spoke again it was out of the side of his mouth and heavy with an irony she hadn't heard from him for a long time. 'Now. Come on. Didn't I say he can't move.'

'I could go to him,' she said, though she knew it was a useless thing to say, but she had to say something to make Denis say more.

'It's only been a few weeks,' he said, quietly. 'Are you that desperate?'

He looked up at her then, and she could see the fear stretched tight on his face.

'I'm in trouble,' she said, very fast.

It came out as a whisper but as soon as she'd said it she put her hand up to her mouth as if she would shove the words back in.

He said nothing.

'Denis,' she said, in a low voice, because he wasn't looking at her, and he wasn't speaking, and she would fall down, she thought, if he didn't answer her.

He shook his head, no, no.

'Denis,' she said, again, louder.

He looked at her then. His eyes were glittering with hard tears, she thought, but that was impossible – it was impossible that Denis should be crying.

'Ahh,' he cried, and he threw his arm up at her. The horse, startled, stepped back from him, his head up and his nostrils flared.

'Get away, you stupid animal,' he shouted, and raised his hand up at him as if he would hit him, and the horse, panicked, stumbled back and then galloped away to the corner of the field. He pulled himself up before the ditch and whirled about and stood watching them, breathing heavily in and out.

Denis walked over to the fence and leaned on it, his head hanging down between his outstretched arms. She stood watching him. She didn't know what to do, or say.

'Have you told anyone else?' he said, eventually.

She shook her head, no, even though he wasn't looking at her.

'Denis,' she said, after a moment.

He was the workman on the farm. She was the farmer's daughter. He would not keep his back to her.

'You'll get word to him?' She said it as coldly as she could manage.

He half turned around with his head down – still he would not look at her – and waved her away.

'I will and that's it, now,' he shouted. 'Go on, out of it. Go on, I'm telling you.'

He spoke to her like she was nothing – like she was a beggar at the door keening for scraps. It would have been better, she thought, if he had struck her, or if he had taken her by the shoulders and shaken her and she had been able to hit him back with all the anger that was in her. Instead she had to pick up her dress and walk across the field away from him; she went as fast as she could without running, but the grass was rough by the river, and more than once she stumbled and nearly fell. The horse came towards her, shaking its bridle. She mounted him and rode back up the hill. When she was at the top she turned back to look down at Denis. He was standing quite still, facing the river, and the mountains beyond it, which were dark blue even in the brightness of such a morning.

All things are ending now, before they have even begun for me: the thought came to her with such a sudden violence that she almost cried out in fright.

She had planned to go into the woods and to lie on the grass under the golden-leafed oaks but she turned the horse towards the house instead. I want to go home, I want to go back to my bedroom and get into bed and never leave it again, she thought. The world felt too big for her, the domed sky too high and everything beneath it strange and threatening and misshapen like in a dream. In the distance she could see the grey house, sitting quietly. She kicked the horse into a trot. I want all of this to stop, she thought. I want everything to be as it was before they came. I would be a good girl, then, a good quiet girl and not a word to anyone. I'd stay in the house and make no trouble if only . . . if only everything could be as it was again.

The horse broke into an easy canter. They went through the low field and back into the orchard. She rode him through the yard and to the stable door. She got off and took the saddle and bridle off him. She led him into the stable; he was strangely quiet, and easily led. She went out of the stable, and put her hand out to him over the half-door.

'Goodbye, my friend,' she said.

He put his head over the door and rested it against her hand. She put her face down against his muzzle and he breathed his sweet grass smell out to her.

There was a noise from the yard behind her. It was the boys. They were early, earlier than usual.

'Hannah,' called Liam, seeing her.

She walked over to them. There was something wrong – she knew it from the way they were holding themselves.

'We were told to go out,' Liam said to her. Eoin gave him a shove.

'Who told you to go out?' she said.

'Don't push me,' said Liam to Eoin. 'Mammy,' he said to Hannah. 'Get out, she told me. We'd no time for breakfast. I'm hungry.'

'I told you we'd have it with Denis,' said Eoin.

She looked at Eoin, but he would not meet her eye.

'Mammy's crying,' said Liam. He looked up at her for an answer.

She put her hand on his warm head.

'Go on to Denis,' she said. 'I'll see you at dinnertime.'

She went into the kitchen. Her mother was sitting at the table with her hands clasped in front of her, like she was in prayer. She didn't look up at her. Her face was blotched red and white and swollen-looking.

'I was waiting for you,' she said, looking at the table.

Her voice sounded thin, like it would break, easily.

'I went out on the horse,' she said.

'Come here with me a minute,' she said.

She stood up and went through the door and up the stairs. Hannah followed her. Her mother's skirts brushed the steps in front of her with a scratching sound and swished from side to side like a slow pendulum. She tried to think only of that, the scratching sound, the swinging. She could not think beyond that.

They went very quietly and carefully past the bedroom where her father slept, like they were thieves, or lovers hiding away together. She looked in the door as she passed by. She wanted to cry out to him but she said nothing; she went on after her mother, like she was being carried along on the wave of some terrible sea.

Her mother went into the small bedroom and she went in behind her and stood in the middle of the room with her hands hanging to her sides. Her mother closed the door behind them. She went to the bed. She pulled back the blankets and threw them on the ground. She threw the pillow on top of them. Then she lifted up the mattress. It was a blue mattress, thin and old, with the springs poking through in places – she had learned to sleep curled up so the vicious springs didn't cut her legs. Her mother lifted the mattress with ease and threw it back off the bed.

On the wire frame, in two neat rows, lay the pads, white as snow, untouched.

Hannah's mind was narrowing now into a little black tunnel. She started to back towards the door, but her mother caught her by the arm. She was standing very close to her, too close, and breathing fast, in out, in out.

'What is it?' said Hannah.

Her mother's eyes were blazing, burning.

'Oh, she's going to pretend,' she said, slyly. 'She's going to pretend now she doesn't know.'

'I don't know what you're talking about, Mammy,' she said.

It was nearly impossible not to cry – her voice was shaking with the effort of it.

'You think I'm a fool,' her mother said. 'You think we're a load of old fools here.'

She started to squeeze her arm tighter, tighter, and put her mouth next to her ear, and whispered, poisonously, 'You think I never had a child? You think I don't know the signs?'

You counted the pads, she wanted to say. That's all you did. You've seen no signs in me. You haven't looked at me properly since I was a child. She tried to shake her mother's hand off her arm; she pushed at her hand with her free hand.

'Let me go, Mammy,' she said, desperately. 'I don't know what you're talking about.'

'You don't know,' she said, slyly, mockingly. 'Oh,' she cried to

the room, 'she doesn't know what I'm talking about, the poor innocent girleen.' She leaned back from her, holding her at a full arm's
length, considering her, and then with a strength Ellen couldn't have
imagined her mother had in her she threw her across the room, onto
the floor. 'Get out of this house. Get out onto the street where you
belong. We want nothing more to do with you. Nothing.'

'Mammy,' she said, crying now and trying to stand and falling
backwards and onto the edge of the bed. She half sat, half kneeled
by the bed and she put her hands down between her knees and
began to turn them over and over each other as if she were trying
to wash them clean of something. She was wearing her white dress
and her black boots and she could see herself as if from a distance,
the white dress against the black bed frame and her black feet against
the ground. She hadn't cried properly since she was a child but the
cries came now in great jagged heaves and she was shaking, terribly,
all over. Her mother stood watching her. Then she walked towards
her as if she'd just decided something. She took hold of her elbow.

'Get up,' she said, pulling her up. She began to propel her towards
the door. 'We'll have to tell Daddy.'

She pulled back away from her mother.

'No,' she said, 'no, no,' but her mother was strong, stronger than
she could have believed, and she was dragging her now down to the
bedroom where her father lay, shouting out, 'Sean,' and Hannah
shouting, 'No,' and everything was splintering about her, the house
was shattering about her, everything was falling away from her. Her
mother pulled her into the bedroom. Her father was sitting up in the
bed with the blanket pulled up to his chin and he was white with fear.

'Noreen,' he said, 'what in the name of god is wrong?'

'Tell him,' she said, and she pushed Hannah forward towards him. 'Tell him,' she shouted, when Hannah said nothing. She couldn't; all she could do was shake her head at her father, no.

'Ahh,' cried her mother, suddenly, furiously, and she stepped around her so that she was standing directly in front of her father.

'She's going to have a child.'

There was a terrible silence in the room. They were all afraid of the words, she thought, afraid of the sound they made out loud. Her father wore a black patch over his bad eye; his good eye was a terrible green unblinking bulbous ball that he swung towards her now.

'It's true,' said her mother. Her voice was shaking. 'Ask her.'

'Hannah,' he said. 'Is it true what your mother says?'

'I think it is, Dadda,' she said in a whisper.

'But . . .' He turned back to her mother and raised his hands up with the palms out flat in supplication. 'It's not possible.' He turned back to her. 'It's not possible, Hannah, is it?'

'I don't know,' she said, in desperation.

'Tell him who,' said her mother.

She shook her head. She would not say his name.

'Ah, we know who it was,' said her mother. 'Don't we?' she said, turning to her father.

He looked at her, blankly.

'Oh,' she cried, as if his stupidity were a thing that she could no longer bear. 'It's that Jimmy O'Leary from the dairy. He's had his eye on her for long enough. You said it yourself.'

Her mind was flying away from her now like a bird.

'No,' she said, in shock.

Her mother put her hand across her mouth, as if she were trying to hold her face together. The tears were running down her face now, and she made no attempt to wipe them away.

'No, what?' she said, through her hand.

Hannah shook her head.

Her mother walked over to her and put her face in front of hers. Hannah could smell her stale breath. Her eyes were wide and red and mad-looking and she screamed at her, 'No what?'

She felt like she had taken all her clothes off and that she stood before them naked.

'Not him.'

'Well, who, so?' said her mother, in a terrible mocking voice. 'Who?'

She shook her head again.

'Hannah,' said her father. 'You tell us who now.'

'No, Dadda,' she said. 'I won't say.'

Her father dragged himself out of the bed, pulling up his old white nightshirt and putting his naked twig-thin bare legs on the ground, and then standing up, staggering, his arms flailing about. He came towards her, very slowly. He stood in front of her and put his hand on her shoulder.

'Were you forced, Hannah?' he said.

She made herself look at him.

'No, Dadda,' she said.

'Oh,' cried her mother. She fell backwards as if she had been hit.

Her father turned away from her. He went to the window and began to bang on it as if he would fight the world outside.

'I have lost my child,' he said. 'I have lost my best child.'

Hannah went past her mother, towards her father.

'I have lost my child,' he said again, but it was a dull cry now, a lament for all that was gone.

She put her arms out towards him.

'Dadda,' she cried. 'Please.'

'No, no,' he roared, flapping at her with his arms.

He turned away from the window, spinning on his heels, rocking backwards and forwards like a baby learning to walk who might fall down at any moment. He went to the chest of drawers and opened the top drawer and took out the pistol. It was loaded – she had loaded it herself the day after the Tans had come. Out of the side of her eye she saw her mother retreat back into the corner of the room. She was holding her skirts in her hands and pulling them up to her mouth and her eyes were little darting pinpricks in her head.

Hannah did not move. She stayed perfectly still – she stopped her breath, even – but he did not look at her; he was fixed on something beyond her, outside the room. He went past her on his stiff legs, and out the door, and down the stairs, sideways, sliding his back along the wall. She went after him. It was the first time he had left the bedroom since the Tans had come, and he would fall down the stairs, she thought – he was too weak to get down them, surely. If he fell, she could get over him and get the gun, maybe, or if she got close enough behind him, she would push him over – she had to get the gun.

But he made it down the stairs, half falling all the time, and went through the door at the bottom, into the kitchen. She heard Mary shout out, 'Oh my god.' Hannah was running now, down the stairs, and into the kitchen. Mary was standing, frozen, with her back against the range and Hannah put her hand up to her – stay there – and went out into the yard.

He was crossing the yard at speed, the nightshirt flapping around his thighs, his arms sawing away by his sides. Was he going to go across the fields and the rivers and into the mountains and after O'Riada, perhaps, like this? Did he suspect it was O'Riada? Then she saw that he was going to the stable. He meant to take the horse. He would go after O'Riada on the horse.

The horse heard them coming, and put his head over the half-door. Her father stopped running. He stood with his legs wide apart, to steady himself, and then he raised his arm up, pointing the gun at the horse. His arm was shaking so much that he had to put both hands on the gun to steady it.

She said it first in her head, No, Dadda, no, and then out loud, 'No, no.'

At the sound of her voice the horse lifted his head. 'No,' she cried, in horror, but the shot rang out all the same. The sound of it hit her like a physical sensation more than a noise: her whole body jumped with the shock. The shot echoed around the yard and over the stones and bounced back at her from the walls, breaking the air, splintering the morning light.

A cloud of crows lifted from the trees on the hill like so many black rags and spiralled away across the sky, calling back sadly to each other as they did, come away, come away.

She ran past her father to the stable and opened the door. The horse was on his knees, with his head nodding down, like he was about to fall asleep. It had been a good shot – he'd got him straight between the eyes. He couldn't have done better if he'd taken all day at it. She got down on her knees and put her arms around the horse's neck. She had the idea that if she could get him to stand up she could do something to help him, so she tried to pull him to stand, saying, 'Get up, get up,' through her teeth, but he was shaking badly now, and beginning to fall down, very slowly, down onto his side. His eyes were open wide and unblinking and there was a single trail of blood running from the hole between his eyes, down his nose and into his nostrils, and there was darker blood starting to come from his nostrils, too. His whole body was convulsing, and she tried again to get him to stand, because his legs were twisted and unnatural-looking underneath him. They will break, she thought. That was what she had always feared: that he would break a leg, because they shot horses when the leg was broken, and then the thought hit her like a sluice of cold water, but they've shot him already, they've shot him already.

She put her face against his face. His breathing slowed a bit, she thought, when he felt her. Later, she realized that the shot had killed him instantly and that the rest of it was just the life leaving him. But just then, in the stable, she thought that he was still with her, that he could hear her, that she could help him.

'Pangur,' she said. 'There's my good boy.'

She began to stroke his face, rhythmically, and under her breath she tried to hum the song she used to sing over and over to him when she was teaching him to turn on the rein. His nostrils were flared and red and terrible and his unblinking eyes were fixed straight ahead but his breath was getting quieter, she thought, and after a while she made herself lift her head up to look at him. His eyes were open but he was still, unmoving, and she knew that he was gone. She closed his eyes.

'Pangur,' she said in a whisper, and it was the last time she'd say his name, she knew.

She stood up and looked at his broken body on the ground. How will I get him out? she thought. He's too big for me to get out, and I can't leave him here. If I leave him here, they will have his body cut into pieces and fed to the hounds. At the thought of that she began to back out of the stable, away from him. Her father was standing behind her. She turned around. He still had the pistol in his hand but he was shaking so hard that he would drop it, she saw. She put her hand out and he gave it to her without hesitation. It was still warm. She lifted it up so it was pointing to the sky and then she rested it against her forehead, between her closed eyes.

'It was O'Riada,' she said, without opening her eyes.

It was completely quiet in the yard, but for the lonely calls of the scattered crows. She opened her eyes.

'Did you hear me? It was O'Riada. It is O'Riada's child.'

She watched with an almost detached interest as her father's face collapsed inwards. She turned away from him and began to walk back towards the house. Mary and her mother and Eily were standing at the door, in a huddle, watching. As she approached they stood to one side to let her pass.

She went through the kitchen and up the stairs and into her bedroom. She put the gun into her dress pocket and opened the wardrobe and began to take her things out. On the bed she put her two dresses, her good shoes, her stockings and a cardigan, all the underthings that she had, and her hairclips, a facecloth and her comb. She looked at everything, and then she picked up the shoes and put them back in the wardrobe. She left her coat hanging there, and her felt wool hat on top of it. She went into her parents' bedroom and from under the bed she took the small cardboard suitcase with the cracked leather trim that her father had used the time he'd gone up to Cork. She went back into the bedroom and put the clothes in the suitcase, and she put the gun on top of them and her calendar too and a pencil and then closed it, click. She picked up the suitcase and looked around the room. This is the last time you'll be in this room, she said to herself, say goodbye to it. Goodbye, room, she said, in her head, but she felt nothing – the words meant nothing to her. She went down the stairs.

Her mother and Eily were sitting at the table. They were whispering to each other, but they stopped as soon as they saw her.

'Hannah,' said her mother. She put her hand out to her, but she didn't stand up – she would always remember that, when she thought of that moment. 'Sit down.'

She stopped and looked at the two of them. She was glad that they looked white, and drawn, and afraid.

'No,' she said, and began to walk to the door.

Eily stood up and moved towards her and put her hand on her arm, holding on to her.

'Where will you go?' she said.

She looked down at Eily's hand, and then back up at her face. Eily took her hand away.

'I'm going away from here.'

'Don't be mad,' said Eily. 'There's nowhere for you to go. Stay here and think about things, will you, Hannah?' Then she said again, quietly, 'Hannah.'

Hannah looked at Eily. It wasn't her fault, any of it. She was her only sister and in their own way they loved each other, she thought, or they had loved each other once. When they were children they had shared a room and at night they would fall asleep holding hands across the space between their two single beds. Things had gone sour between them, somehow, and she was suddenly sorry for that. She leaned towards Eily and kissed her on her pale cool cheek and almost smiled at the shock on her face.

'Bye, Eily,' she said, and then she went out the door, leaving it wide open behind her.

Her father was standing with his back to the wall of the house, bent over like a broken thing; out of the corner of her eye she saw him stand up and try to walk after her so she began to run, with the suitcase banging against her leg and the blood going bang, bang in her head. She ran across the yard and climbed over the wall and into the field, and then kept going, into the world beyond.

XIX

SHE FELT LIKE SHE'D run a race, and lost it. She couldn't catch her breath. She sat on the floor with her back to the bed and put her hand on her heart to try to steady it. She was about to have a heart attack, maybe – she would have a heart attack here on the floor of this awful hotel, in her knickers. The idea began to grow in her head and the panic with it until her heart was racing even faster. I'm having a heart attack, she wanted to shout, help, and then, like an answer, there was a knock on the door.

She sat up like she'd been shot at.

'Who is it?' she shouted.

'It's Dorothy Flood. From the hotel.'

She looked around the room. She couldn't climb out the window – it was too far down – and there was no point hiding in the bathroom with the shower turned on, pretending she couldn't hear, when she'd already answered. She stood up and began to try to put on the dressing gown that was on the end of the bed but it had been folded by some kind of origamist – it was impossible to unknot the waist cord and the sleeves were rolled into themselves and the whole hateful thing was an impenetrable box that defied her.

'Will you open the door, please?' said Dorothy, loudly, so she threw the dressing gown on the ground and flattened her hair down and went to the door and opened it an inch.

'I came to check that everything is all right,' said Dorothy, putting her hand on the open door.

'Everything's fine, Dorothy, thank you,' she said.

'Well, everything didn't look fine a minute ago,' said Dorothy. 'If you don't mind me saying. Could I come in, please?'

She couldn't stop her – that was clear to both of them. So she opened the door and stepped to the side and Dorothy came into the room and closed the door behind her. They looked at each other, assessing each other, and then Dorothy looked around the room, before turning back to her.

'Did you have some sort of accident?' she said.

'You could say that, I suppose,' said Ellen.

She wished she'd tried harder to untie the dressing gown: it was terrible to be standing here in her big knickers. She turned around – there was nothing else to be done – and went to the cupboard and took out a pair of jeans and began to put them on. All the time, she was conscious of Dorothy's sharp eyes skating over her thighs, her big bottom.

'But I'd prefer not to talk about it, Dorothy, if that's all right.'

'Come on, now,' said Dorothy. 'I'm concerned, and I have a right to be concerned, I think.' Her voice was going up and down; her accent was getting stronger. She'd dropped her refined receptionist's tone. She put one hand on her chest and the other one on her hip. She began to tap her chest with the tips of her fingers, lightly, quickly. 'I mean, I have to look after our guests, it's my responsibility.'

She would have to tell her something to make her leave.

'I went to see the house again,' she said. 'And I went for a walk down by the river and I slipped into it. My jeans were soaking so I took them off. That's it, Dorothy, there's no more excitement than that, I'm afraid.'

She buttoned up her jeans and put her hands on her hips to try to steady herself. Her neck was hurting badly, and it took a moment for her to remember why. Then she remembered her head whipping back as she'd hit John's car. She would not cry. She would not crack. She put her hand to her mouth and blinked hard. Dorothy was breathing heavily through her nose and looking straight at her. Ellen could see her preparing herself for what she was about to say next.

'Now, we both know, Ellen, that I saw you coming up to this room only two nights ago with John O'Connor.' She paused, but she kept looking at her. 'I saw him leaving half an hour later in a fine temper; he nearly took the door off the hinges below when he left. And I know that John O'Connor was going to the O'Donovan house today; the new girl from the office came in and told us. He's gone for a couple of hours, she said, I can have my lunch in peace now. He was in the bar here from midday and he'd a good few drinks and I saw him drive off myself, not long after you'd left. They must have another appointment out there, I said to myself, and I thought isn't it strange the husband and the mother aren't going too? And now here you are back and looking like this and there's no sign yet of John, of course.' She stopped. 'No sign of John.'

Ellen sat down on the bed.

'You're a real Miss Marple,' she said, and then she started to cry.

Dorothy went to the cupboard under the TV and took out two

tiny bottles of whiskey, and a glass. Ellen watched her unscrew the little bottles and pour them both into the glass. Dorothy walked back to her and handed her the drink, silently.

'Thanks,' said Ellen, wiping her nose with the back of her hand.

'You're welcome,' said Dorothy.

She sat down on the bed next to Ellen, crossing her ankles; it creaked in surprise at the weight of both of them.

'I've known John O'Connor since he was a child,' she said. 'And he was always a vicious fecker.'

She put her hand out for the glass. Ellen handed it to her and watched as Dorothy finished the drink.

'What happened?' Dorothy said. 'Do you need to see a doctor?'

'No, no,' said Ellen. 'It didn't go that far. I fought him. I gave him a good kick.' She gave a small laugh.

'Right,' said Dorothy, and Ellen could hear the relief in her voice – she was too shy to press her for any of the details.

She stood up and went back to the minibar and took out two more bottles of whiskey, and a jar of jellybeans, and a Kit Kat. She walked back to Ellen and filled up her glass and then sat back down next to her.

'Do you want to phone the guards?' she said.

'No,' said Ellen. 'I probably should, but I won't. I just want to go back to London now, I think.'

'You should phone the guards,' said Dorothy.

'No,' said Ellen.

Dorothy sighed.

'Think about it. You might feel differently tomorrow.'

'I won't,' she said. She could not go to the guards, because she would have to tell them about the night in the hotel, and Simon would find out then.

Dorothy opened the jar of jellybeans and began to eat them delicately and very quickly, as if she were trying to finish them before she changed her mind.

'Will you still buy the house?' she said eventually.

'I don't know, Dorothy,' she said, wearily. 'I don't know what I'm doing at all, really, to be completely honest with you.'

'I know what you mean,' said Dorothy, looking at the wall in front of her, and eating the jellybeans.

Ellen kept drinking the whiskey; she felt warmer, and the shaking was easing now.

'Do you know anything about Hannah O'Donovan and Padraic O'Riada?' she said after a while.

'Bits,' said Dorothy, turning to look at her. 'You're interested in all of that, are you?'

'I don't know,' she said, and she sounded sad, even to herself. 'I suppose I am. Charles O'Connor said you'd know about Hannah, he said to talk to you.'

Maybe I'm trying to steal a bit of glory from the people who went before me, she nearly said. It would give me some weight to come from someone who counted for something. And I don't want to move forwards, I don't want to get any older, or fatter, or more tired – I want to go back to how I was, I want to start again, I want it all back again. The best part of my life is behind me, Dorothy, and I'm not ready to accept that yet, so I'm trying to look at the bigger picture here and see how I can fit into things and make some sense of it all.

'No one knows what happened to her,' said Dorothy. 'We know all about O'Riada, of course. After the killing of the Tans on the O'Donovan farm things were very bad here; the British had their revenge on the local people, of course. O'Riada fought through all that and fought bravely, brilliantly they say, and after the War of Independence he fought with Collins during the Civil War – they fought for the Treaty. By the end of it all he was known to be a terribly cold-blooded man, he was renowned for that. They say he was a ruthless killer during that time, which was a terrible period, of course – it was brother killing brother by the end of it. But O'Riada survived it all, and he rose as high as junior minister when it was all over. He had a distinguished career up in Dublin. But we know nothing about Hannah. Of course, she had the baby and her unmarried and the disgrace of that would have been huge, they'd have wanted to get rid of her, I suppose, and forget all about her.'

Even as Ellen listened she thought, I am not interested in Michael Collins, or the war. I don't care. I was only fooling myself when I believed that all of that was of interest to me. I am interested in myself, really, and that has always been my weakness. I have never been able to see beyond myself.

'We know so much about him, and nothing about her,' she said, almost to be polite to Dorothy.

'Sure, isn't that always the way?' said Dorothy. 'We know all the stories about the men, told by men.'

They sat on the bed in almost companionable silence, Dorothy holding the empty jellybean jar and Ellen drinking the whiskey, both of them watching the golden evening light move across the window.

'She must have been a very strong person,' said Ellen after a while, 'to have gone to America with a baby and made a new life for herself out there on her own.'

She felt Dorothy give a little start.

'What do you mean?' she said.

Ellen looked at her. 'To have gone with a baby, alone.' She hesitated. 'It's not easy, I think.'

'She didn't take the baby,' said Dorothy.

I have an expression of complete stupidity on my face right now, thought Ellen, wildly, trying to rearrange her features into something approaching normality.

'What did she do with the baby?' she said, trying to stay calm.

'She left the baby here,' Dorothy said, looking at her with something like alarm. 'Didn't you know any of this?'

I didn't, no, Dorothy, she wanted to shout. The list of things I don't know seems to be growing by the day.

'Why didn't she take the baby?' she said, too loudly.

'I don't know, Ellen,' said Dorothy. 'Who knows?' She gave a heavy sigh. 'My mother was an O'Donovan. Her grandfather was Eoin O'Donovan. He was the brother of Hannah and Eily. He was still alive when I was a child. He was a small old man then; he used to sit by the fire in the kitchen and smoke and watch the horse racing on the television all afternoon.'

Ellen wanted to shake Dorothy, hard.

'Right,' she said, very slowly. If I say anything more, she thought, or speak too quickly, even, we will never get to the bottom of this.

'And he told my mother about the baby, and about Hannah, and Eily. I thought you knew. I thought that's why you were so interested. ' She lifted up her hands. 'I thought you knew,' she said again, looking sorry now. 'Everyone here knows.'

'She didn't take the baby,' said Ellen. Why, Hannah? she thought. Why, why did you leave the baby?

'No,' said Dorothy. 'She didn't. She went on her own.'

'And we don't know what happened to her,' said Ellen, as much to herself as to Dorothy.

'We only know what happens to the ones who stay behind,' said Dorothy. 'Of Hannah we know nothing. We know that Eily married, of course, but the place was always known as O'Donovan's. Even Hannah's child was always known as an O'Donovan – Rose O'Donovan. That'll tell you something.'

'Rose O'Donovan?' said Ellen. 'My grandmother?'

Eily had taken the baby. Eily. And raised her. And that baby was my grandmother, Rose.

'Oh my god,' she said to Dorothy.

I am Hannah's great-granddaughter.

I am drunk now, perhaps, she thought, or I am stupid, which would explain, really, quite a lot, but I cannot understand it, the whole, big picture – Hannah going, Eily staying behind with the baby. And Eily ended up in a terrible terraced house in the city on her own, ended up as a cook in a hotel and Rose grew up a servant's daughter and what happened to Hannah, why did Hannah never come back?

Rose was Hannah's daughter. So my mother . . . She sat up a bit straighter. My mother. Does my mother know? Does she know that her own mother was Hannah's daughter?

Did Rose know? Am I the only one who knows?

She stood up from the bed very suddenly and turned so that she was facing Dorothy.

'Are you all right, Ellen?' said Dorothy.

'Ahhh,' she said, to make some kind of noise. 'It's just all very interesting. It's a bit much to take in, really.'

'It's very interesting, it is,' said Dorothy. 'The history of it. It's complex. One thing I never understood, for example, was why the O'Donovans switched sides after the War of Independence, why they switched to the De Valera side in the Civil War. They turned their back on Michael Collins. That was a strange thing I never understood, and that was the undoing of them in the end, I think, because this was Collins' territory, and they'd never have been accepted again here after doing a thing like that. The boys eventually all left the farm and set up a shop in the town but no one would go to the farm to work, and no one would buy from the O'Donovans or sell to them and in the end they couldn't keep going. Once the father and mother died – and they didn't last long after the Civil War – Eily and the husband and the child had to go. They were made to go. It was sad. All these old stories are sad.'

'God almighty,' said Ellen. I am going to be sick, she thought, I am going to be sick, possibly all over Dorothy.

'Well, yes,' said Dorothy. 'That's history for you.'

It's not history to me, Ellen thought wildly. Or to my mother. This is our life, our present. Hannah was my mother's grandmother. My mother's grandfather was O'Riada. This is not the past for us, Dorothy.

Dorothy held a Kit Kat out to her.

'You need a bit of sugar,' she said. 'You've had a shock.' She tried to give her a smile. 'Have a break, have a Kit Kat,' she said, and she winked, and she gave her big shoulders a comedy wiggle.

Ellen laughed and then she was crying again, great big jagged embarrassing heaves that wrenched her in two, nearly, as she tried to hide them. She sat back down on the bed next to Dorothy.

Dorothy put her arm around her shoulders and squeezed her and she sighed, sadly.

'You'll be all right,' she said.

'Thanks, Dorothy,' she said, wiping her face. 'Thanks for being nice to me.'

'Ah,' said Dorothy. 'I've daughters of my own and you'd like someone to be kind to them if they were in trouble,' she said. She looked at her. 'Are you in trouble?'

In all the worst ways, she thought. I pretended to myself and to everyone else for a long time that things were bad and hard for me and now I realize it's true. I'm in a tunnel now, she thought – my life is narrowing down and down and behind me is every wrong decision I've ever made and ahead of me is only fear, and I can't move forwards, and I can't move back. And now I've found this out, about Hannah, about me, really, and that's because I made another wrong decision, I think, to look for things which should not have been found, and I've made everything worse now, not better, not easier. There's no way out of for me, Dorothy, really, because I think Simon is going to leave me and if he does, I won't be able to survive in London, and I can't stay here – I've been gone too long, and no one wants me back. I don't fit in here, and I never did. Take me home with you, Dorothy, she wanted to say, so I can live with you and your girls forever and eat sausage sandwiches for my tea and pretend I'm someone else entirely.

'I'm OK,' she said. 'Generally speaking.'

'Do you have children in London?'

'No,' she said. 'I can't have children. We've tried for a long time but we can't. The doctors don't know what's wrong with me.'

Dorothy slumped forwards a bit and tutted, sadly.

'That's very hard,' she said. 'Very hard altogether to bear.'

'It is,' said Ellen.

'You're young still, though. And we don't know what the future holds.'

'That's right,' said Ellen. 'I suppose.'

She kept her eyes on the ground. She wanted Dorothy to be pleased with her, she realized; she wanted to say the things that Dorothy wanted to hear. She had always been a good girl, she thought, or at least she had always wanted people to think of her as a good girl, and that had been part of the problem. You're a great girl, her mother had said to her once, when she was very little, aren't you a great girl? She still remembered how embarrassed her mother had sounded, saying it.

Dorothy stood up.

'I'd better go back down or they'll be sending out a search party for me.' She looked worried. 'Will they be up soon?' she asked. 'Your mother, and your husband?'

Ellen knew what Dorothy wanted to hear.

'Any minute now,' she said. 'I'll have a shower and a rest before I see them.'

'Right,' said Dorothy. Ellen could hear the relief in her voice. 'I'll

see you, so, tomorrow. Just ring down when you want some food,'
and she backed away from her, smiling and nodding encouragingly.
She closed the door very gently behind her.

Ellen sat on the bed for a long time after Dorothy had left, looking
out the window at the darkening light. She stayed sitting even after
the night had come in, and the room was in darkness.

Then she stood up, and without even looking in the mirror, she
went out the door and down the stairs, looking for her mother.

HER MOTHER WAS IN the bar, sitting at a high round table in the
corner, eating her dinner. The light in the room was low and golden
and there was a fire in the shining grate and all was ordered and
rich-looking and Ellen, encouraged, heartened, went to the table
and climbed up on the stool facing her mother. For a long moment,
neither of them said anything. When her mother spoke first, it was
as good as an apology – she has given in, Ellen thought, she has
spoken to me first.

'I'm having something to eat,' said her mother, 'before I drive
home.'

'You'll have to drive in the dark,' said Ellen, quietly, looking
down at her hands on the table.

'I know,' said her mother. 'I'll head off soon.'

'Were you going to say goodbye to me?' said Ellen. Still she did
not look at her.

'I told Simon to tell you I was leaving,' said her mother. 'He's gone
to the pub in the village. He said he'd see you later.' She stopped,
hesitating. 'He looks very tired.'

'We're both very tired,' said Ellen. She looked up at her mother.
'I'm very tired, Mammy.'

She put her hand on her forehead. She had not wanted to say this
or anything like it – she did not want to sound weak, or defeated.
I have had no one to rely on for as long as I can remember, she
thought, only myself, and if I begin to show her that I am not strong,
I am lost, I am lost.

'Ellen,' said her mother, 'what are you doing to yourself, at all?'

Ellen put her hands on her lap. She clenched them together,
tightly, like she was praying.

Now, she thought.

'Rose was Hannah's daughter,' she said, very quickly. 'Did you
know that, Mammy? Hannah left her with Eily. Your mother was
Hannah's daughter. Did you know that?'

Her mother put her hand up to her mouth. She did not speak.

'Did you know, Mammy?'

Ellen was crying now, and oh, the shame of it, and she could not
stop the terrible hot tears that burned her eyes and burned the back of
her throat and then she saw that her mother was crying too, that her
eyes were small and red and swollen and full of tears that did not fall.

Her mother shook her head.

'No,' she whispered.

'Dorothy Flood said that everyone here knew.'

'I didn't know,' her mother said. She put her arm across her chest,
as if she were trying to hold herself together. 'And my mother didn't
know, I'm sure of that. She would have told me. We were great friends
and we told each other everything, everything. She would have told
me.' She looked almost grey in the face. She is old now, thought

Ellen, I have just realized that she is an old woman, now. I've been fighting her for so long that I did not see her, I could not see her.

'Oh my god,' said her mother, and she began to cry properly then. 'Mammy.'

'You said that Eily always talked of Hannah to your mother, that she told her to wait for her,' said Ellen. 'You never suspected? There was no sign?'

She had not expected her mother to respond like this. I have never seen you cry, Mammy! she wanted to say. Don't cry! I don't know what to do! I wanted to tell you because you wouldn't listen to me and you didn't want to talk about Hannah or about Eily or about me, all you wanted was silence, and denial, and I thought this would make you see but I'm sorry, Mammy, and I think I have done the wrong thing – I have taken your past and changed it, and it was not mine to take, to reshape. I'm sorry, Mammy, I'm sorry.

'No,' said her mother. 'Nothing. I was a child when Eily was alive – I knew nothing at all.' She shook her head. 'I can't believe it,' she said. 'I can't believe it.'

Ellen put her hand out and took her mother's hand in hers.

'Are you all right?' she said, awkwardly.

Her mother pulled her hand away from Ellen, slowly. She sat up straighter.

'It's a big thing in the family. It's upsetting. But I'm fine.'

You don't look fine, she wanted to say. You look like you've been hit in the face.

Her mother sniffed hard and picked up her fork, and speared a potato, viciously.

'She's sure, this Dorothy, is she?' Her voice was cold now.

'She is,' said Ellen.

'And O'Riada was the father?'

Ellen nodded.

'Well,' said her mother. She put the potato, and the fork, down, and regarded them sadly. 'That's that, I suppose. I've no more appetite.' She pushed her plate away from her.

They both sat in silence, looking at the plate of potatoes.

'Do you want a drink?' said Ellen, eventually.

'I'll have a port,' said her mother. 'I suppose you'll have something.'

'I'll have a coffee,' said Ellen.

'Oh,' said her mother with a small, bitter laugh. 'A coffee.'

Ellen got down from her chair. She started for the bar and then she stopped and turned around.

'Do you feel sorry for Hannah now, Mammy?'

'Sorry for her?' said her mother. 'Why would I feel sorry for her?'

'Because she left,' said Ellen, 'she never came back, she never saw her baby again.' Why is she angry? she thought. She is flaming with anger, and that has always been her chief emotion – anger – and it's only now I see it, that everything else has come from this anger.

'I do not feel sorry for Hannah,' said her mother, and Ellen saw that she had to speak quietly to keep the anger down, to manage it. 'I feel sorry for Eily, stuck in a miserable house raising her sister's child, living with that secret all her life and dying with it, too. That's who I feel sorry for. And I feel sorry for my mother, never knowing who her mother was, and I feel sorry for myself finding out here, now, but I don't feel sorry for Hannah. I do not, no. She left – she could have stayed, presumably, or she could have taken the baby with her. She made a choice. We all make choices, to go, to stay. Like yourself, Ellen. Like yourself, and the choices you made.'

Don't ask, Ellen thought. Don't ask her.

'What are you saying to me, Mammy?' she said.

'I'm saying that you left like Hannah left, left us all here, because it was never enough for you here, was it? And now you come back and dig all this up and here you have it, what you wanted, and the rest of us have to deal with it now, what you've dug out. Because this is what you wanted, isn't it? You didn't want a boring old story, and now you have your excitement. Now you have your sad, special ending. Isn't that what you wanted all along, Ellen?'

Her mother was breathing very fast, and her face was flushed dark red.

I feel nothing at all, thought Ellen, her words do not touch me. I am beyond them, now, perhaps, at last.

'I'll go to the bar, Mammy, I'll get you your port,' she said, and she turned and walked away so that her mother could not see her face.

XX

SHE WAITED FOR HIM in the woods. It took her a long time to walk there, and when she finally sat down under the trees she realized that she was so tired that she could sleep, so she lay down on the grass and fell asleep almost immediately, and slept for hours. When she woke the sun was low in the sky and dipping fast towards the horizon. He would come soon, she expected, while it was still light. She went to where the stream was and drank deeply and washed her face and her neck as best she could. She had no food and she was very hungry – she wished she had brought some bread with her. She didn't know when she would eat again; not until the next day, perhaps. She drank more water, cupping it in her hands and bringing it up to her mouth hungrily. It was sweet, cool water, and for a moment she felt almost satisfied.

She went back to wait by the young oaks. The woods were quiet: the day still had a heavy heat to it and there was no wind. She'd hardly sat down when she heard the low whistle. She stood up. He came through the trees quickly, his head down and his hands deep in his pockets. He walked straight up to her and for a minute she thought he would walk past her and on into the woods, but he stopped next to her.

'Eoin told you,' she said.

'He did.' He let his shoulders relax a bit. He shook his head. 'The poor old horse.'

She started to cry. She had cried more on this day than on any day she could remember.

'I can't go back,' she said.

'No, no,' he said, and then he said, with a sudden violence, 'He shouldn't have done that to the horse.'

'Will you get him out of the stable, Denis?' she said. 'I don't want him left there. They'll feed him to the hounds.'

He rubbed at his nose and gave a small, empty laugh; there was something possessive about the way he was looking at her, like he was proud of her.

'Still thinking of the horse she is,' he said, and he threw his arms out as he spoke, as if appealing to unseen listeners. 'You've to forget all that, now, Hannah. We've bigger problems on our hands than that, now, I'd say. You'll have to leave them to do what they will.'

The words were cold but her heart lifted a bit to hear the old affection in his voice. He went to where she'd lain and picked up her suitcase.

'Come on,' he said.

'Where are we going?'

'To May Fitz's tonight, and then we'll see.'

They said May Fitz was a witch, that she'd give you the evil eye if you looked at her wrong.

He walked away and then stopped and turned.

'Are you coming or are you staying here waiting for the Tans to get you?' he said, and so she walked after him, through the woods, to the witch.

IT WAS LATE AT night when they got to May Fitz's. Her cottage was at the foot of the mountains, and by the time they arrived they'd walked up and down fields and through a bog and by the lonely peat bog lake where they'd seen a pair of swans sleeping in the rushes, their necks twisted together into a white heart. The night was warm and not dark and more beautiful than any day she'd seen, and the further she walked the more she felt that she was walking into a kind of dream. I will keep on walking, she thought, away from it all, towards him, and it will all be all right. She could taste the sweetness of the night on her tongue and her heart was nearly bursting from the beauty of it all and she was happy, she realized, with a shock. I'm happy to be free and on the way somewhere, to be moving, and I'll remember this night for the rest of my life, when I set out for something and the world turned its face to meet me.

They walked for hours. By the end of the walking she was nearly asleep as she walked and Denis had to pull her after him and push her and all the way he didn't speak, he never said a word until he saw the cottage in the small valley below them.

'You'd know it by the trees,' he said, nearly to himself: the cottage was ringed by a few heavy conifers that were darker than the night around them.

She started down the hill.

'Wait,' he said, and put his hand on her arm. He crouched down low and nodded at her to do the same and for a while they watched the cottage, and then, when he was satisfied, he stood up and headed down the hill. A fox barked with laughter in the distance, and the door of the cottage opened and a figure appeared in it.

'May Fitzgerald,' Denis called out in greeting.

The figure in the doorway signalled to them to come on. They went down the hill.

'You're welcome here,' said the woman, in Irish, and she stepped forwards. She was white-haired but broad-shouldered and as tall a woman as Hannah had ever seen. She wore a black dress and had a shawl over her head and shoulders in the old style and in her hand she had a blackthorn stick.

They went into the cottage. It was one-roomed, windowless, and spotlessly clean. May went to the fire and began to stir it.

'You'll have food?' she said, still in Irish.

'We will, May, thank you,' said Denis, in English. He understood the Irish but he couldn't speak it. 'And I'll be off then and I'll leave Hannah here with you.'

'They came last week,' she said. 'O'Riada and the other one. They stayed the night with me before they went up the mountain.' She pointed her stick to the back of the house. 'They're up there still.'

'I'm going up there tonight myself, May,' said Denis.

'Ah,' she said, with resignation, and she raised her hand up in a surrender but she kept her back to them, and said no more.

They sat on the step by the fire in silence and waited while May prepared the food. When she turned to them with two bowls Hannah shook her head.

'I can't eat,' she said, realizing it suddenly. She had been hungry all day, but the hunger had left her now.

'You're too tired is what it is. You're beyond hunger,' said May. 'Sit down on the bed.' She took hold of her arm and led her to the bed and sat her on it like she was a child. She took her hand and squeezed it. 'We'll mind you here,' she said to her, shyly.

Hannah felt light-headed and weak now. Her eyes were closing. She could see Denis outlined by the low fire, and then him standing and coming slowly towards her. The fire behind him made him glow bright. He kneeled down by the bed, in front of her, and put his hand out to her.

'Goodbye, Hannah,' he said, and then he added, too quickly, 'Will you give me a kiss for luck?'

He was trying to smile at her, and thinking he was making a joke, she laughed and sat up and took his hand and they shook hands, gravely, formally. His hand was warm and dry in hers, and he kept holding on to her hand, not dropping it, and then he looked at her and her heart gave a terrible thump as she understood something suddenly, completely, from the hungry, searching way he was looking at her.

How could she not have seen this until now?

She had been blind, blind and stupid to have not understood this before and her face burned red to the roots of her hair and he looked at her and she saw that he knew what she had understood. He dropped her hand and stood up and stepped away from her.

She had only ever known Denis as a man about the farm who did what her father told him to do. Once as a child she'd been playing too loudly in the yard when there was a sick ewe lambing in the stable and he'd come out and shouted at her to be quiet and she had told him, she remembered now, not to speak to her like that or she would tell her father and he would send him away. She had always thought of him as belonging to her father, belonging to her – until the Tans had come she had not even thought of him as a person with desires and thoughts of his own. Denis had nothing. He had come from nowhere. That he should think of her as anything but her father's daughter was a corruption of the order of her world.

She tried to look at him like she was seeing him for the first time. He was not tall, but he was barrel-chested and as strong as a bull, with hair cropped close to his skull and small neat ears and she didn't even know what colour his eyes were – such a thing had never concerned her. May Fitz had turned from the fire and was watching them. Denis inclined his head towards her.

'I'll go now, May,' he said, backing away.

'God bless, Denis, god bless,' May called after him, sadly.

Hannah went out the door after him. He was already walking away from the cottage, towards the mountain.

'Denis,' she called.

He turned around.

'Will you be all right?'

She couldn't see his face in the darkness.

'The divil a know,' he shouted out, wildly, and she was so shocked that she laughed out loud with something like delight.

IT WAS WARM WEATHER while she was in May Fitz's cottage, waiting for Denis, and the valley below them and the fields beyond that, where her house was, were more often than not shrouded in mist, though the sky above was a clear pale blue. She spent the days in the sun, bringing water up from the stream, watching over the few chickens that scrabbled about in the dust in front of the door. One whole day was given over to picking gooseberries from the small garden and making jam from them. They pulled the table out from inside the cottage and set it against the wall in the sun and worked late into the evening. May was fastidious in her habits and everything was done slowly and carefully but with great good humour and she praised Hannah excessively, it seemed to her, for even the smallest undertaking. There was relief in being busy – she suspected that May had her making the jam to keep her occupied – and she was almost happy, she found, in the sweet warm air. Everything that had happened before she came to the mountain seemed unreal to her now, and when she tried to think of it all, it was like trying to see her house through the distance and the fog: it was there, but all of it as distant as an old dream.

They spoke in Irish – the English hurt her head, May said, tapping it on the side with her knuckles – about the business of the day, and that was all; why she was there was never mentioned. They hardly spoke of her family, though May said once that she had known her mother as a girl, and she had rolled her eyes comically, and then given a little apologetic half-shake of her shoulders, and Hannah had laughed, guiltily at first, and afterwards, with relief.

They rose at first light and were busy all day, and they went to sleep before it was dark, and after two days Hannah began to feel that perhaps she would stay on the mountain with May forever, beyond time, beyond thought, suspended, but on the fourth day, in the evening, Denis came back.

She was lying down already, nearly asleep, and May was in the rocking chair by the range when he came in. He was unshaven and he smelled stale – she could smell him from across the room – and his face looked hollowed out.

May gave a small cry and stood up.

'Are you on your own?'

'I am,' he said, sitting down at the table. 'Do you have any food in the house?'

Hannah stood up. He didn't look at her. May brought him a bowl of potatoes and a cup of milk and they both watched him as he ate.

'You've a fierce hunger on you,' said May, carefully.

He didn't answer. He'd poured the milk on top of the potatoes and was using his hands to eat. Hannah watched him, half appalled. When he'd eaten in her kitchen he'd done it quietly and quickly, bent over the plate to hide the way he held the fork. He was hiding nothing now.

'Do you have any meat?' he said.

'I've eggs,' said May. 'I'll get you a couple of eggs.'

Hannah sat down in front of him.

'Did you see him?'

'I did,' he said.

May put the eggs in front of him and he cracked them on the table's edge and ate them raw.

'What did you tell him?'

'I told him what you wanted me to tell him,' he said.

'He didn't come back with you.'

'No,' he said, and he looked up at her then. He looked very tired; his face was black, almost, with exhaustion.

'Am I to meet him somewhere?' she said.

He shook his head.

'Am I to wait here for him?'

He wiped his mouth with his hand and pushed his chair back from the table. When he spoke again, he didn't look at her.

'He said for you to do as well as you might, for in him is no trust to trust in.'

May was standing next to her, though she did not know it until she felt her fingers digging tight into her shoulder.

'What does that mean, at all?' said May. 'That means nothing to her. What's she to do? That's what we want to know.'

Hannah put her hand out and May took hold of it and squeezed it tight, tight. She did not speak. She stayed sitting completely still, with her eyes down, and her hands folded in her lap, and her breath going in and out like a piston. Her life until this summer had been regulated and ordered and private and empty of anything but the smallest excitements, and it seemed to her that it was beyond her understanding now to absorb what was happening to her; she could no more make sense of it than she could understand a foreign language.

'I'm just telling you what he said,' said Denis, and he slammed down his open hand on the table. 'A day it took me to get to him and a day back and the Tans are all over the place like flies. I couldn't close my eyes the whole time I was on the mountain.'

'What's that to us, Denis Mulcahy?' said May. 'We're waiting here for news and this is all you have for us.' May let go of Hannah's hand. 'What is to become of her now?' she said. 'And the child? Will her uncle the priest be coming looking for her? 'Tis not so far we are now from your own story, Denis, is it?'

'We're far enough from my story,' said Denis. 'And we're far enough from your story too, May, and the child they took from you because you'd no husband of your own, so don't be worrying yourself about that now.' He stood up. 'He won't come back. He has notions for himself. Michael Collins has big plans for him. He's off up the country soon. So we've to look after our own now.'

Black fear was opening up through Hannah now like a yawn. She stood up. She could not stay sitting down, listening to this. She would run up the mountain to him, rending her clothes as she went, before she continued to sit here listening to Denis. It is not true, she thought, it cannot be true. She began to repeat his name in her head, O'Riada, O'Riada, and the rhythm of it was like a prayer she might say on her rosary beads, every letter of his name a hard bead.

'What is she to do?' she heard May say, as if from a great distance.

'What can she do,' answered Denis, 'but marry? Sure, she has to get married.'

He stood up. He walked around the table so he was standing in front of Hannah. She was as tall as him – taller, nearly. Her mother's voice came into her head, unbidden – the poor people were always small, short in stature, not tall, like our people. She tried to make herself look at Denis. She could see that he was preparing to speak. He was searching for the right words; she watched his face contort with the effort. He turned to May, and spoke to her.

'She can marry,' he said, suddenly, with force, and then, in a rush, 'She can marry me.'

She saw May's face go slack with the shock she herself felt. Denis? It was unthinkable that she would marry Denis. The idea was ridiculous. He looked at Hannah for a second, furtively, and then his eyes slid away from her. He was afraid of her response, she knew, and she despised him for that, and for thinking that he could marry her, and another part of her admired him, for his bravery, and his mad optimism. And it was not nothing to be wanted, even by Denis.

'Ask her, so,' said May, angrily. 'She's there in front of you. Don't be thinking you can make plans for her and not even be asking her.'

He moved to stand closer to her. If he touches me, she thought, I will strike him.

'Hannah,' he said.

He was trying to make his voice softer.

She couldn't let him go on.

'Ah, Denis,' she cried, in desperation.

'Right,' he shouted, turning away from her. 'Right. Forget it.'

He picked up his cap from the table and put it on, pulling it down low over his eyes. He went towards the door and then stopped and turned around. He is going to say something hurtful now, she thought, to relieve himself a bit, and I will have to take it quietly – I will do that for him, at least. He looked at her, and then his face sagged a little, and he nearly gave her a smile, but he nodded at her instead, goodbye, and then he went out the door, closing it behind him.

She sat back down at the table.

'Look up at me now.' May was standing in front of her. 'It's no use, at all, looking like that. What's done is done. I learned that myself the hard way. You have to think now of what to do.'

May walked around the table so she was standing behind Hannah and put her hand on her shoulders and leaned down, pressing her soft thin cheek against hers.

'You can stay here as long as you'd like. I'd welcome the company. Stay here,' she said, sounding decided, 'and sure, we'll see what happens.'

'They say you're a witch, May,' she said with a cry, not caring anymore what was said. She would think of that afterwards, of her deliberate weakness in that moment.

'I know that,' said May. 'If you're out on your own, they can say what they want about you.'

'You came up here on your own,' said Hannah. May had been brave, she thought, braver than she could ever have been.

'Ha!' said May. 'You think I wanted to come here? They sent me up here, girl, when I was no older than you. They put me in this cottage and told me never to leave it. In the beginning they dropped off the food every month by the front door. After a while I learned how to manage for myself. I was sent here, and here I stay.'

Hannah couldn't speak.

'Take it day by day,' said May. 'Day by day from here on in, we'll do it together, and we'll see what's in front of us. You can't do more than that.'

WHEN SHE WOKE THE next morning, she took her small calendar from her suitcase and looked at it as if it held the clues to her future. But the days and the weeks ahead of her were as a river that wound off into the distance, to an unknown end. Perhaps she would stay at May's always, she thought, and always be warm in the sunlight, doing easy work around the place, the days as long as weeks to her, the past forgotten, and the future, too. But even as she thought it she knew that what was ahead of her was altogether more tumultuous. We can all see the shape of what is to come for us, she thought. We all know, somewhere inside ourselves, what will be.

XXI

'I DON'T WANT IT,' HANNAH said, in Irish.

May was bent over the fire with her back to her; Hannah could see her black outline against its low flames. There was light from the fire and light from the candles – so many candles, she thought, all of the candles in the house alight and they would be in darkness tomorrow night surely with all the light gone.

'I don't want it, May, do you hear me?' she said, more loudly.

May turned and came towards her. She leaned down to her and put her hand on Hannah's forehead. Hannah could hear her breathing heavily and quickly, in and out, in and out; she could feel her warm breath on her cheek.

'I hear you,' said May. She pushed Hannah's wet hair back from her forehead.

'It's too late now, anyway,' Hannah said, turning her head to one side away from May's hand. 'Too late.'

'What's she saying?' said her mother, in English.

Her mother and Eily were standing by the table. They had been sitting earlier, she thought, but now they were standing, and she didn't know why. Why didn't they sit down? She turned her face towards them to tell them to sit, that they were bothering her by standing there with their heads sticking forwards like two mad chickens, and she nearly began to laugh at that thought but then the pain came again, a terrible tightening pain that made her grab at her stomach and it was worse than before, worse each time, surely, and almost a thing beyond pain now – it was a white-coloured flame that she was burning and breaking on. She bent her legs and lifted her head and tried to push but she didn't know where to push from – she was doing it wrong, she knew; she had been pushing for hours and nothing was happening. She gave a cry then that frightened her; she hadn't thought it possible that such a sound could come out of her. I am become a stranger to myself, she thought, as the pain lashed her. Even my mind, now, is strange to me. What I was before is gone, is dead, is dying, so that the baby can live.

She tried to sit up to ease the pain but it was impossible – she was too big to move. The only thing that would help her was to move and she could not. She gripped the bed and tried to push herself up but she fell back down, beaten, breathless. There was something wrong, surely. The pain was too much. It was not meant to be like this.

'May,' she said.

'I know,' said May.

May had her hands on her stomach. She was pushing against the baby, shoving at it like she was looking for something. She was making the pain worse, and Hannah tried to tell her this, but she found that she could not speak.

'The baby is lying wrong,' she heard May say then.

'What does that mean?' said Eily.

'It means we have to turn it,' said May. 'She's been labouring for twelve hours, since this morning, and she's still like this. We have to do something now.'

The pain was moving away from her like the sea running out from the shore. I am fading away, she thought. Each time the pain goes it takes some of me with it and I am less and less each time. It will leave nothing of me.

She closed her eyes, and found that she was beginning to drift into something like sleep. It was as if a gate had been opened to her and if only she could pass through it and be free of the pain, and all of this . . . She threw her head back in longing so that her mouth fell open and something clicked in her throat.

'What's happening to her?' Eily said.

Eily and her mother were at her head. Go away, she wanted to say to them. Leave me be. When they'd arrived first she had been ashamed that they were seeing her like this, with her legs open and bent up on the bed and only a thin old sheet to cover her, her huge terrible breasts clear through the shift and the shift bunched up around her waist leaving her more naked than not. She was beyond shame now. If only she could sleep, she thought. If only they would leave her be so she could sleep.

'Why are you here?' she said, in a whisper, turning to look at Eily.

'To help you,' said Eily.

'No,' said Hannah.

'No, what?' said Eily. 'No, what?' she said to May and her mother, when Hannah did not answer her. 'Well? Why is no one answering me? What should we do? Should we get her up and walk her around?'

She sounds afraid, thought Hannah. What is she afraid of?

Her mother had moved to stand next to May at the end of the bed.

'I'll hold her legs and Eily will hold her arms and you turn it,' she said to May.

'I'm not holding her arms,' said Eily in alarm.

'Eily,' shouted her mother.

Hannah heard Eily mutter something under her breath in reply and then she took hold of her wrists and pulled them above her head. Her mother took hold of her legs, one leg in each hand.

She lifted her head up to look down the bed at May and her mother. I must get off this bed, I must stand, she thought. I will not be held down. She pulled her hands free from Eily with one motion, but she had forgotten how strong her mother was and she had to get herself up on her elbows and kick out and twist her legs and when her mother began to lose her grip she pulled one leg free and back and kicked her as hard as she could in the chest. Her mother fell back from her. She leaned over and put her hands on her thighs and Hannah could see her back going up and down as she tried to catch her breath. After a minute her mother straightened up. Hannah saw her and May look at each other. They will do something bigger now, she thought. That is what that look means.

There was silence in the room for a moment.

'Hannah,' said May then. 'The baby is lying across you. It can't come out like this. Do you understand me?'

She lay back down. The pain will come for me again soon, and I am done for then, she thought, I am at the end.

'We have to turn the baby,' May was saying. 'Will you let us do it, Hannah?'

'No,' she said. She began to shake her head. 'No, no, no.'

'If we don't turn the baby, you will die, Hannah, and the baby too,' said May. 'Do you understand what I'm saying to you?'

'Too late,' she said. She fell back on the bed.

'It's not too late,' said her mother. 'The baby is still moving. If we turn it now, it will be all right. We have to turn the baby.'

I don't care if the baby is all right, she would have said if she could have. I don't want the baby. I feel like I'm tied to train tracks and the train is coming and there's no way out for me. I want to go back to before all of this happened, back to before O'Riada came that first night, and if I can't go back, I don't want to go forwards, because there's nothing left for me now.

'No,' she said.

'What will we do?' she heard her mother say to May.

'We have to tie her,' said May.

SHE HAD KNOWN THAT the baby would come at the blackest hour of the night. Since the end of the summer the baby had been still during the day, sleeping, she thought, and stirring only occasionally, but at night it was awake. At first its movements had been no more than a strange quickening, but as the winter nights drew in the baby had occupied her, had rolled in her, calamitously. Through the long, lonely hours, when even the dark hills seemed to breathe with sleep, the baby turned and pushed, increasingly restless. It was looking for something, she thought, it was not at ease; once, even, she had seen its hand pressed up against the thin, stretched skin of her stomach, reaching out to her. She had almost put her hand against its hand, in a hello, and afterwards had wondered that she had not, and was sorry for that, almost.

The days after these sleepless nights passed in a haze of great tiredness for Hannah; often, she fell asleep as she sat in the chair by the fire, and more than once, as she walked the lonely fields, she was compelled to lie down in the long grass by the ditch and sleep. And when she did sleep she was disturbed by strange and unsettling dreams. Once she had dreamed that there was something like a thread sticking out of the palm of her right hand. She had pulled at the thread and it had spooled out and she'd found that the thread was the branch of a tiny, perfectly formed tree whose roots went deep down into her hand and she dug down then into her hand, digging up the tree and the earth around it until there was a terrible hole in her hand, and the more of the tree she dug up, the less of her hand there was and down she went, into the earth, pulling at the tree that came out of her, that should never have been there in the first place.

MAY HAD THE SHEET off her now and was tearing it into strips. She handed her mother a strip. She took one of Hannah's legs and her mother took the other and they began to tie her ankles to the short posts of the bed. She tried to fight, but it was impossible to fight against both of them, and anyway, she was growing weaker, she realized, she was losing her strength quickly.

'Keep your legs bent,' said May.

When they had finished tying her legs May said, 'Do I have to tie your hands, Hannah, or will you let us turn the baby? It will be worse if you fight it and you don't have your hands free.'

'Don't tie her hands,' said Eily. She put her hands out and took Hannah's in hers. 'See?' she said. Hannah looked up at her. Eily was completely white in the face. Her hair was tied back in a tight bun on the back of her head and in the candlelight she looked almost spectral. 'You don't have to tie her hands.'

'Do you know what to do?' her mother said, very quietly, to May.

Eily dropped her hands.

'Has she not done it before?' she said, in great alarm. 'God almighty. Do we know what we're doing here at all?'

'Would you be quiet, Eily, for once in your life,' her mother cried.

Eily took hold of her hands again.

'I'm only saying,' she said, and then she caught Hannah's eye and cocked her head in her mother's direction and gave a comical grimace and Hannah tried to shake her head at her, stop, and then they smiled at each other and Eily was crying she saw, and she marvelled at that.

'Eily,' she said.

'Don't leave me on my own, Hannah,' said Eily, so quietly that only Hannah could hear her. 'I've no other sister. I've no one but you. Don't leave me here alone.'

I am dying, she thought, and what a waste it has all been, everything thrown away so carelessly with no thought given to a way forwards, and I'm sorry to leave Eily, isn't that amazing that after everything the love was there all the time, and I never knew? I never knew because I would not see. She could not speak, and she tried to squeeze Eily's hand to make her understand, but the strength was gone from her. I am dying, she thought, it's all too late, and oh, the pity of it.

May had moved the three-legged stool from its place by the fire and put it at the end of the bed. She took hot water from the pot on the fire and poured it into the bowl on the table. She pushed her dress sleeves up to her elbows and washed her lower arms in the bowl and dried them. Hannah watched her as she did all this. She was very tired now and it was becoming hard to stay awake. She closed her eyes and felt her mind begin to swim away from her.

'Hannah,' said May, and then she said again, loudly, urgently, 'Hannah.'

Hannah opened her eyes.

'Are you ready?' said May. She was standing at her side, looking down at her.

Hannah put her face to the wall and nodded. There was nothing else to do now. She had lost, she felt. She had been defeated. She could feel the tears pricking at the back of her eyes, but she would not cry.

May went to the end of the bed and sat down.

'I'm turning it now,' she said.

The pain was so great that she vomited, almost immediately. She could not lift her head to be sick so Eily had to turn her face for her and the foul-tasting vomit ran down her neck and into her hair. After she had vomited she continued to retch and she began to struggle to breathe so Eily stood behind her and took her head in both her hands and pulled it up against her chest and pulled her hair back from her face. May's hands were in her now, pulling and turning, and the baby was struggling to get free from her hold and it felt wrong – dangerous, and unnatural. She began to cry then and she called out, 'Stop,' and Eily said, 'Stop, stop, this can't be right,' but May kept on tugging and then she said, 'I have the ankles.' She felt warm liquid run from her then – she knew from the strange, sweet smell of it that it was not blood.

'You have to bear down now, girl,' said May.

'Push, Hannah,' said her mother.

She lifted her head up and pushed but the effort was coming from her chest. She could push harder, she knew, and better, but she was very tired, and she didn't want to, she didn't want to make the effort. She wanted it all, all to stop.

'No more,' she said, and lay back down.

'She has to push now,' said May, 'or I'll have to let go,' and there was something in her voice that she hadn't heard before – anger, she thought, or desperation.

'Push, Hannah,' said Eily. 'For god's sake.'

She looked up at Eily. She had to decide now, she knew. She had to choose. She closed her eyes. She remembered being a child and running down to the river on the long summer nights. She remembered the sound the horse made when it cantered across the land, the feel of its mane whipping against her face. She remembered the light through the trees as she lay underneath them with O'Riada, and how she had put her hands up to touch the light, as if she could hold it, the innocent thing that she had been then.

'Lift me up,' she said to Eily.

Eily put her hands under her arms and heaved her up so that she was half sitting, then she leaned her body in against Hannah's back, pushing against her, taking the weight of her. Hannah put her hands down flat by her sides and took hold of the bed as best she could. The pain would come soon again – she could feel it rising up. If she did not act now, it would be too late.

She lifted her head up and looked down the bed at May, and nodded at her.

'Now?' said May.

'Yes,' said Hannah, and she was surprised to hear that her voice sounded strong and clear.

This is my last chance, she thought. The end is near now, one way or another.

'Untie her ankles,' May said to her mother, and when her legs were free she pulled her knees up as near to her chest as she could and then she began to push down.

'That's it, girl,' said May.

'Will she tear?' she heard her mother say to May.

'She's torn already,' said May. 'Come on, Hannah.'

Eily leaned in against her. Hannah pushed again – down and forwards – and Eily pushed at her and she felt something shift in her. There was a vital loosening somewhere, a movement. She was making terrible noises, low and guttural, and she kept her chin on her chest and held on to both sides of the old narrow bed and pushed. No more, she thought, I can do no more, it is finished, and then she heard her mother say, in wonder, 'It's coming.'

Her mother was standing behind May, and Hannah saw her face change, become filled with light.

'It's coming,' her mother cried again, and this time her voice was filled with triumph.

It was easier, suddenly. May pulled – she felt her turn the baby one more time as it came down – and she had to push again but she had momentum now and within a moment May said, 'I have it,' and the baby came out of her with an unexpected, glorious rush, all at once.

'Oh my god,' said Eily, dropping her so that she fell back down flat on the bed.

The baby was silent. It should cry, surely, she thought, it should make a noise.

'Is it all right?' she said.

No one answered her. She struggled up onto her elbows. Eily and May and her mother were standing together at the end of the bed with their backs to her.

'Where's the baby?' she said, and she could hear the urgency in her voice.

Her heart was beating very fast now. She was afraid, she realized, more afraid than she had ever been in her life before.

Everything was perfectly still. No one breathed.

Then the baby gave a small cry and all the blood in her body seemed to run – whoosh! – through her veins with a great loud bang.

Her mother threw her hands up in the air and gave a laugh of pure happiness.

'She's alive,' she called out to the world.

It was a girl.

She watched them wrap the baby in a blanket that she remembered: it had been Liam's blanket when he was a baby. It had been her blanket, probably.

Her mother came towards her holding the baby in her arms.

'Oh, Hannah,' she said. 'Congratulations.'

She had never seen her mother look so happy. She looked fundamentally changed. She looked young.

'Hold your baby,' she said to her, and Hannah lay back down on the bed and her mother put the baby on her chest.

She moved the blanket back from the baby's head and looked at her face.

She looked like her.

Something turned over in her chest. She leaned down and kissed the baby's blooming cheek and oh, the smell from her, and the small hopeful noise that she was making in her throat, and the feel of her hand in hers. I have met you before, she thought. You have been here before.

'It was a long night,' May was saying, 'all behind us now.'

'You're right, May, you're right,' her mother called out in response, half laughing, and half crying.

The first light had come into the room like a blessing, and Hannah turned her face towards its benediction.

She is mine, she thought. I will protect her, I will make her life easy, I will do whatever is needed to make her safe.

I will do whatever I have to do.

XXII

ILY CAME AT FIRST light. Hannah was on the bed with the
baby and May was starting the fire when the door opened slowly
and there stood Eily, pale as a ghost.

'Hello,' she said, and May called out, 'Jesus,' in fright and crossed
her hands across her chest.

Eily came into the room. She was breathing very fast and she had
a wild, almost feverish look about her. Hannah got up from the bed,
and, holding the baby against her chest, went to stand next to May
by the fire. They stood together watching Eily, and waiting. After a
moment she gave herself a shake like a cat shaking off a smell and
then she seemed to come into herself and she became still and calm
enough to speak.

She'd left straight after the dinner, she said; she'd told them all
that she was tired and going to bed and she'd gone up to her bedroom
and taken a sheet off the bed and twisted it into a rope and tied it to
the leg of the bed and let it down out the window, and then she'd
slid down it and gone across the yard, making sure no one saw her
– no one did – and down the lane she'd gone and into the fields and
she'd kept going all night until she came to May's. She seemed as

surprised to be telling the story as Hannah was to be hearing it: it didn't seem possible to either of them that Eily had done such a thing.

'I only stopped once to have a rest,' she said in wonder, 'but as soon as I sat down I got up again.'

'Won't they be looking for you?' asked Hannah.

'I left a note,' said Eily, 'saying, "I have been called away on family business and I will return shortly."' She gave a laugh of delight at her impudence.

The baby stirred then, raising her hand in the air.

'Can I have a look at her?' Eily said.

Hannah came to her and held the baby so that Eily could see her but Eily put her hands out, opening and closing her fists impatiently, until Hannah handed her the baby.

Eily put her face down low to the baby's. For a moment, she said nothing.

Then she said, very gently, 'Hello. Say hello to your lovely aunt who came over a mountain to see you,' and she leaned down and kissed her forehead. Stop that, Hannah wanted to say. Don't touch her. She is mine.

'I'd better take her,' she said to Eily. 'She might be hungry.'

Eily looked at her and then she looked back down at the baby and smiled at her.

'Eight weeks today,' she said. 'Lovely girl.' She gave a small sigh. 'Back to your cranky mammy.' She handed the baby back to Hannah. 'She's getting big,' said Eily.

Hannah turned away from her and went to sit back down on the bed.

'I thought you wouldn't come for another few weeks yet,' she said, being careful not to look at Eily as she spoke. 'That's what we said, I thought, that you and Mammy would come nearer the summer to see her.'

Her heart was beating very slowly, steadily, banging at her chest like a closed fist.

'I know,' said Eily. 'But I've news.' She sat down at the table and began to help herself to the bread. 'I'm starving,' she said. She looked up at Hannah and May. 'Is there any milk?'

'From the goat,' said May. 'Will that do you?'

'It'll have to,' said Eily, too brightly. May handed her the cup and Eily drank it down, all the while watching them with her still, light eyes. When she'd finished she licked the drops of milk off her lips with a small, darting tongue. 'Sit down over here with me,' she said to Hannah. 'I'm hurting my neck trying to see you.'

Hannah came across the room and sat at the end of the table, facing Eily. She was eating the bread in great chunks – she had never seen her eat with such enthusiasm. There were two red spots on her cheeks, high up.

'Take it slow,' Hannah said to her. 'You'll choke.'

May brought her more milk and she drank that, too.

'I'm tired now,' she said, when she'd finished.

'You've come a long way,' said May. 'And all on your own, too. Did you not have trouble finding your way, in the dark, on your own?'

'No,' said Eily. 'It wasn't hard. I ran most of it. I'm fast.'

It was true, thought Hannah. She had never been able to beat Eily in a race. Her father used to say she was built like a greyhound, for speed.

May was standing in front of Eily, examining her.

'And what's put this great hurry on you?'

Eily turned her face away from her and looked across the table at Hannah.

'I've news of O'Riada,' she said.

'What of him?' said May.

'I heard Denis telling Daddy,' she said. 'They didn't know I was listening. There's to be a great meeting of the Volunteers at our place and O'Riada and the other one, Tiernan, will be there. They're coming off the mountain now, they're all coming back in from Kerry. Plans have changed, Denis said.'

'When is the meeting?' said Hannah.

'Tonight,' said Eily. 'Denis told Daddy that we are all to hide out in the fields well before the men come.'

Hannah went to the bed and lay the baby down on it. She began to dress. She put on her dress over her shift and then on top she put her cardigan and buttoned it up to her neck. May and Eily watched her without speaking. She bent down and pulled her suitcase out from under the bed. She put the suitcase on the bed next to the baby and opened it and picked up the gun. She clicked open the barrel and counted the bullets. From the suitcase she took one of the dresses and wrapped it once around the gun and then tied a knot to make sure the bundle was secure, and then she tied the dress as a belt around her waist. She sat on the bed and put on her heavy stockings and her boots.

'Where are you going?' said May.

'Back,' she said, not looking up from the lacing. I want to stay here forever, May, she wanted to say, but I have to go back to get his name for the baby, to lay claim to his land and make what is his hers.

She stood up and stomped in her boots, testing them out. She'd been barefoot since she'd come to May's and the boots seemed tight and extraordinarily heavy on her.

'With the child?' said May. 'She's only weeks old and you're taking her across the mountains in the wind and the cold?'

'I won't leave her here without me,' said Hannah. She tried to steady her voice. 'She has to be fed.'

'Cool your heels,' said May. 'I've questions to ask here, questions you'd be asking yourself if you had any sense left.'

She looked at Hannah, and when she didn't speak, she turned to Eily.

'You won't mind me asking you, now, Eily, and you'll forgive me for being rough in the English and not able to say easily what I want, but how are we to know that things are as you say they are?'

There was a small silence.

'What do you mean?' said Eily. The high red spots on her cheeks were getting darker.

'How are we to know that O'Riada will be there? And Eily, and you'll excuse me for saying this, but Hannah has told me bits and pieces about the family, bits and pieces, and I have to wonder but were you sent? Who is it that wants her back? Is the priest waiting for her back down there?'

'Whether she comes or not,' said Eily, very quietly, 'is her own affair. I'm not telling her what to do. I'm only passing on what I heard.'

She picked up a piece of bread and began to chew at it, not looking at either of them.

'It's the baby I'm thinking of,' she said, almost to herself. 'Is she to stay hidden up here all her life?'

'Do you know what you heard to be true? Do we know what you say to be true?' shouted May.

'I don't understand you, at all,' said Eily, in a low, dangerous voice that Hannah recognized as a warning. 'I'm only telling you what Denis said. Are you saying we shouldn't believe Denis? If we can believe anyone, we can believe Denis. All these years . . .'

She stopped and turned away.

'Eily,' said Hannah, and she gave a half-laugh, turning away to pick up the baby. 'Anyone would think you were soft on Denis.'

'Oh, leave me be,' cried Eily, and she stood up from the table, knocking over the chair behind her. 'You know nothing of it.'

'What?' said Hannah. She had turned around so she was looking at Eily. 'Nothing of what? What are you talking about?'

'Oh, what, what,' shouted Eily. 'You see nothing outside yourself, Hannah. You're blind to all the rest of us. All these years Denis has been looking at you, watching you, and you never saw it and there's me like the big fool waiting for him to see me and he never did, he never did, he only ever saw you.' She put her hands over her face, leaning over into them. 'Ahhh,' she shouted, into her hands.

Hannah sat back down on the bed as suddenly as if she had been pushed. The baby, startled by the sudden movement, began to cry, and Eily was crying too, she saw, her whole body was shaking. Hannah watched her as she bent to pick up the chair. She did it slowly, and then took her time setting the chair in against the table. She is trying to hide the crying, Hannah thought: that is why she is slow. She was always proud; she could never bear to be seen crying.

'Eily,' said Hannah, standing up.

If I am with O'Riada, I cannot be with Denis; that is why Eily is here, though she has perhaps not admitted that even to herself. In some deep part of her heart Eily wants me to be with O'Riada so that Denis is free.

Before she believed it, before she understood it, she knew this to be true.

I have been blind, and only now do I begin to see.

'It's all right, Hannah,' said Eily. 'Really. Don't look like that. And it doesn't matter anyway. It's not like Mammy and Daddy are going to let me set up with Denis. Mammy would have me sent off to the convent first. It's all right.'

Everything I have known is wrong, thought Hannah. How is it possible to have got everything so wrong?

Eily sat down at the table and folded her hands in a little tight fist in front of her. She looked very tired, and pale, as if she had been emptied out.

'What will you do, Hannah?' she said very quietly.

She would not stay here, hiding. She had to do something to change the track of things – that much was clear to her now. She went to May and put her hand on her arm.

'I've to go, May,' she said simply.

May put her hands up to her head. Her face was folded up with grief.

'There was a bad moon last night,' she said. 'Blood on the moon, I says to myself, and then I heard that old fox coughing out on the mountain, telling me of trouble to come. The old spirits are stirring. Is there a curse on us all, and all of us dancing to the old spirits' song?'

She began to sway very gently backwards and forwards, and to keen quietly under her breath.

Eily was watching her, appalled. She pushed her chair back from the table, as if she would slide out of the door unseen if she could.

'I've to go now, May,' Hannah repeated. 'I've been waiting long enough. You know that yourself.'

May kept swaying, and keening quietly.

Hannah took her hand.

'I'll be all right,' she said.

'I'll do a powerful enough spell this day,' said May, 'to hold you to this world, but it may not be enough, it may not be enough.'

'SHE'S A WITCH,' EILY whispered. 'I heard talk of it before and god, but isn't she an old witch.'

They were standing outside the cottage. May would not come out to see them go; she had stayed sitting in front of the low fire with her back to them as they left the room.

'Don't say that, Eily,' said Hannah.

'She is, though,' said Eily. 'And the old black shawl on her and the look she'd give you, the blood would run cold in you.'

'Behave yourself and she won't give you any look,' said Hannah.

'Oh, she's the wise woman now,' said Eily loftily, to the sky.

Hannah didn't reply. She looked down the mountain, towards the valley. There was a sharp wind rising; the day would be cold and unsettled and the light was poor. She had tied the baby to her chest and fixed the blanket over her head and unbuttoned the top of her cardigan so that the baby's face was against her skin. I have nothing, she thought, but this old blanket and the milk in my breasts to give her.

Eily was watching her; she looked down at the baby, and then up at her face, and then away again, and there was something like sympathy in her face, and even, terribly, sadness.

'You're tired,' she said.

'I'm all right,' said Hannah.

She tightened the dress around her waist, pulling at the knot that held the gun.

'You should mind yourself,' said Eily, shortly, in a way that reminded her of her mother.

'I'm doing my best,' said Hannah, and she began to walk away from the cottage, with Eily behind her.

They moved fast. The morning was fresh and in the beginning she felt strong and able for the journey. She ran as far as she could manage, with her hand behind the baby's head, holding her against her. She had always been able to keep up a slow, steady jog for a long way, but her body was tired now, and too soon she found that she had to slow to a walk, so she and Eily walked side by side, as quickly as they could, and in silence, down the mountain. She remembered the summer night when she had walked up these fields with Denis and she wondered then at Eily's coming through them in the darkness, on her own. She looked across at Eily, walking alongside her with her head down. It is astonishing, she thought, that we have come to this, that we have so much to lose. She felt her heart begin to constrict with fear then. Stop, she said to herself. There is no use to such thoughts. Do not weaken now. She tied her hair up on top of her head – it had come loose on the long run down – and started again onto the path.

They didn't stop until they came to the brackish lake she'd passed with Denis.

'I've to feed her,' she said.

They sat down on the dark sandy shore. She unwrapped the bit of sheet she had tied to her chest and unbuttoned her dress and put the baby to her bare breast. She could feel Eily watching her.

'Does it hurt?' said Eily.

Hannah could feel her face burn red with embarrassment. Eily could see her breast, her nipple. She was exposed, vulnerable.

'It hurt in the beginning,' she said. 'Not now.'

'She's hungry,' said Eily. Then she said, 'Is she?'

She is still unsure of me, thought Hannah. She is careful when she speaks to me. I did that, I was unkind to her for years because it was easy, because it made me feel better.

'She's always hungry,' said Hannah, and she could hear the pride in her own voice. She was proud of her strong baby, and she was desperate, she realized, to talk about her. 'You could feed her all day and she'd look for more.'

'What will you say to him when you see him?' said Eily suddenly.

'I don't know,' she said. 'I'll say, look at your child, I suppose. I'll say, here we are.'

A hope began to rise in her like a small white flame, easily extinguished. Surely when he saw the baby he would understand. Would he not want to give her then what was his — his name, his land? It was unthinkable that he would not.

'Are you sorry it happened?' said Eily.

'I'm not sorry I had her,' said Hannah.

It would have been impossible to regret the baby's existence. It would have been like wishing she herself had not been born. It was not a thing that was open to question. The baby was here, she was part of her, she was meant to be.

'A pity she has him for a father, though,' said Eily, and as she spoke she touched the baby's face with great gentleness. 'They say he's from a farm in Kerry,' she said, after a moment.

'He is,' she said.

'And he's the only son.'

'That's right.'

'Well, that's something, I suppose,' said Eily, with great sarcasm. Hannah laughed.

'It's a long time since I heard you laugh,' said Eily.

'It's a long time since I had anything to laugh about,' she said.

The baby pulled away from her breast.

'Will you hold her?' she said to Eily.

She handed her the baby and began to button up her dress and fix the sheet but she did it deliberately very slowly so that she could watch what Eily did. Her head was bent low over the baby's and she was crooning to her and the baby put her hand out and held on to Eily's loose golden hair and would not let go, and Eily laughed as she held the baby's tiny fist in hers and shook it very gently. Blood is blood, she remembered her father saying. Blood will out.

She looked away from them and out across the lake. She was looking for the swans she had seen with Denis, but they were gone, or hidden from view. It was hard to remember the night she'd come by here; it seemed like a memory from another life, or like a fragment of a dream. In her time at May's she'd realized that she was a person who didn't like to think of the past. The past seemed more unreal to her than even the unknown future; she was interested, indeed, only in the future – in the baby's future, really – and in the present in as much as it was a path to the future. The past, to her, was a thing without use, and it was almost a gift, she suspected, to be able to discard the past so easily, as if she were throwing off an old coat. The swans were gone; whether they had ever been there, or whether she had only imagined them, was of no importance to her now.

IT WAS EARLY EVENING when they arrived at the dark whispering trees on the hill. The light was beginning to fail; Hannah could smell the night coming in. They moved slowly through the trees, not speaking. When they came out of the wood they stood on the crest of the open hill and looked down at the house in the small valley below them. There was something wrong. She knew this, instantly. Eily had said that the men would come after nightfall but she could see that there was a great tumult already there. They stood stock-still for a moment, watching. There was a lorry in the yard, and Hannah could hear shouting, even at this distance. The dying sun was bouncing off the backs of glinting rifles. She tried to understand what they were seeing. The men in the yard were the Black and Tans, she knew that, but she couldn't understand why they were there, or what was happening; her mind wouldn't let her. Where were the Volunteers? Where was O'Riada?

'What's happening?' said Eily.

'Black and Tans,' she said. Her mind was racing away from her.

Eily stood back, pressing herself against a tree.

'Get back, Hannah,' she hissed.

They cannot hear us, thought Hannah, though they might see us if they look up. She moved back, slowly, and stood next to Eily. She put her hand against the baby's soft head.

'We can hide here for the night,' said Eily. 'Or we could try to go and get help. What should we do? Hannah, what will we do?'

'It's too late to go for help,' said Hannah.

They were standing side by side with their arms pressed together. Eily put her hands up to her mouth, and Hannah understood that she was trying to stop herself from shaking, or crying. As a baby she had sucked her thumb for comfort – she remembered that now, and she remembered her fat golden curls and how red her cheeks would become when she was warm, like there was a little fire burning inside her. She had always liked the heat, and when she was afraid, or tired, she became very cold and pale – all of this came back to her, unbidden.

'The baby,' said Eily in a whisper. 'The poor baby,' she said, too loudly now, and she began to cry, and to shake, violently.

She will begin to scream, thought Hannah, or to run. With both of her hands she took hold of Eily's and pulled them down from her mouth. She held her hands in hers and began to rub heat into them.

'Eily,' she said, as calmly as she could, though it was hard for her to speak – I want to scream myself, she thought, I want to run away – 'Are you all right?'

Eily nodded at her, though Hannah could see her teeth chattering. She let go of Eily's hands and began to untie the sheet across her chest. She lifted the baby and handed her to Eily. Eily looked down at the baby, and then up at Hannah, uncomprehendingly. Then she cried out, 'Hannah, no.'

'I have to, Eily,' she said. 'Eoin is down there, and Liam, and Daddy. We can't turn away from them.'

'You're doing this for him, for O'Riada,' said Eily. 'Don't be trying to fool me. What about your baby, Hannah?'

'I'm doing this for her,' said Hannah.

'How is you getting killed good for her?' said Eily, desperately. 'They'll kill you. What will become of her?'

'Eily,' she said. She put her hand against Eily's face. 'We can't leave them down there. What would we think for the rest of our lives? I have to do it. Don't you know that, Eily?'

'I don't know that, at all,' cried Eily. 'No, no.'

'If I don't come back, will you look after her for me?' She had to say it quickly, quickly, so that the words were out of her.

Eily was crying now, and the baby, taking fright, began to cry too.

'Don't, Hannah, please,' she said.

'Will you look after her for me, Eily?' she said. 'If I don't come back. Will you keep her?' She could hardly speak – she would choke, she felt, on the words; they would strangle her.

Eily nodded. She was crying hard now, in great jags.

'Say it,' said Hannah, furiously. 'I have to hear you say it.'

'I'll look after her,' said Eily, looking up at her. 'I'll keep her. You know I will.'

'Take her back to May's,' she said. 'Run there, Eily.'

She put her cheek against Eily's hot cheek and kissed her. Then she put her forehead down to the baby's, and the baby, sensing her, stopped crying, and began to move her head from side to side, smelling the milk, and looking for it. Hannah felt the familiar sharp pang in her breasts and stepped back.

'Jesus, Hannah,' shouted Eily, desperately, but Hannah was gone already, away from her.

*

THE ONLY WAY TO the house was down the open field. If they turned and looked up to the field, she would be spotted, but there was nothing else to do. She could not cut across the field and come to the house by the lane: it would take too long. She could not hide in the trees and wait. She could not go back for help. The only thing to do was to go down the field, fast and low, and so she went.

She made it to the orchard.

She fell onto the blessed ground, face down. She put her face in the earth and opened her mouth to it. Salt in the earth, blood on the moon. She put her hands in the earth and clawed at it. If only she could sink into the earth, she thought, if only she could become a part of it and the trees and the lowering heavy light and belong no more to this world of men, at all. A cry broke out from her, and she kept her face on the sweet, kind earth that called to her so the cry ran into it. No peace, she thought, no peace – that is not what the world holds for me. She pushed herself up onto her knees and then onto her haunches. She wiped the earth from her face and spat onto the ground. Then she unknotted the dress around her waist and took the gun out and loaded it. Her hands were steady, she noted, as if she were noticing something about someone else, entirely. She tied her hair up and checked the laces on her boots. She was beginning to feel calm now, and steady. When the blackbird screamed out its brittle warning she put her head down on one side to listen for the blackbird three fields away call out its answer, and when it did she closed her eyes and in her head she said, I know, to the bird talking to her, to the whole world that thrummed and rattled and held her in it. She lifted her face to the wind. I know.

She got down onto all fours and began to crawl forwards as quietly and as quickly as she could manage it. She didn't dare to lift even her head, and that was the worst part of it – keeping her head down when she was desperate to look up, but amongst the low trees of the orchard it was too dark to see much, anyway. It was wet amongst the trees and the ground was rough with roots and stones and holes but she pushed with her feet against the earth as she crawled and she pulled herself along on her elbows, and in this way she was able to move fast. She kept one fist clenched tight and in the other one she kept the gun pointing straight up at the sky. She could hear shouting, and she could hear screaming now, too, but she could see nothing, yet.

She came through the orchard to the low wall that bounded the yard. She sat with her back to the wall and lifted her face up to the sky. The evening sun was almost warm on her face; she was conscious of that, and of the pleasure of it, but her mind was empty, clean. She was beyond thought, almost. She breathed in, and out, and took hold of the gun with both hands. She would turn now and climb the wall.

'Hannah.'

It was a low whisper. She looked down the length of the wall and saw that Denis was coming towards her, on all fours. He put his finger to his lips and sat next to her, so that they both had their backs to the wall, facing the orchard. In his hand he had a gun. He pointed to her gun and shook his head, no.

'Give me the gun,' he said, very quietly, but his voice was shaking, and his hands too.

She moved back from him.

Why was Denis here? Why was he not with O'Riada? She saw

then that there was something wrong in his eyes, and that there was fear in his tight, contorted face.

'They came too early,' he said, and now the tears ran freely down his face, and he was hardly able to speak. 'Too early. They were supposed to come after dark, and to take O'Riada only.'

He began to move towards her.

'Hannah,' he said, desperately.

No, she thought. No no no. This cannot be.

'After what he did to you . . .' He stopped. 'I could not let it stand. Please, Hannah,' he said. 'Do you see?'

'What have you done?' she said. 'What have you done to us?'

Then she stood up and climbed over the wall.

THERE WAS A SINGLE lorry in the yard. She counted eight soldiers – no more than eight, she was nearly sure, and one of them an officer. They were running to the house and around the yard and it was difficult to tell for sure with all the movement, but eight, she thought. Some soldiers – she wasn't sure how many – went into the house; three of them stayed in the yard, dancing about, almost, with the excitement, and shouting instructions at each other. After a moment two of the soldiers came out of the house dragging her father between them. He was in his white nightgown still, and they were pulling him along on his knees. His legs stuck out beside him like white sticks and as the soldiers pulled at him the nightgown rode up above his hips and he was naked, his body a bright milk-white stick thing, and the soldiers laughed terribly at his humiliation. Her father's head was hanging down very low, almost to the ground, and he didn't react to his nakedness; he didn't look alive. Behind him came two more soldiers holding Eoin by the elbows. They were almost lifting him off the ground and they were laughing too and Eoin was writhing and kicking out with his legs and crying out, 'Dadda, oh Dadda.' Then came Tiernan, and O'Riada. They were walking with their hands behind their heads and they were followed by a single soldier who had a rifle touching the back of O'Riada's neck. She counted again: two and two and one, and there was the officer directing it all, and the two others with guns on the house and the yard. Eight.

Then her mother and Ciaran and Liam and Mary came running out of the house with another soldier behind them – nine – and her mother was screaming, and with the shouts and the cries and the noise of the lorry it was hard for her to think.

She had to think.

She closed her eyes and put her hand over them. Then she opened her eyes and put the gun behind her back and began to walk across the yard. The soldiers were pulling her father and Eoin towards the wall and she saw that her father was alive; he had been hit in the head and there was blood running from it, but he was alive. The noise was getting worse now, the screaming, the shouting, and she would never forget it, she knew, the noise, and the way she felt as she made her way towards them. Everything began to slow for her and become very clear and sharp and something in her head said, Now, and then she began to run.

One of the Tans saw her and shouted out in confusion and they all turned towards her. She began to run faster and she saw the childlike surprise on all their faces as she pulled the gun out from behind her. She fired as she ran. She shot one soldier in the face, and the second one in the side of the head, as she swung left. Out of the corner of her eye she saw a soldier lift his gun and point it at her. She heard a shot, and then another shot, in response. He has shot me, she thought, and then immediately thought, I feel nothing, why do I feel nothing? and then a great roar of horror rose up from behind her, and she knew: he has shot someone else, someone has been hit, and where did the other shot come from? Through all this she kept running. In front of her the officer was standing completely still and staring at her with his mouth open a little so she went straight up to him and put the gun to his forehead and pushed at him. He was holding his gun by his side, pointing it at the ground. Why did he not shoot at her?

He had a red face and a mark on his cheek from where he'd cut himself shaving. She had seen such marks on her father's face in the morning, she thought, almost absently. Imagine seeing such a thing, she would think long after, with the smoke from the guns and the blood and with all the noise, imagine seeing that, and remembering it, too.

'Drop that gun and get back against the wall,' she said.

When he didn't move she pushed her gun further into his forehead. He looked at her and she looked back at him, very calmly, and he dropped his gun – she heard it fall on the ground, softly – and began to move backwards.

'You should have shot me when you had the chance,' she said to him, not turning around. 'Why didn't you shoot me?'

He looked at her and shook his head and smiled, sadly.

'I could not shoot a woman,' he said.

Out of the side of her eye she was aware of things happening: O'Riada and Tiernan were taking the soldiers' guns and kicking the legs out from under them so that they fell to the ground. O'Riada was shouting, 'Get away, get away,' and Eoin was pulling her father back across the yard towards the house and her mother was screaming and Liam too and who had been shot? Who had been shot? With her gun still pushing into the officer's forehead she half turned to look: she had to see. Mary was on the ground with her arms and legs sticking out from her at odd angles. Her eyes were open and there was black-looking blood running from her ear.

Mary.

Near her lay a soldier, and standing over him was Denis. Denis had followed her, of course, over the wall, across the yard, and he had shot the soldier who had shot Mary.

She turned back to the officer.

'You should have shot me when you had the chance,' she repeated, very quietly. Too late now, too late.

She pushed at him with the gun again and he stumbled backwards and kept moving backwards until he was against the wall.

The soldiers were lining up next to him now. She began to back away from them, with her gun held high. Only when she was standing next to O'Riada did she let her arm drop by her side. The soldiers stood with their backs to the wall and looked at the men on the ground, and at her, and at O'Riada and Denis who stood on either side of her with something like dumb surprise, she thought, as if they could not quite believe what was happening. Then the officer took a step forwards. He stood up very straight, with his chin up.

His hat was crooked on his head and he took it off and put it under his arm. He had golden hair that fell forward onto his forehead in a wave and he pushed it back impatiently, and then smoothed it down behind his ear with a flat hand.

'Take the family in the house,' O'Riada said to Tiernan. 'Stay in there with them.'

He still hadn't looked at her. He was staring straight ahead.

'What are you going to do, chaps?' the officer said, cheerfully, looking only at O'Riada.

'You know what we have to do,' O'Riada said. 'Our duty. Do you have messages you want sent?'

She felt, suddenly, very far away from everything, as if she were floating up in the sky and they were all a million miles away from her, little black doll figures playing at a game. She couldn't see out of one eye, she realized, and put her hand up to it, and she staggered a little to one side then.

'Go way into the house,' said O'Riada to her. He was next to her; she could smell his shockingly familiar smell. 'Don't have it on you.'

'I have it on me already,' she said.

She had killed two men. She had their blood on her face where it had sprayed out towards her in a fine mist.

'Get in the house, woman,' roared O'Riada.

She took a step back, and then another, and then she stumbled and almost dropped her gun and then she was half running, half falling into the house and closing the door behind her. She put her back to the door and tried to steady her breathing because it was coming out of her too fast; her mouth was hanging open and her heart was hitting against her chest like a trapped bird banging against a glass window. Her parents and her brothers and Tiernan were standing in the middle of the kitchen, facing the door. They looked at her when she came into the room, holding the gun, and they were looking at her still, like they were looking for an answer, when the shots rang out around the yard.

XXIII

THEY HAD BEEN TO a party the year before, Simon and she, and the hostess had had a Polaroid camera and amused herself by going about taking pictures of her guests when they did not suspect it. She'd pinned the photos she had taken to the front door, so the guests would see them as they left. Ellen had made Simon wait as she looked for theirs – she had wanted to see how fat she looked in her new dress. She had found the photo and she'd pulled it from the door and studied it as they waited outside the house for a taxi. In the picture Ellen was talking to someone out of shot, and Simon was looking at her and on his face was an expression of such dislike, such disgust, almost, that she had cried out in fright, almost.

In that moment, she had known that his love for her was gone. She had torn up the picture and put the pieces in her pocket, and had never spoken of it, or thought of it again, even. She had continued, blindly, as if everything was all right, as if nothing, at all, had changed.

*

EVERY LOVE STORY IS a great love story in the beginning, and then the middle comes, and then, an end.

ELLEN PARKED THE CAR by a low wall overlooking the beach. It was a small beach, horseshoe-shaped. It finished, on both sides, in black rocks; beyond the rocks were the cliffs and more rocks and more small empty beaches that ran on into the headland and the headland gave onto the sea and the sky, and after that was America. She thought of Hannah getting on a boat to go across this sea to America. She wondered if she had stood on the deck watching Ireland fade away. If it had been her, she would have turned her back to it and faced America: she wouldn't have wanted to look back and think of all that she was leaving behind. But Hannah would have faced the shore, she thought, and maybe Eily would have stood there holding her baby up so Hannah could see her as they pulled away from the land for the last time. She imagined Eily bending down to kiss the sweet-smelling soft head and smiling into the radiant face and the baby laughing back up at her and Hannah watching all this as she moved away into the darkness.

It was nearly night, and the sea was coming in fast, a great high wall of it sucking at the sand like a hungry yawl. She opened the car door. The air was heavy and wet with spray from the sea and it was raining – a vicious, horizontal rain that came at her like an old enemy. The noise the sea was making was tremendous, an awful frightening banging sound, like it was knocking something down.

She closed the door and the sea roared sadly at her. She took off her boots and socks and rolled up her jeans as far as they would go.

She put her socks in her boots and put them on the floor of the car, with her handbag. She got out of the car – she had no coat and she was wet to the bone, almost instantly. She walked across to the steps that led to the beach and started down them. They were too narrow and in the rain it was nearly impossible not to fall down them. She held on to the mean metal handrail and slid down them like some kind of cartoon character, talking to herself, out loud, as she went. 'This is ridiculous. For god's sake. Stupid steps.' She was a person now, apparently, who spoke out loud to herself. That was new.

She made it down to the beach. Without pausing, she went towards the sea and then walked into it. The roar it gave, this close up, filled her head. She was only in up to her ankles and already she felt unsteady – it was pulling at her, urgently, and it was hard to stay standing up with the rain blinding her and the wind pushing at her like a bully and the noise from the waves all around her and the wind confusing her. The sea was drawing out at a gallop. If she stepped a little further in, she would be pulled under and then out and the sea would have her then. It would be very fast, she saw.

She took a step back. If she didn't take a step back, she would fall forwards into it, like someone falling off a cliff. It was calling her in, it was calling to her like it had a secret to tell her. She had to make herself take another step back. She stumbled, and nearly fell, and that woke her up a bit, and then she turned away and began to walk towards the beach and away from the sea, it calling all the while after her, forlornly.

Simon was coming down the steps.

'Marvellous weather.'

He had to shout to make himself heard. He was holding himself against the wind, with one shoulder to it, angled right. He came to stand next to her and she took out a cigarette and a lighter. He made a cup with his hands so she could light the cigarette in the wind. She took one drag and then held it out to him, almost as a challenge. They used to smoke together, years ago, before they had tried to have children, before Simon had started doing triathlons fuelled by kale and protein shakes. All those years of running: he'd been running away from her, of course. She saw that now. He gave her a hard stare and then took the cigarette and began to smoke it, slowly, all the time looking at her quite coolly.

'They used to bring ships onto these rocks,' she shouted. 'When there was a storm and a ship was looking for harbour they'd tie lights to a few old donkeys and walk them up and down the strand and the ship would follow the lights in and it'd finish up on the rocks. The people would have the cargo then from the ship. They say the sea would run red with the blood of the crew.'

What she did not say was it was my people who did that. They were a hard people, she thought, made hard by this world.

He looked out at the sea, smoking, saying nothing.

'I'm sorry,' she said.

'For what?' he said, without looking at her.

'For everything. I haven't been the same since the baby and I take it all out on you. There's something wrong with me, I think, Simon.'

He put a hand up to stop her.

'Ellen,' he said.

She looked at him and took in his perfect profile, his golden hair, hardly ruffled by the rain and the wind, the set line of his mouth.

'You're not exactly perfect yourself,' she shouted, suddenly angry.

He knows nothing of the night in the hotel with John, she thought. He has no right to be so angry with me.

He threw the cigarette down.

'It's too windy,' he shouted. 'Come back to the car.'

They went back to the car and got in and turned on the heating. Simon took off his jacket; underneath he wore a paper-thin T-shirt that was perfectly dry. He pushed his hair back with one hand; his skin was glistening golden with the rain. Her hair was stuck to her head and she had mascara all down her face, she knew. She wished she could take off her soaking, steaming jumper, but that would mean sitting in her bra. Neither of them said anything for a while.

'Simon,' she said. 'I mean it. I'm sorry.'

He said nothing, and the fear started to spread through her like dark ink.

'Do you still love me?' she said.

It was a mistake to ask this now, so early in the argument, but she couldn't stop herself. Usually when they had an argument or he was distant with her she would push him and push him until he capitulated and said what she wanted to hear and what she always wanted to hear, what he always said in the end, even impatiently, or bitterly, was, 'Of course I love you.'

But this time he said, 'I don't know,' and then stopped, as if he had shocked even himself.

'Simon,' she said.

He sighed. 'I suppose I do love you, in a way. But you're not the person I married. I know I'm not supposed to mention it but you've put on all this weight and you do nothing to try to lose it, and it's not the same for me, now. You're angry all the time, and stressed. I don't enjoy your company anymore, and that's the truth of it. The fun has gone out of it.'

They both said nothing for a moment, lost in the wash of his words.

'Is it because of the weight?' she said. 'The weight is because of the hormones.' She looked away from him, down at her hands. 'I can try to lose the weight,' she said quietly. It was so unlike her to be so compliant, to suggest such a thing, that she thought it might throw him momentarily off guard.

'You can't blame the hormones anymore, Ellen,' he said. 'It's the crisps and the wine and the no exercise.'

'Right,' she said. It felt as if a hand had moved in her stomach, turning things over.

'It's more than that,' he said. 'I think things have gone so far between us that we can't go back.'

Her heart was beating so fast that she had to put her hand up to her chest to try to steady it.

'So what do you want to do?' she said.

She couldn't look at him; she looked instead at the lonely wild sea before her.

'What do you want to do?' he said. 'You can't say you're happy with me. What do you want to do, for once? Why does it always have to be on me? Don't you want to change things, or do you want to go on like this?'

He began to rustle with something and then he pulled a sheaf of folded-over papers out of his pocket and handed it to her. She began to go through the pages, but she was immediately blind with panic:

all she could see were their names in bold print, everywhere. These are divorce papers, she thought, he's divorcing me.

'It's the contract for the house, Ellen,' he said. 'I went to the agent's after you phoned me today and I closed the deal. Maybe this is what we need; it will give you a new interest, and we'll be able to spend some time apart and think about things. You'll be closer to your family, and that's a good thing. It's all done. I told them to cancel your deposit, and it's all in my name, but it will be your house, of course, yours.'

Oh no, she thought, no no no.

'What will you do?' she said.

'I'll go back to London tomorrow,' he said.

'Is it because of the baby?'

She could not go on without Simon. I love him, I love him and now I've lost him, she thought and panic began to rise up in her. All this time I've been living in the past and thinking I should have done things differently and I've been cruel to Simon, I've ignored him and belittled him and made him fall out of love with me. But without Simon I don't know who to be, or how to be. I am only something with him.

When he did not answer she said, 'We could try again, Simon. The doctor said that's all we can do. We could make another baby.' She took hold of his arm, too tightly, she knew. 'We could get her back.'

'She's not coming back,' he said. 'We've been over and over all this and she's never coming back, Ellen. She's gone. And I'm tired of thinking about the whole thing. We've tried and tried and maybe, now, we need to admit that it's not going to happen for us. Don't you want to move on with your life? Aren't you tired of the misery of it all?'

We have seen our child live and die, she thought, and that has broken us. He associates me now only with loss, and failure, and sadness, with death, even.

'Will you stay in the hotel or at your mother's?' he said. He was determined, she saw, to push on with this. He knows I cannot stay at my mother's, she thought, but he does not want to pause to consider that.

'You'll need to be here for the survey, and I think you should start looking for builders, and getting quotes.'

'OK,' she said.

'Right,' he said, sounding relieved. 'Good.' He had a plan now, he was making things happen. 'And property is property, never a bad investment, even here.'

She took out another cigarette. He said nothing: he didn't seem to mind her smoking anymore.

'I was thinking I might go to America,' she said.

This was her last chance.

'You always liked America,' he said, very calmly.

That's that then, she thought.

They both sat in silence for a while, looking out the window at the rain coming down and all the world bulbous and distorted beyond the car windows.

'What do you think happened to Hannah O'Donovan?'

It was the last time she would ask him the question.

'I think she went to America, and made a new life for herself. She was brave enough, Ellen, to leave things behind, and she was all right in the end, I think.'

'I always thought of her as this great heroine,' said Ellen, 'who did things that I could never have done. But she left her baby. I wouldn't have done that. I'd have fought it out, I think. I'd have made a different choice.'

I would have stayed with my baby, she thought. But I never had the chance. I never had the chance.

She looked at Simon and he looked back at her and she was amazed to see that his eyes had filled with tears.

'You would, Ellen,' he said. 'You would have done the harder thing. You were always brave. You were always the bravest person I knew.'

He had loved her once, as best he could, and she had loved him – she loved him still, she knew – but the love had been under the weight of the bad things that had happened to them for so long now that it had just drifted away from them like a sad little ghost and now here they were in this rented car, in the rain, trying to find a way out.

'I'm sorry,' she said, and she meant it this time: she was sorry for Simon, she was sorry for herself, she was sorry for the whole mess.

He let the words hang in the air between them for a moment, and when he spoke again it was with a studied cheer; the tears were gone now.

He was going to drive back to the hotel, he said – he had come to the beach in her mother's car – and pack, and maybe they could meet later in the bar for a drink, but she said no, it had been a long day now, and she just wanted to sleep when she got back. He should go to the bar on his own, and maybe not wake her when he got in. They could have breakfast together, tomorrow, before he left. So he got out of her car, and she waved him goodbye, but she didn't watch him drive away; she looked out the window instead, at the sea.

Beyond the sea was America. She put her head down on the steering wheel. America.

'Should we go to America, baby?' she said out loud, to the listening silence. 'Where should we go? What will we do?'

She had no one to talk to; she had been lonely forever, she thought. All the things that had happened to her, all the lives she had lived – there was no one person who had shared it all with her. Her life was a series of boxes, all neatly packed, stacked, and each time she changed her life she left behind the people who had occupied that section. She could not bring the past into the present with anyone, because there was no one who had been with her through everything. What was gone for her was gone, as if it had never happened. If you cannot remember something with someone, with anyone, she thought, it is as if it never happened. My reality is a fiction of my own making. I am without a history, almost, beyond history, and I was wrong to think that history could save me.

She began to bang her head very gently on the steering wheel. Then she lifted her chin up and shouted, 'Argghh,' and began to hit the steering wheel hard with the heels of her hands, again and again and again. She fell back in her seat, her chest rising and falling, her breath tight in her throat. Her hands were stinging with pain. She lit another cigarette, and picked up her phone, and dialled a number.

She took a very deep inhalation, filling her lungs with smoke, and then she exhaled, slowly, through her nostrils.

'Hello?'

'It's Ellen,' she said.

'Oh my god, Ellen, how are you?' said her sister.

It was such a shock to hear her, to hear the joy in her voice, that Ellen began to cry.

'Oh, you know,' said Ellen. 'Not great.'

'Where are you?' said Fiona.

'I'm in Lisarna,' she said. 'Near the old farm. I've bought it back, and the land too. Didn't Mammy tell you I was back?'

'No,' said Fiona. 'She'd tell you nothing. You know that. How long are you here for? When are you going back?'

'I don't think I'm going back,' said Ellen, 'for the time being.'

It is easier to leave, to disappear, she thought, sadly. The harder thing is to stay and face yourself.

'Come home, Ellen,' said Fiona. 'Come back here. I want to see you.'

She stopped. It was difficult for them to speak openly, properly to each other because they had grown up in a house where love was not shown, but hidden, denied.

'Come home,' Fiona said again. 'Come back. I've been waiting for you to come back.'

'All right,' said Ellen. 'I will.'

XXIV

DENIS AND O'RIADA CAME into the dark kitchen.

'We need the donkey and cart,' Denis said to Eoin. He sounded very tired, thought Hannah, he sounded like an old man who had seen and heard too much.

When Eoin didn't move O'Riada shouted at him, 'Move, will you, boy,' and Eoin jumped then and ran out of the kitchen and into the yard.

'And you,' O'Riada said to Tiernan, 'for Jesus's sake, wake yourself and go out and give him a hand.' He turned to Hannah. 'Give me that gun,' he said, not looking at her. 'It needs reloading.'

'Where's Mary?' said her mother, dully.

'Mary's gone,' said O'Riada.

Denis sat down heavily at the table. He lit a cigarette and began to smoke, his head hanging down against his chest. The cigarette paper and then the tobacco crackled and sparked against the silence in the room.

'He was aiming at Hannah,' said her mother in the same flat voice then. 'I thought to myself, Oh my god, that soldier is going to shoot Hannah, and then he saw Denis with the gun on him and he swerved to shoot Denis and he shot Mary instead.' She put her face in her hands. 'God almighty,' she said, with a cry. 'Mary.'

'She was a soldier for Ireland,' said O'Riada. 'God bless her soul.'

He had lit the oil lamp in the window and now he was sitting at the head of the table taking Hannah's gun apart and cleaning it with a bit of rag and reloading it as he spoke. His hands were very steady, and his voice was level. He might be going out to shoot rabbits for the dinner, she thought, watching him. He's used to this. It costs him nothing at all.

'Why did this happen?' said her father.

'We were given the wrong information,' said O'Riada, without looking up from the gun. 'But we'll sort it all out tonight. There'll be no one else touching this place from now on. We have them on the run. Stay in the house until we tell you otherwise and let us take care of business and not a worry on any of you.'

He does not suspect Denis, she thought. He thinks it an external betrayal.

Many years she and Denis had known each other, and all seasons they had passed together in the fields, in the woods, and always there had been an understanding between them. Denis looked up at her, expecting her to speak, and she looked back at him steadily until she saw the wonder and the joy spread across his face as he began to understand what she had just begun to understand herself – that she would not speak of what she knew. I understand why he did what he did, she thought. I would have done the same, maybe – maybe I would have done even more.

She stepped forwards into the light of the oil lamp. Still O'Riada had not looked at her. Why did he pretend she was not there?

'I'm leaving tonight,' she said. 'So I'm not staying in the house.'

His face burned dark red. She saw him draw breath, and then he met her eye and she saw, immediately, that there was no hope. He did not want her: that was clear. I will think about that later, she said to herself. I will not think about that now. I must act now, I must do something.

'I'm going back to May's.'

He came towards her and put his hand on her arm and leaned towards her in the way that she remembered so that his face was next to hers. He spoke quietly in her ear.

'We have to have a discussion,' he said.

'There's no discussion to be had,' she said, pulling away from his hand. 'I've everything planned. If you mean the baby, you'd plenty of time all along for discussing but you weren't in too much of a rush, you took your time.'

'I knew nothing for sure,' he said to her, 'only what Denis Mulcahy told me.'

'Many months ago he told you,' she said. 'I've been waiting on that mountain . . .'

She wanted to say more, but she found she couldn't – the words were stuck in her throat. She was too conscious of everyone in the kitchen watching them, and listening, to be able to speak freely. The humiliation of having to talk to O'Riada like this was nearly too much to bear. All this time she had fostered the idea that he had been kept from her by some force beyond his control, but she understood now that he had not come to her because he had not wanted to, because it did not suit him. What Denis had told her on the mountain had been right, after all. He was not interested in her, or in the baby.

He looked at her coldly. Such coldness he has in him, she thought, and only now I see it. Too late, too late.

'We've been fighting for the likes of you and yours, while you waited,' he said, 'in your warm cottage.'

'And you the hard man,' she said, trying to keep her voice even. 'Saving us all.'

She took a step back from him. 'You broke a promise you made to me, and you brought a crowd of Tans down on us here not once, but twice. So good luck to you now. Go away from here.'

He grabbed her arm so hard that she had to stop herself from shouting out in pain.

'What is it you want?' he said. He was about to say more, but he stopped himself; he let go of her arm by almost pushing her away from him. She watched his face change. 'How do I even know what you say to be true?'

Did he deny the existence of the baby? She would bring him the baby to make him see – that was simple, easily done. Surely when he saw her he would understand.

Then her mother gave a gasp and called out, 'No.'

The breath stopped in her. He was suggesting that another could be the father.

He turned to the kitchen.

'Mrs O'Donovan,' said O'Riada. He stood up very straight. He is composing himself, thought Hannah, controlling himself. 'She can't go back up the mountain to that woman. She has to stay here, surely, with the family, until an arrangement can be made for her. We have to call the priest, Mrs O'Donovan.'

'I told you that I will not stay here,' said Hannah.

He stood up and spun around to her and she saw that he was pale with fright, perhaps, and with anger, certainly. He doesn't like to be defied, she thought. He does not accept it.

'It's no use asking my mother or my father to tell me what to do. I'm going back to May.'

'And the baby?' said her mother. 'You will keep the baby on the mountain, with no father, and you with no husband?'

Her face had reddened, as if she were ashamed to even speak of such a thing. She stood up from the table as if to step away from her embarrassment.

'You will stay here and marry, Hannah,' she said. 'And that's all there is to it, now. All there is to it.'

'Who will I marry, Mammy?' Hannah cried. 'There has been no mention of marriage, that I see.'

She flung her arm towards O'Riada and he turned away from her, as if she had struck him. He cannot even meet my eye, she thought; he will not.

'I wouldn't marry for the sake of it. I won't, Mammy,' she said.

I want to get out of this dark room, she thought, and go back through the fields and up the blue mountain and back to my baby. She will be looking for me. She will be hungry now. At the thought of the baby she felt a sharp stab in her breasts. The milk is coming in, she thought, in a panic. It will soak through this thin dress, I will have to stand here before them all wet through. I must go to the baby. She began to move towards the door. I must get away from here. I must be free of this room and all the people in it.

'You both might not think it ideal, but many a marriage started with trouble,' said her mother. 'You'll not go back up the mountain,

Hannah,' she said, and she sounded angry now, 'and do what there, what will become of you?'

Her mother had understood, Hannah saw, that she meant to make for the door, and she too had begun to move towards it, to cut off her escape.

'We can talk to Father Michael tonight,' she said, 'and he might help us, we might be able to hide what has happened here today and we could start again then, we could put all, all of what has happened behind us, all behind us, and start again.'

Hannah was at the door now and her mother grabbed at her, her sharp fingers scrabbling at her.

'We could find a solution for the child, even,' she said, softly, almost slyly. 'There are places for children who have difficult starts and for the mothers, too. Father Michael will know of such places.'

'No.'

Her father's hair was dark and hard with blood, and there was blood on his blind eye, on his face, on his hands, on his white shift. He was standing, holding on to a chair for support, and his whole body was shaking terribly.

'No, Noreen,' he said.

There was a terrible, waiting silence.

'She has killed men,' said her father.

'To save you,' shouted Denis. 'All of you are saved because of her.'

'Denis Mulcahy,' said her mother, and she put her hand over her own mouth as if she would stop such words coming out of Denis's mouth.

'She cannot stay here,' said her father, so quietly that they all had to almost hold their breaths to hear him. 'They will come for her, and even if they do not, it would always be on her. She will have no chance here.'

He looked down at his white hands gripping the back of the chair.

'She has to go to America.'

'America?' said her mother, appalled. 'You don't know what you're saying. What will become of her in America? And the child? If she stays here and marries, she could settle down, Seanie, couldn't she? Haven't many done it? Haven't they, Seanie?'

'I have a cousin in America,' said her father, 'who could help her to get a position. We will find the fare for the journey. She can start again in America.'

'With a baby?' cried her mother. 'Are you after forgetting about the baby?'

'She can leave the baby here until she is settled. We will look after her. She will stay with us. Hannah will send for her when she is settled.'

'I will not leave her,' said Hannah. Her voice was shamefully, hatefully, shaking.

'There is no life for you here, Hannah,' said her father, still not looking at her. 'You know this. And there is no life for the child there. You cannot take her now. We will look after her until you send for her.'

And the thought came to her then, and as soon as she thought it she felt herself collapse almost with the sadness and because she knew that this is what would happen: I could leave the baby with Eily. Eily would have her.

'If I went to America,' she said, almost distractedly, 'Eily would have her.'

'Hannah,' said her mother. 'Eily is eighteen years old. What would she do with a child?'

'Eily made me a promise that she will not break. She promised that if anything happened to me she would look after the baby.'

'Eily has no husband!' screamed her mother. 'Will you ruin her life as you have ruined your own? Where are we to say this child came from? This child from outside a marriage?'

'Eily and I would have the child. Eily and I would marry,' said Denis. He looked at Hannah until she looked back at him, and when she did she saw that his face was twisted and almost black with emotion. 'So Hannah could go to America.'

'Well, this beats all,' cried her mother. 'You? Who do you think you are, to marry Eily O'Donovan? You, the workman? Is it gone soft in the head you are? Are all of you gone soft in the head?'

'Sit down, Noreen,' said her father. 'And shut up.'

Her mother stumbled to a chair, and sat, her face white and pinched with the shock.

'Seanie.'

O'Riada had his back to Hannah now, and spoke to her father, only. 'We've to think what people will say when they hear about this, and hear they will. I can't have this hanging over me. I can't have the child left on this farm and all knowing its story.'

'Step back,' said her father.

He drew himself up and raised his face so that he was looking down at O'Riada as he spoke. He is from an ancient people, Hannah thought, as if in a dream, and there is in him the blood of the Gaelic chiefs – that was what he had told her when she was a child. We were the kings of this place, he used to say, before it was taken from us, before they took the land from us and all that the land meant.

O'Riada stood very still. He is holding my gun in his hand, against his leg, Hannah saw – why is he holding the gun like that? She looked at Denis and saw that he, too, was looking at the gun.

'We will look after our own,' said her father. 'You leave this house today and we won't speak your name again, you need not fear that. We'll make no claim on you.'

'How can I know for sure?' said O'Riada quietly.

'You know because I say so,' said her father. 'You leave here today and after you'll have no right to the child or what belongs to the child. You'll be a stranger to us. You'll never come to this place again.'

O'Riada didn't answer. He was breathing heavily, his shoulders rising up and down and his head hanging slightly forwards, as if he had been hit a body blow and was stunned from it. Then he lifted his head up and at the same time lifted the gun so that it was lying flat across his chest.

'Give me my gun,' said Hannah.

O'Riada spun around to her.

'That's my gun,' she said. 'Give it back to me.'

He put his head back, considering her, and then he smiled at her in the same slow way he had smiled at her in the orchard that night when she had surprised him by putting her hand across his mouth to stop him speaking. He is the most beautiful man I will ever see, she thought, and then, I am mad, I am mad to think such a thing now, and to feel the desire tighten in me again like a knot, and I am glad that he has broken with me, for if he had chosen to stay with me he would have destroyed me, and I would have let him, willingly. I would never have been free of him. At least, now, I am free.

O'Riada held her gaze for a moment, watching her, and then he nodded at her, all right, Hannah. All right.

He held the gun out to her, flat on the palm of his outstretched hand. They looked at each other. There is something in him that I know, she thought. That first time I saw him in the kitchen, I recognized him, almost. In some fundamental, terrible way, we are alike.

She took the warm gun from him with both hands. Step away from him, Hannah, she said to herself, don't stay standing where you can hear him breathing, where you can smell him.

She moved back to stand next to her father.

'What do you say?' said her father to O'Riada.

'I'll go,' O'Riada said. He was still looking at her. To break the hold of the look, she looked down at the ground. He will not look at me again like that, she thought. I won't let him. 'I won't be back, if that's what you all want. You have my word.'

'All here are witnesses,' said her father, and he raised his arm and pointed at him. 'All here, O'Riada. Go on now away from this place.'

She looked up at her father. He was crying now – the tears were running down his ruined face, silently. He let go of the chair, and lifted his head to look at her and when he found that she was looking back at him he smiled at her his old crooked shy smile, the smile that she had loved more than everything, always, and then he turned away from her and walked up the stairs, alone.

EPILOGUE

1920

'WE WERE MARRIED LAST week,' said Eily. 'By Father Michael. So we can have her now and no one can do anything. Do you see, Hannah?'

Hannah did not answer her. She had not spoken since Eily and Denis had come into May's cottage. Instead, she sat silently, considering Eily, who had put her hair up so that she looked older, and was wearing her best dress, and a new cardigan. She dresses so carefully, as if she is going to High Mass, thought Hannah, now that she is a married woman. It was hard to watch Eily and understand what she was saying to her at the same time. It had been three months since the shootings, and all of that time she had spent on the mountain with May and the baby. I am unused to people, she thought. I am become strange.

'The same Father Michael on his way up the mountain?' said May.

'The same one,' said Denis. 'One is enough.'

'How long does she have?' said May.

'She'd want to be on her way tonight,' said Denis, 'so that she's well clear of here by morning. Eily will leave with the baby now and I'll take Hannah by the back roads to Skibbereen, and from there we'll get to Cork. There's a ship leaving for Boston on Friday. She'll have to be on that ship. The priest knows about the baby, and about the shootings, about what she did, so we've to move now.'

Denis took off his cap and put his hand on the back of his head, as if he were trying to hold it up. His forehead was bevelled with a line from the pressure of the cap; his face was red.

'Who told him?' said May.

'Who knows,' said Denis, sadly. 'But he found out after we were married, and married by him more's the better. The child has never been seen – we will say the child is ours. He will rail, but he can do nothing, now, about the child, if we say she is ours. But Hannah has to get away from here.'

If she stayed, Eily had said, if she were found here on the mountain with the baby, Father Michael would take the baby away and put her in a place where she would never be seen again and then he would put her herself, Hannah, in another place that they had only ever heard speak of. She had said this to her very slowly, and in language that Hannah understood to be deliberately simple. You have no choice, Hannah, Eily had said to her. You have to leave for America tonight.

'Hannah,' said Eily, again. 'You have to go.'

Hannah was sitting in the chair by the fire, feeding the baby. Without giving any sign that she had heard what Eily had said she turned the baby around and moved her from one breast to the other, swiftly, with ease, arranging her dress so that she was covered.

They are mad to think I can go tonight, she thought. Who would feed the baby if I went? The baby needs me; she doesn't know Eily, and cannot be left with a stranger. She will not feed properly with a stranger. She will not settle to sleep. I have understood all along, of course, that I will have to go, but we need time before I can think of going – preparations will have to be made, plans will have to be drawn up.

She felt a wave of terrible panic rise up in her then. I am going to scream, she thought, and I will choke on the scream and I cannot breathe, and to stop herself making a noise she leaned down so that her cheek was touching the baby's head; her heavy hair fell over the baby's face so that they were both hidden behind it in a dark, private world.

I cannot leave her. If I leave her, she will forget me; when she opens her eyes and sees Eily she'll think, there's my mother.

I cannot. They are mad to even imagine such a thing.

Eily was kneeling down in front of her now and pushing her hair back from her face and putting the soft palm of her hand to her cheek. I am crying, Hannah realized, and then she lifted her face and looked at Eily and shook her head, no, no, and the tears were coming from her nose, from out of her mouth, and she gave a great cry, 'No.'

Eily took her by the shoulders.

'You cannot let them take you,' Eily said. 'And you cannot let them take the baby. What will become of her, Hannah, if you let them take her? You have to do this for her. Do you understand what I'm saying to you?'

'I understand,' said Hannah, very quietly. 'Now let go of me.'

She stood up. The baby, disturbed, cried out, and Hannah settled her to her breast again.

No one spoke.

'She'll take goat's milk,' Hannah said then.

She looked down at the baby's perfect face.

'Her name is Rose,' she said. She was unused to saying it out loud; it was, for her, a private, almost blessed word that beat in her blood like a drum.

Rose, Rose.

May was by her side now, with her hand on her elbow.

'If you don't want to do it, Hannah, if you think you can't go, you can say no now and we can hide, we can leave here and hide on the mountain. I know places where we won't be found, and time will pass and we'll be happy as the day is long, the three of us, free under the sky.'

She looked at May, at her dark, beseeching eyes.

'No, May,' she said.

She stepped away from her, and towards Eily.

'We are taking the farm over from my father,' said Eily. 'Me and Denis.'

Eily blushed red as she spoke: she is shy yet, thought Hannah, to speak of her and Denis, but she forces herself to do it. She is determined that we all acknowledge what is the truth: she and Denis are one, now. She is laying claim to what is hers. She is proud, thought Hannah, and she is strong. That's good. Rose will need that.

'She'll grow up on the land, Hannah,' said Denis. 'The land will be hers.'

She would not hide the baby in a ditch on the mountain. And she could not take her to America now. She would not have her be a servant's child in America. She would have her be free as she herself had never been free. Her child would have ownership of the land, and the farm, Denis and Eily would see to that: she would start life as a person of significance, and her life would be her own. She would have the land behind her, and America before her, and she would be free.

She herself would go to America, go into the dark unknown, and when she could, when everything was ready, she would send for her, and they would be together again then, always.

'I'll be back for her, Eily,' she said.

'You will, Hannah,' said Eily, very quietly, as if she didn't trust herself to speak more loudly.

'And until I come back will you tell her about me? As soon as she's big enough to understand? So she knows me when I come for her. So I'm not a stranger to her when I come.'

'I will,' said Eily. 'We'll be waiting for you here, Hannah. You'll come back to us. I know you'll be back soon.'

The baby called out. They all looked down at her.

'Isn't she a beautiful child?' said Denis, in wonder.

'She is,' said May. 'Beautiful like her mammy.'

ACKNOWLEDGEMENTS

This book wouldn't have happened without the help and encouragement of Jonathan Myerson, the Director of the Creative Writing MA at City University.

Thank you to Julie Myerson for believing in me.

I am lucky to have the support of two brilliant Irish women: my agent, Sallyanne Sweeney, and my editor, Niamh Mulvey, who is my perfect reader. Without them this book would be a much poorer thing. My debt to them both is great.

Thank you to my writerly friends, Jennie Walters and Debra Hills. Thank you to Caroline Conway Pendrill, for all these years of inspiring friendship, and to Lucy Gibson, who kept me going.

Thank you to my sisters, Claire O'Mahony and Louise O'Mahony, and thank you to my first and most loyal supporter, my mother, Lola Lewis.

My father, Jack O'Mahony, didn't live to see me write this book, but he would have been happy that I made it. I write, always, in memory of him and of all the O'Mahonys of West Cork, who persisted.

Thank you to my children, Louis, Allegra, and Gabriella, who showed me what love can be.

Thank you to my husband, Mike, beloved by all, and as constant as the northern star.

A NOTE ON THE TYPE

In 1924, Monotype based this face on types cut by Pierre Simon
Fournier c. 1742. These types were some of the most influential
designs of the eighteenth century, being among the earliest of the
transitional style of typeface, and were a stepping stone to the more
severe modern style made popular by Bodoni later in the century.
They had more vertical stress than the old style types, greater contrast
between thick and thin strokes and little or no bracketing on the serifs.